THE JERSEY

A STORY OF LOSS AND REDEMPTION

JAMES ROSENBERG

The Jersey
A story of loss and redemption

ISBN 978-1-7327612-1-6

NOVEMBER OF THIS YEAR

CHAPTER 1

My labored breath, coming in short bursts, stalls at the back of my throat as I guide the car to the curb in front of our house. I attempt to collect myself and trudge up the concrete steps as the three-story Victorian looms above me. The shrubs we planted the past two summers spread across what had been an unsightly, empty expanse in front, mockingly offering a supposed cheerful greeting. I appreciate the irony of their glad tidings, wondering why Jill and I spent so much time digging and planting these bushes.

I am jolted by the intense silence that greets me when I open the door. I enter and stand in front of the brown suede chair Jill had placed by the picture window. Framing the chair are the molding surrounding the window and the floor-to-ceiling bookshelves she insisted we put in even after we'd blown past our remodeling budget.

The leathery smell subtly lingers in the air. The piano sits to the right, and I can almost hear Charley playing his scales.

Jill bought the chair over a year ago when she announced it was time to fix up the entryway and give away Charley's toys strewn in plastic buckets since he was a toddler. I didn't share Jill's enthusiasm and worried the cost of the chairs she was considering was more than the price of my first car.

The chair has served as the prime spot to watch Charley play piano, the place where he relaxes when waiting for a ride, and Jill's favorite reading location. The slight depression in the seat, according to Charley, "Is a conglomeration of all our butts."

My hands hang at my sides with my head bowed slightly, feeling a form of weariness I have never experienced—an unbearable, jarring, and devastating exhaustion that impedes every move I make. If I sit, I will be unable to move; but I have no interest in wandering upstairs, as the stillness emanating from its depths prevents me from venturing further inside.

I collapse in the chair, its warmth and softness offering little comfort. I close my eyes while emptiness consumes me.

Every muscle in my body tenses, and I force myself to exhale. Memories bounce around my head in a random, chaotic mess. The images slow for a moment so I can briefly control them. Then, just as suddenly, they gain speed, hurtling through my consciousness, randomly pinging back and forth. It will be a methodical, deliberate process, but I must force myself to figure out how I arrived at this moment.

AUGUST OF THIS YEAR

CHAPTER 2

I'M CALM, EVEN THOUGH the crowd is on its feet screaming at a fevered pitch. The bat feels firm in my hands, and I slowly swing it back and forth waiting for the pitcher to begin his windup. The dull roar of cheering rings in my ears.

This dream is so real. One hit and our team will be victorious. My body is young, nimble, and able to do almost anything. The ball comes floating toward me and I'm ready to smash it.

The bat begins its trajectory into the flight path of the ball but never makes contact. I feel a jolting pain as the wind is almost knocked out of me. I am awakened by the crush of 60 pounds of 11-year-old boy. The slight disappointment of not getting my chance to bat dissipates immediately when I hear the excitement in Charley's voice.

"Dad, get up. We have to play some soccer. Our first practice is today. I want to make sure I'm ready." He shakes my shoulders. I roll over to see his blue eyes staring at me. His face, small and round, with hair falling over his eyes, is six inches in front of mine.

"Come on. Let's go outside."

I glance at the clock. It reads 7:15. At least the sun is up.

"Give me a few minutes," I groggily request.

"How many is a few?" He is right in my face and unrelenting. I will not be returning to sleep.

I put my index finger to my lips and reach over my shoulder to point at his mother lying wrapped in the sheet with her back facing us. She creaks, "Don't worry. I'm up."

Jill rolls over and glances at Charley, giving him the look moms hold in reserve for when they want their kids to do something important. "Charley West, don't you have something to say to your dad?"

Charley's face constricts. He's supposed to remember something, but his mind is only on one track. "Can we practice soccer?" He shrugs sheepishly at his mom, knowing that wasn't the right response, but not wanting to play her game.

Jill sits up and seizes her son's attention. "What day is today?"

He smiles. He can almost get to the answer, but it's too much effort. He narrows his eyes and slowly responds, "It's the day Dad and I practice soccer in the backyard."

Jill's face displays no emotion. She lowers her head while keeping eye contact. "What day is it?" she repeats, emphasizing each word.

Charley delays. He takes his time and thinks, knowing he's stuck until he gives the right answer. Gently bouncing up and down on the bed, he gazes at the ceiling. His rhythm increases in tempo while a sly grin consumes his face. He has our attention, both of us, so he pauses before happily announcing, "Happy birthday, Dad!"

"Nice job, buddy," says Jill, quietly laying her head back on the pillow. My birthday is not Charley's top priority at the moment. He stands on the bed and yells, "It's now time for soccer. Come on."

She tries to slow him down. "Wait a little. Why don't you get yourself some food? Dad and I have to talk, and then he will be down. Okay?"

He somersaults off the bed and spins to face us. Energy radiates from his body. "It's a plan!" He bolts from the bedroom, and we are alone.

Jill grabs my T-shirt to yank me closer to her and kisses me. She's wearing the pink and black pajama set I gave her for Valentine's Day. My thoughts quickly move away from soccer. She switches our positions and gets on top of me while pinning my arms over my head.

"Are you ready for your present?"

I nod and mumble, "Yes I am."

I stare into Jill's deep brown eyes. Her long hair falls onto her shoulders. I touch her soft, smooth skin.

"Happy birthday Mr. Forty-Two-Year-Old Man." She says, "I think we have about ten minutes before he finishes eating."

"I'm ready to go. Anything we should discuss first?"

"Nope, it's down to business. Skip the small talk."

She kisses my neck, and my thoughts focus on the task at hand. I rub her back and feel the strong muscles underneath. She begins to take off my shirt when Charley's squeaky voice rises from downstairs. "Dad, let's go. We need to practice."

A scarcely audible groan escapes from Jill. We smile at each other. Nothing's happening now—hardly the first time. She winks at me because she doesn't blame me when things don't go as planned. "Go play with him. He loves it when you make him work hard. Just remember we're finishing this tonight, and you will enjoy it."

Don't worry. I will.

"You're awesome," I say before heading to the bathroom.

"Happy birthday, Sweetie. Try not to hurt yourself."

Springsteen's "Badlands" surges from the speaker tucked into the corner of the vanity as I stare into the mirror, letting the water warm. I tilt my head and squint my eyes. I'm not thrilled about turning 42. My taste in music hasn't changed much since my college years, which are getting fainter in my memories. Some people still look a lot like they did when we met them in school, but others are starting to age or are putting on weight. Some of our friends' relationships are closer to the end than to the beginning.

Jill and I often talk about the demands careers and kids put on marriages. Every day our life is a buzz saw of activity. We both work full-time, and yet we have to deal with Charley's life. Jill manages to return home to take care of Charley after school and make us dinner. Some days we only muster enough energy to say about three words to each other. At the end of the evening, we are often only able to fall onto the couch to watch 30 minutes of TV before crashing.

I assess what reflects back from the mirror while brushing—straight teeth, blue eyes with perhaps a few creases forming around the edges, and some gray sneaking into the once jet-black hair. I step back to examine my full body. I'm not ashamed, although I won't be jogging through the neighborhood without my shirt. Turning 42 isn't the end of the world after all. I commit to reassess when I hit 50.

I don't like birthdays, but I can't waste time feeling old. Soccer season starts now.

It's the weekend, time to hang out with the family. Whatever Charley wants is fine with me. At this moment, I'm not a lawyer and I will ignore any reminder of the piles of paper sitting on my desk at work. I love Arthur Spinelli, and I know he needs my help, but I promise not to worry about him until Monday. Today is for soccer, relaxing, and a birthday dinner with Jill.

CHAPTER 3

I come downstairs and Charley is already outside dribbling a ball around two cones. I love watching him play soccer. He's always played it with enthusiasm and demonstrated foot skills from an early age. Not only does he have the technical ability to move the ball deftly around obstacles or past opposing defenders, but somehow, he's unwittingly developed a style that accentuates his moves without appearing like he's trying to showboat.

In my eyes, he's always been an excellent soccer player. Jill, the more pragmatic of the two of us, doubts it when I suggest he is the best in his group of friends. Either way, Charley, who generally has troubles mustering enthusiasm for most activities, loves to play soccer, which is apparent anytime a ball is at his feet.

Jill beat me downstairs and is gathering ingredients to make breakfast. I pull her over to the window overlooking the backyard, so we can spy on Charley. He practices a dribbling drill he learned on the internet and then starts whacking long kicks against the retaining wall. The ball makes a satisfying *whomp* whenever it collides with the bricks and returns to him, where he stops it with his foot. He stares at the ball and dances a circle around it. He repeats the kick, stops the ball with his other foot, and dances around it in the opposite direction. Jill leans her head on my shoulder while we stand enraptured.

Images of our son running around the backyard when he was a toddler flash in my head as he chases after an errant kick. From the day he was born, Charley was filled with personality, smiling and engaging with anyone who held him. While Jill was pregnant, we secured childcare for him, as neither of us wanted to give up working. Jill couldn't sleep for days right before she had to return to work, consumed with guilt over deciding not to stay home. He started at daycare at 3 months old. The teachers loved him immediately.

We noticed the first time we dropped Charley off that he was, by far, the tiniest baby. This didn't change as he got older—the new babies were always bigger than him. He was, without fail, the smallest in his group of friends, and on every team he has ever played on since.

Jill's family tree is devoid of tall people. Her dad, amiable and caring, is 5'4." Her brother tells everyone he's 5'7", but that's only if he stood on Webster's Dictionary. Jill barely cracks five feet. The only conceivable evidence of height in Charley's lineage comes from me, and I stand 5'10". We knew from the beginning our son wouldn't be tall.

Charley deflects when kids mention his height, making the situation non-confrontational. The first thing his best friend Sam ever said to him was, "You're not the tallest kid, are you?" Charley's immediate reply was "No, but I have every *Star Wars* movie—let's go put one on." Sam stared at him, forgetting how the conversation started, and went with him to watch the Jedis battle. Their friendship is now almost seven years old.

No one outside of the family knows how much comments about his height bother him. He may smile and say something to make the kid laugh, ending any potential conflict, but after such an interaction, he lets us know how hurtful it was. Nobody wants to be short, yet someone has to be the smallest, and that perpetually is our son.

Doctors have examined him, and luckily there is nothing wrong. They say when he gets older, he might have a growth spurt. Right now, he is four inches shorter than the next-shortest person in his class. We tell him there is little we can do about it, but our hearts break when we see the pain this causes him. I wonder what will happen in a few years when girls become as important to them as sports.

I venture into the backyard and am greeted by the warmth of a late summer day. Charley runs over and asks me to put him through some drills. I set up a different obstacle course and tell him to start by juggling his soccer ball, dribbling through the cones, and finishing with twenty push-ups. He does this at lightning speed and repeats the pattern. I think he would keep doing the drill all morning, but I tell him he should save something for the real practice this afternoon. He smiles and runs back over to the wall for more long kicks.

Charley continues to pound the ball, and I gather in the basketballs and baseballs strewn throughout the backyard. He loves playing soccer, but he doesn't do it to the exclusion of other sports. .

Like many kids his age, Charley started in organized athletics at a young age. His friends were bigger and stronger, but their size came with gawkiness that contrasted with Charley's quickness and agility. He competed on nearly an even level despite the height differential. Watching him play basketball, running around the court among relative giants, could be humorous, but Charley got as many rebounds as the bigger kids because he possesses uncanny field awareness and always out-hustled everyone to the ball.

He's played with his buddies since they were 5. With them, sports become a mixture of athletic endeavor and social event. The tightness of his friend group is also part blessing and part curse. They have competed together for so long, they usually play well as a team. During their games, however, they might spend lots of time discussing those things important to eleven-year-olds, rather than having complete focus on the action.

Charley has played baseball, basketball, and hockey, but soccer *is* his love. He liked playing the other sports with his friends but never cared too much if he missed a basketball game or baseball practice.

Soccer has been different for him since the first time he kicked a ball. At 2 years old, he insisted on sleeping with his ball. He could maneuver it walking down the sidewalk at 4, when the other kids could barely get a foot on it. He developed a style and grace to his game and displayed moves the older boys couldn't duplicate. It takes my breath away when he dribbles the ball at full speed.

I coached Charley's team a bit years ago. His soccer league utilizes parents as coaches, so I was in charge of his team for a short time. Never having played the sport much, I didn't know how to run a practice, which wasn't a problem because when they were young, it was more about keeping them moving than teaching skills.

I place the balls back into the proper racks in the garage and notice last year's participation trophy sitting on a table with a variety of other mislaid items. Charley displays his prized trophies on the bookcase in his room commemorating his athletic accomplishments. Apparently, he didn't value this one.

Last season, his soccer team struggled. They won two games, and one win came because the other side never arrived. The losing got worse, and the kids stopped trying. The parents got upset, and the coach, the father of one of the players, said he couldn't handle another season like the last one, informing the parents the boys needed new direction.

Not a lot of people volunteered to coach the team. In fact, no one did. Many of the parents wanted a voice in the process of picking a new coach, but none would accept the responsibility to lead.

Sally Madden, one of the outspoken parents, offered unrelenting criticism last year and got the moms in an uproar when she sent out a series of emails suggesting our coach taught the kids inconsistently with the coaching techniques of English soccer. In all of her diatribes, she never once offered any type of solution.

The parents met three weeks ago at the rec center to discuss who should coach the team. I didn't attend the meeting, but Jill informed me everyone wanted someone who could get the boys to play with heart and passion. Remembering how they quit last season, I laughed. She told me the consensus was I could handle the job, causing me to chuckle louder. My laughter stopped when she informed me she accepted on my behalf. That's when I realized I shouldn't miss any more soccer meetings.

I grip Charley's trophy in my hand and think back on the painful games we sat through last season. I turn to walk back into the house and drop the trophy into the trash.

CHAPTER 4

A SWEET VANILLA SMELL GREETS me when I return to the kitchen. Steam rises as the skillet on the stove sizzles. I grab forks and dishes and set the table, assuming some food is for me.

Jill comes up behind me. "You hungry? I made a stack of French toast. We should start. I don't know when Charley will join us."

I toss pieces of the steaming French toast on plates for both of us and grab syrup warmed in the microwave oven.

Jill eyes flash after we sit, when I start to pick up the newspaper. She wants some adult interaction, so I say, "Today should be interesting."

"What do you mean?" She cuts her French toast with the side of her fork.

"This is the first soccer practice I've run since the boys were little." I stuff my last bite in my mouth and reach to grab another piece.

"Don't worry, the kids will love you."

I frown at Jill. "I'm not worried about that. What I want is for them to improve and to care. I know they were only 10 last year, but they quit. I won't coach if they don't play hard."

"You played lots of sports when you were young." Her hands wrap around the coral-blue mug of coffee. "You know what to teach them."

"I hope so. Those boys are smart. They can sniff out a fraud at five feet."

"Honey." Jill tilts her head slightly. "In the last three weeks, you've read four books and watched every video on YouTube having anything to do with coaching soccer. You're legit."

I shake my head. "I need to get these boys excited, but kids today are different."

"Now you sound like your dad."

"He would understand. The kids don't want to dedicate themselves to anything—only to their video games. The reason they play sports is to hang out with their friends. They're not looking to put in the effort to be the best."

"Charley is."

"Don't be so sure. Whenever the kids practice, all they do is mess around. I watched enough last year, and our son is as guilty as any of them."

"So, what are you going to do?" Jill smiles.

I think for a moment but can't come up with a decent answer. I put on a brave face and announce, "Rules. I will make rules."

"Such as?" Her smile broadens.

"I don't know. They must listen, and they will improve."

"Brilliant! Tell them it's your mandate they have to get better."

I stand to clear my plate and face Jill. "I have to think about this more. Practice starts in a couple of hours."

Charley bounds down the steps to the garage and practically leaps into my little hybrid. He wears his shin guards, soccer socks, and cleats, and carries his water bottle. "Dad, this is going to be a great season."

"Why do you say that?" I ask as we pull out into our street.

"Because."

"Not helpful. Why?"

"Because we're going to be better."

"So is everyone else."

He pauses for a moment. I'm not sure where his thoughts will lead us.

"Do you want the team to improve?" I ask.

"Yeah."

"Well, how do you get better?"

"Practice."

"True. How else?"

"Hard work." He looks at me, grinning. "And cool shoes."

I laugh—he and I may not exactly have the same expectations for how to get his team to improve, but at least he's putting a little thought into it.

The ride to the soccer field is short, and Charley is energized and talkative. We talk about school. I find out Andrew cut his hand at recess. We discuss video games. He informs me the new Megazone game comes out soon. We converse about the weather. He tells me once it flooded so badly in Texas, it created a river of cows. I enjoy his excitement for soccer, because he can't stop giving me tidbits about his life.

A few of his teammates are running around when we arrive. Practice is scheduled to start at noon, yet there are only four players ready five minutes before the starting time. At the anointed hour, seven kids chase each other on the far side of the field.

I yell to them, yet they ignore me. I put my fingers in my mouth and whistle. They still don't respond.

I run across the grass, yelling it's time to begin. One of the boys responds, "We'll be there in a minute." Five minutes later, they're still chasing each other.

Carter and Stephen show up as I'm preparing a plan to gather the wayward children. I ask them if they want to start. They respond by asking where everyone else is. I point across the field to the mass of bodies rolling in a pile. The allure of the scrum is too much. They bolt to join in the melee.

I stand fifty feet from the ongoing chaos with my hands on my hips as the boys continue to throw each other to the ground and run around like maniacs. I pull a whistle out of my pocket and raise it to my mouth. The shrill sound catches their attention, and they pause to glance in my direction. Like a pack of jackals eating their prey, they aren't bothered by anything not in their immediate vicinity. They ignore me and begin jumping on each other anew.

I walk toward them, crossing the white line that marks the edge of the field. I watch in amazement. They have no concern for anything other than what occupies them at that moment. A couple of the kids glimpse at me but pay no mind. They will continue for the next hour unless I do something. I again put the whistle to my mouth and blow it as loud as I can. Finally, I have their attention.

"It's soccer time, gentlemen. Care to join me?" I ask sarcastically.

"Not really," responds Nate, a tall defense man, who is holding Stephen's ball while Stephen tries to retrieve it.

I swallow my rising anger. "Let's go. It's time to start."

The boys gather their gear and straggle across the grass. I instruct them to stand on the white line. They gingerly walk to the chalk and begin conversing again.

I want to refocus the group. "Who's here to practice?"

A couple of hands rise, but most haven't heard the question as a new round of stealing soccer balls begins. I blow the whistle again.

"Sit on the line!" I demand, pointing to the ground. Desperately trying to salvage some practice time and hoping to demonstrate my authority, I stare at the group. I have their attention, I think, until my hopes are dashed when four of them, including Charley, begin chasing each other on the field. This encourages three others to revert to climbing on top of their neighbor.

"Stay on the line," I yell at the five kids who remain seated, as I to leave to corral the wayward boys. After another five minutes, the entire group is finally together. I pace in front of them, my anger barely dissipating. "Who's here to play soccer?" I again ask them.

Everyone yells, "We are!"

"I'm glad to hear it. Let's talk about what we are going to try to accomplish this year. First...."

A hand in the air interrupts my flow. "Should we call you Dan or Coach?" asks Lance, his high voice almost cracking.

"I think either is fine," I reply. "I want to see if we can figure out what went wrong last season. From what I saw, we should address a few issues. For example...."

Another hand rises. I nod.

Jacob asks, "When is our first game?"

"In two weeks. I think we should start, so we are ready."

The inquiries begin without any hands being raised: "What position am I going to play?" "Who's bringing snack?" Why are you wearing a green T-shirt?"

The boys want to ask questions just to hear their own voices. We might spend all practice playing this game, so I change tactics.

"Stand, please," I coax the group. They all rise, but soon three of them are kicking other kids' soccer balls.

I want them to focus, so I instruct, "Put your balls behind you." The words are barely out of my mouth when I recognize my mistake.

The boys begin to snicker until Hunter yells, "He said, 'Put your balls behind you.'"

"Yeah, I heard that," Ricardo responds.

"Watch this," says Sam, as he puts his hands down his pants. "My balls are behind me, now."

"Hey, Coach, how are we going to play with our balls behind us? It's not comfortable," laughs Carter.

The boys all attempt to put their testicles behind them. Each has his hands down his shorts, demonstrating to his neighbor how difficult it would be to play soccer with his balls behind him.

I've lost control and make a mental note always to refer to the item they kick as a soccer ball. The boys laugh uncontrollably while rolling on the ground. I pull out the whistle again and blow. They stop. "On the line," I yell.

They return to their original positions.

"Nobody's putting up with this crap again." They stare, finally quiet.

I meet their gaze. "Don't give me that wounded routine. I will swear at you if you act like babies again. I'm here to teach. I'm not your babysitter. There's one of me and twelve of you. You will win this battle every time if you want. You're lucky I told your parents to stay away from the field today. You don't want to learn today, and if you don't, I'm won't coach. We're done."

I stop and tap at a ball at my feet. "Next time, if you want to play, show up on time. If you intend to screw around, don't come. This isn't social hour. This is practice. We're done. Your parents are over by the pavilion. Go tell them you weren't ready."

I turn and leave them staring at me. I'm mad but in control of my emotions. Last season they trampled their coach. Not this time. I suspect some parents will call. I rehearse in my mind telling them their kids must be prepared for practice the next time.

Charley runs over to join me as I walk toward the car. "Get the message to the team this is not last year. If you're here, you will focus on the drills—no more social hour."

He stares at the ground. He won't walk next to me, and I'm just as happy to walk alone.

CHAPTER 5

THE SUN SHINES THROUGH the front window of the car, highlighting the dried rain spots. Charley is visibly upset over how I had abruptly ended practice.

"Dad, how could you do that?" he wails.

"Do you think I wanted to?" I say, answering his question with my own.

"I don't know."

"I think if you intend to play soccer, you should play soccer. You see your friends a lot and there's enough time for screwing around, but not during soccer. It felt rude to me, like you and your buddies didn't care I was trying to run a practice. All you cared about was doing your thing. I was disappointed when you joined in with everyone. It needs to change."

I let the speech hang in the air as I focus on the reasons I was coaching. I was on board now and expected the same out of the kids, even though I hadn't originally signed up to be coach. The boys may be young, but they had to dedicate themselves during the times they are playing soccer. I thought that coming into the season, with at least some commitment, signs of significant improvement would emerge. The reality of today's practice is already making me re-evaluate my expectations.

Charley thinks for a moment and questions, "How can I get them to play if they don't want to?"

"Fair question. It's called leadership."

"I'm not a leader."

I look at him in the rear-view mirror. "You're the best player. That's enough to make you a leader. Don't you want to help make your team better?"

"Sure."

"Well—talk to your friends. Get a couple of the other kids on board with the idea to focus during practice, with the goal being to improve."

"Okay. I will try," he replies. It sounds a little feeble, but at this point I will take all help offered.

Light music plays in the background as we sip our first drinks. We sit in McIlvoy's, a small, out-of-the-way restaurant on Murray that is quiet and, arguably, romantic. The small booth is cozy. I play with a sugar packet while listening to Jill. Her glass of wine rests between her fingers.

We don't take many opportunities to have an evening to ourselves, but I'm ready to relax. Jill reminds me constantly to mark our milestones. Tonight, Charley is staying with his grandparents, so he's happy and well-fed. We won't rush.

Jill and I avoided leaving him with others when he was little because we felt time away somehow meant we weren't adequate parents. We still don't leave him with a sitter often, but there are positive benefits to changing our patterns. Tonight, he will watch a movie with his grandparents and stay up late. In the morning, he will eat rainbow pancakes and play video games. When we pick him up, he will be happy and so will his grandparents—they love spending time with him.

The small, black dress Jill wears is perfect. In the far corner, the Pirates game is on a flat screen, but it's easy to ignore.

"Applying for grants is so much more difficult than it was a few years ago," she begins. "I'm always thinking of the next amazing project. It's hard."

I nod my head as she continues, "So many people in my department aren't getting funding. The government isn't committed to behavioral research. It's so shortsighted and depressing. Another grant review is in a couple of weeks. I guess we'll be having a lot of pillow talk at 2:30 in the morning."

I roll my eyes—she sleeps poorly during the review process. Jill spent years studying for her doctorate, followed by learning how to conduct proper research trials that can happen only if she gets money from the government. She amazes me—she's received three fully funded projects while many of her colleagues struggle to find any money. Her work, unfortunately, is all about now, and if she doesn't continue to find grants, she'll lose her job.

"You've heard this before." She deflects the conversation toward me. "What's new at the firm?"

"Don't stop talking about your research," I say.

"Nobody cares about getting three hundred participants for my postpartum obesity study. I want to hear about the inner battles at Hadley and Hart."

"Same old stuff. I stay in my office in the bullpen and shuffle papers."

I've worked at my firm for nearly fifteen years and Jill knows the players. She understands the main reasons I work there is because people don't look over my shoulder and I try cases in court.

She hones in. "Anything you're taking to trial just because of the principle?" She smirks.

"So unfair. We went to trial because our client wasn't about to let a shoplifter claim the store had improperly stopped him, even though he was caught stealing."

She gets that gleam in her eye when she knows she is right and responds, "The thief admitted he had stolen the towels and agreed to dismiss the case. But the store insisted on defending itself in court—just for the principle."

I blush a little. "When you put it that way, somehow the concept gets lost. It seemed smart at the time."

She puts her hand on mine and drinks a sip of wine. "Tell me about some new, exciting fact scenario."

"There are always new cases, most of them are run-of-the-mill. Primarily, I'm focused on Arthur's case. You know we go to trial soon."

Jill purses her lips and takes in a gulp of air. Family members fighting over a successful company and claiming each other stole cash from the business sounds intriguing, except when my client is also one of our close friends.

Arthur Spinelli founded Spinelli Enterprises decades ago and grew it into a sprawling success. His nephew unceremoniously dumped Arthur after accusing him of cooking the books. His nephew and the company sued him for the money they claim he had stolen. Arthur hired me to win back the company and protect his legacy. We're staring at an impending trial.

The skin above Jill's eyes furrows as she scrunches her nose. "You're going to kick butt. You know I love him. He's one of the good people. Make sure you don't blow it," she jokes and forces a smile. Despite this, I see worry all over her face.

Ordinarily, Jill is an excellent sounding board for my cases, evaluating them through her internal prism of balancing people's motives with how their actions benefit others. I can't describe her thought process, but she predicts the outcome of my cases with amazing accuracy. Arthur's case is different—she is way too invested, and unable to remain objective.

The waiter interrupts our conversation. I consciously order the type of pasta we both like, and she selects a fish I will enjoy.

We sip from our glasses, ignoring the packed tables surrounding us. I like taking a little time to touch base and reconnect. Jill's work life is separate and distinct from what she does at home, and it helps to sort through the details of her life. Her genuine interest in what I do during the day connects me to her.

Jill leans forward, ready for her next subject. "You appeared unhappy coming home from Charley's soccer practice."

"I was. Can't we talk about something else?"

I didn't want to discuss kid issues yet. We focus on our son the vast majority of time. Mostly, we deal with problems surrounding Charley and his life. Too often we ignore everything else. I love being an involved parent, but not one hundred percent of the time.

Jill's life takes a backseat to everything in Charley's life, but that's her plan. She wants to be the best at her job, but it's more important for her to assist Charley through his daily landmines.

"What happened?" she presses me.

"The boys had no interest in practicing."

"What did they do?"

"They screwed around. They jumped on each other, and they found it funny when I made a reference to their balls."

"You did what?" she exclaims with a slight screech.

"Their soccer balls—I forgot to use the word 'soccer.'"

I describe what happened at practice. She finds the picture of the boys reaching in their pants to put their testicles behind them amusing. She reserves a soft spot for Sam, the leader of the "balls episode," so she's quickly able to forgive.

"Tell me, what are you going to do?" She tilts her head to the side.

"I don't know. How can I make them if they don't want to?" I ask rhetorically. "I need them to want to learn and crave new skills. I want them to be crushed when they lose a game and high as a kite when they win. Now, they don't care."

"It sounds like you have passion."

"They're the ones who should be passionate."

After discussing how to motivate the kids and moving on to parenting issues at school, we are served our meals. We slowly consume our food and order more drinks. The waiter leaves us alone as we linger.

We lost the ability to stay out late once Charley was born. At eleven o'clock, we pay and head to our car. I ignore the automatic locks and open her door the old-fashioned way. She turns to thank me. I put my arms around Jill's waist, and we kiss.

"What did I do to deserve that?" She asks as we drive away.

"So much. I'm rather lucky."

"Me too. Happy birthday."

I think about the present she promised.

CHAPTER 6

In the morning, the sun shines through the trees lining the sidewalk. Jill holds my hand as we walk down the street. Our time alone is coming to an end, so we are in no hurry.

Around the corner, we see the well-kept, two-story bungalow Jill's parents restored. When we arrive, Charley will still be in his pajamas, likely playing a video game, and hot pancakes will be waiting for us.

Russell and Estelle moved into the neighborhood when Charley was little. I had protested they would be too close and were invading our zone of privacy. They ignored my entreaties and purchased a run-down house three blocks away from us.

They spent nearly a year renovating the place, with each room somehow reflecting their varied interests. Out-of-towners from my side of the family often stay at her parents' house because it is quieter and less messy, and the food superior.

Estelle and Russell are tremendous grandparents. Time has proven my worries unfounded as their proximity has been so much more blessing than my predicted curse. They are generous with their time and energy, and Charley is a better person for having them in his life. Their kindness, sincerity, and humor all have in some way rubbed off, and we detect bits of their personalities in what he says and how he acts.

"Hello, it smells amazing," I remark as I open the screen door to enter the house. Stacks of pancakes and steaming syrup in a porcelain jug await us on the kitchen island.

"Hi, guys. You ready to eat?" Estelle responds, grabbing the food and taking it to the family room table. They are pushing 70 but move with the vibrancy of people two decades younger. She says to Charley, who is playing a video game on the couch, "You want more?"

"Can I finish, please?" he replies.

Turning back toward us, she says, "He's already eaten six."

Jill takes a seat at the table and spears her first pancake. "When did he get up?"

"He slept past 7, so we got *some* sleep."

Estelle recounts the movie they watched the evening before—Charley liked the scary parts but turned his head at the kissing. He, of course, consumed a huge quantity of popcorn and went to bed without fuss.

Estelle places a hand on Jill's shoulder. "You know we love having him around."

"You can have him whenever you want," I joke. "We had a fun evening. It's a new experience to get out of bed and not have any worries."

"Careful what you wish for."

Estelle eases into a chair at the far side of the table, and we are joined by Russell, who takes a seat at the other end.

He groans. "I went for a 25-mile bike ride and my back is hurting a little." He's a ball of energy who fits in time for exercising most mornings before leaving for work as a pediatrician. He doesn't appear to be close to slowing down.

"I hope you showered," I remark as I casually lean over and sniff like a hound dog would. He raises his arm and shoves my head into it, remarking, "Do you think I stink?"

I fall off my chair, feigning passing out. Charley glances over from his video game, a fiendish smile emerging on his face. He has witnessed other odd events in this house before—food fights, wrestling matches, and bad puns. He doesn't quite comprehend adults can act more childish than kids.

He runs over and jumps on my back—his goal to join the fray. "What happened, what happened?"

"Your father was attacked by BB's armpit," Estelle answers, deploying Russell's nickname.

"BB, why did your armpit attack my dad?" Charley wants to be a part in the worst way.

"Because he's obnoxious."

"You shouldn't mess with him"

"Then who should get my wrath?" Russell snarls.

Russell leaps from his chair and pins Charley to the ground. Charley giggles, waiting for his mock torture to begin.

"Do you want my armpit?" Russell hovers over his grandson.

"Don't do it," Charley begs, his resistance appearing futile.

Russell sits on top of his grandson, his armpit nearly covering his head. Charley struggles, but is laughing so hard he has no chance of getting loose. "BB, stop. I'm going to pee myself."

"Well, we don't want any of that," Russell releases Charley and returns to his chair. "By the way, I showered. Neither one of you would have survived, if I hadn't."

Charley regains his composure and walks over to sit on my lap. It's rare these days he's willing to demonstrate much affection, so I'm thrilled to have him close by. He stares at his grandfather with an unconditional love he reserves for the people who will do anything for him and who always see him in the best light. I never thought it was important that he finds out most adults act differently from his grandfather.

After eating breakfast, Jill and I clean the dishes. She hands Charley some clothes she brought from home, so he can get dressed. Estelle reaches over, putting some pans back into the cupboard.

"I hear practice never got off the ground," she begins. "He was sad he didn't get to play soccer." I'm not sure if she's chastising me for ending practice, or working to sort out what happened.

"He and his friends were out of control," I explain, trying not to sound defensive.

"What did they do?"

"They were running off, jumping on each other, kicking each other's balls, and not showing the slightest interest in playing soccer."

Russell walks over to listen. Jill's parents are extremely involved in all of our lives. They have two younger grandchildren, so they spend a lot of time attending to everyone's whims. For the most part, we appreciate and consider their opinions about the children.

Russell interjects, "I see it all the time with the families who come to the office. Kids are over-scheduled and their parents do everything for them. They don't get enough time to hang out with their friends. Maybe they're just burning off some energy."

"I get it," I respond, "but they need to focus some. You've seen it with Charley. He tries to do three things at once, which means he focuses on nothing."

We talk for twenty minutes trying to figure how to get the kids passionate about soccer while still having fun. We agree things have changed since we were young, when our parents threw us outside and told us to play and return at dinner time.

I worry this season will be a lost cause for Charley's team. He loves soccer and could be better if he developed his skills with the right coach. I would hate to take him away from his friends, but we might have to get him on a team where the focus was on teaching and not socializing.

SEPTEMBER OF THIS YEAR

CHAPTER 7

"HEY, BUDDY—HAVE AN AWESOME day at school," I yell to Charley, who is scurrying around while he and his mom gather his belongings.

"Bye, Dad, I'll see you tonight." He runs toward the front door.

I put the last dishes in the dishwasher and prepare to leave for work. I picture the piles of paper on my desk I need to deal with today. Mondays suck—I always find it difficult to shift gears from the weekend's activities to the nerve-racking issues awaiting at the office.

Over the past eleven years we have developed a morning ritual that operates with factory precision. Jill and I both love to run. I get up first and go for a quick jog. Forty minutes later I return and hand her the baton, so she can do the same. I shower and get Charley out of bed. After we get ourselves some breakfast, he rushes to brush his teeth. The baton is passed back upon Jill's return. After making sure he has his homework, permission slips, and his lunch in his backpack, she takes him to the bus stop.

Most days Jill does not return to the house before I leave for work. She has become infamous in our neighborhood for remaining after the bus leaves to talk to her friend Liza—the mom of Charley's best pal, Sam. Jill and Liza stand at the corner and gab about school, activities, personal issues, or a hundred other possible subjects. Everyone commuting to work notices them gesturing expressively or laughing uncontrollably. Neighbors often text me to let me know they have spotted them again. Many days I am already at my desk while they are still involved in an animated discussion on the corner.

Liza Austin and Jill have been friends since Sam and Charley met. They bonded immediately and talk, text, email, or snap almost constantly. Liza exudes more positive energy than anyone I know, which probably explains her youthful exuberance, and is also one of the smartest people around. Trained as a lawyer, she clerks for a federal judge in town. She is married to Pete, her classmate from law school, with whom she has two gorgeous children. Through the years, we have shared in the pitfalls of parenting, often lamenting our perceived shortcomings over wine and beer.

Sam and Charley are best buddies, part of a larger gang that attend their elementary school, Brighton. In addition to Charley and Sam, Carter, Stephen, Lance, Ricardo, Andrew, and Jacob are all friends who also play on the soccer team.

These boys have grown up sharing in many of the mile markers of youth. They attend each other's birthday parties, study together, and have all played on many of the same sports teams. Their parents have forged relationships by taking over restaurants, overwhelming picnic groves, and reserving twenty contiguous camping sites for a weekend. Some drama has occurred over the years, but mainly this is a solid group that has helped the kids to navigate the difficulties of childhood.

The fathers have also become friends. We've started a beer night tradition and will often go to baseball games together.

We try to stay away from the drama, and any of the dads would be humiliated if caught gossiping on the street corner in the morning.

Sometimes, driving to work, pressing issues awaiting me at the office consume my thoughts. Today, I avoid the stress and picture Jill and Liza on the corner, and Charley getting off the bus and returning to class. I visualize our next practice and almost make out the kids paying attention and focusing on the next drill. I pull into the parking lot in my building. The images of piles of papers reemerge to wipe away the more serene pictures of soccer and family.

The elevator dings as the door opens to my floor at Oxford Centre. A small hallway leads to where my office is situated. Four lawyers occupy this back area, which we have named "the bullpen" to honor our self-described seclusion from the power brokers. We stay out of sight most of the time, unencumbered by daily visits from the higher-ups.

Stacey, my assistant, greets me while placing a stack of papers on my desk, which is in its normal state of organized chaos. My routine upon entering the office hasn't changed much in the fifteen years I have worked at Hadley and Hart. My first task is returning any necessary phone calls and emails. I shift to focus on the most pressing issues—reviewing a new file or finishing a brief on a case being argued in the appellate courts.

Ordinarily, I represent civil defendants—clients who are being sued or, at least, trying to avoid a lawsuit. Each case provides the opportunity for negotiation and, if necessary, a trial. Most ultimately settle and the defendant pays some money to the plaintiff. Sometimes, my client may elect to go to trial and let a jury decide who is right and who is wrong. My dad practiced law for a long time, and back then many more cases went to trial. Now, not as many end up at trial, as the risks have increased and clients are wary of letting strangers determine the outcomes of their disputes.

Many lawyers who identify themselves as litigators have never been in front of a jury. I have tried bunches of cases and have gained confidence in my ability to convince juries that my client's version of the facts is better than what the other side is selling. Trial attorneys have too many constituencies to please to allow them to sleep at night. My clients, the other side's attorney, my bosses, judges, and jurors have competing interests. Pleasing one group often means antagonizing another. After the haranguing, it's a delicate balancing act to finish a jury trial with your sanity and ethics intact.

Most of my files represent years of work. It takes a long time for cases to wind through the system. After a complaint is filed to initiate a lawsuit, the attorneys must draft pleading, obtain documents, send written questions, take depositions, and prepare legal briefs to raise esoteric arguments.

The parties fight over huge sums of money and argue about differences, often petty, having significance to the clients. Most of the time, everyone becomes emotionally invested in the outcome. Lawyers try to remain unemotional and deal with each other civilly, but sometimes we assume our client's perspective of the dispute. Lawyers, in those cases, get nastier than their clients, leading to unpleasant phone conversations and letters filled with venom. These uncivil interactions hung in my mind for weeks early in my career, causing me to lose sleep and focus. I have developed better relationships with opposing counsel since, and learned my clients may not be the best judges of what had happened.

My goal every evening is to leave the emotions in the office and deal with my family with a clean slate. I'm not always successful. I feel most guilty when I get angry at Charley or Jill when I am really reacting to something stressful from earlier in the day. My dad was a lawyer for nearly fifty years. He passed away a few years ago but always told me to try to separate work and family. He spent too much time working while I was growing up. I don't want Charley to think of me in the same way, so I am determined to get home as soon as possible and leave the wrangling behind.

The stuffy, established firm I worked for right out law school didn't mess with my style. I hated it. The lawyers who got ahead were the ones adept at office politics. Superior legal skills didn't matter. At Hadley and Hart, where I fled after fifteen months at my first job, it's more important to service our clients than to make face-time. My bosses don't care what hours I keep as long as I get my work done and get good results.

I move papers into new stacks, trying to get organized for the day. "Your desk is a mess." Jana Larihall leans against the door frame, holding a cup of coffee and smiling. "Want to get lunch later?"

Jana's my closest work confidant. Tall, leggy, and retaining remnants from her athletic youth, she tries to project confidence. She's ten years younger than me, and I have mentored her since she started with the firm five years ago looking to gain trial experience after completing a federal clerkship. She bristles at her failure to try any cases of significance and believes the partners don't think she can hack it. Her office is next to mine in the bullpen, which she thinks reflects the partners' lack of trust in her. She doesn't believe me when I tell her she's here because she's smart, resourceful, and doesn't require constant supervision.

Jana and I often work together on cases, with her tackling the complicated briefs and me taking depositions and handling the trials. In private, she informs me she doesn't mind the legal writing, but she wants to take on more responsibility. I have promised her multiple times to find her the right opportunity to be in charge of her own cases.

"I'm free for lunch," I respond. "Get me when you want to go."

"We also need to talk about Spinelli and what we have to do to prepare for trial," she interjects. "Can we do it now?"

I have other pressing agenda items, but I acquiesce. "Sure, sit down."

Arthur's case provided the perfect chance for me to give Jana the responsibility she craved. Other matters diverted my attention, so she took many of the key depositions. Her questioning of our client's accuser provided us with a lot of the ammunition we will deploy at trial to counter the nephew's claim that Arthur Spinelli was stealing money from his company,

Jana plops herself into the small leather chair in front of the window. She crosses her legs, opens her file, and faces me. Jana's face scrunches when she is ready to bear down and focus. I know she wants to jump right in.

"Jury selection is scheduled next month. The testimony is already digested, but we have to get our exhibits organized. I know you're handling the opening statement, but I think you should have it prepared as soon as possible, so we have a road map for our trial strategy." Jana knows I often wait to the last minute to draft my opening, and she is coaxing me to break my bad habits.

She continues, "We have to exchange witness and exhibit lists in ten days. I already have ours together, so we will have no problems. The other side will delay as long as possible before sending us anything. I don't trust them." Her voice trails off.

"I don't either, especially after the stunts they pulled at the depositions," I add.

A deposition is one of many tools a lawyer utilizes to get information from the opposing side during the discovery phase. Depositions are the only time the other side can question a witness under oath. An attorney's job is to prepare the witness for any possible line of questioning and make sure he is familiar with any documents he may have to review while testifying. Usually the defending attorney doesn't do much. He will make an occasional objection, but his primary responsibility is to ensure the other lawyer doesn't ask improper questions or try to intimidate the witness. Most times, the other attorney acts professionally.

I toss Arthur Spinelli's transcript toward Jana, who picks it up and exclaims, "Carlson's a huge ass." We laugh as we both remember the antics from Arthur's deposition.

Arthur and I had shown up at Keith Carlson's office, the lawyer for Arthur's nephew, Mike Vorat. I was surprised Carlson had a person there to videotape the proceedings. This ordinarily would not be a problem but only if he had provided us with written notice of his intention to film the deposition—which he hadn't done. Carlson also tried to seat me in a corner ten feet way from Arthur.

I informed Carlson I would sit next to my client and he could not tape the deposition because he had not sent us proper notice. Carlson is one of those guys who's amenable when getting his way but blows up whenever someone disagrees with him. I reminded Jana how red-faced he got and how he started yelling and screaming because I wouldn't agree to his terms. He wouldn't calm down, so Arthur and I walked out.

The judge signed an order preventing Carlson from videotaping and making sure I would sit next to my client when questioned. We returned a month later. Carlson attempted to make amends, but within five minutes of beginning, he started to berate Arthur. He tried to question him about documents that he had never given to us, though we had asked previously for every conceivable document. He stood and got in Arthur's face. I stopped the proceeding and we again left.

We went to court a second time, now seeking sanctions. The judge granted our motion, made Carlson pay a portion of the attorneys' fees, and limited him to two hours to ask his questions.

Carlson finally took Arthur's deposition, but he was so flustered by the time limitation, he neglected to explore many potentially fruitful areas of inquiry. He extracted minimal useful information.

I tell Jana we need to focus and finalize our preparations after we laugh about how irate Carlson was when Arthur and I stood exactly two hours after questioning began and left as he was in the middle of one of his questions.

I scan through the file materials quickly. "You have the exhibits and witness lists in order. I have an outline of the opening in my head. We should divide up which witnesses each one of us will handle."

"You mean I get to ask questions at trial?"

"Of course. You did most of the work on this case. The information you gleaned from the nephew is helpful. He's definitely your witness." I raise my eyes from the file and catch hers. "He's an ass, so be ready."

Jana beams. "Awesome. Thanks."

"Don't thank me. You've earned it." I lean forward. "Arthur only says positive things about you. He has confidence in you."

"I'm a big fan of his as well." She stands and puts her notes back in the file. "See you at lunch."

Jana walks out, leaving me with the random piles around my office. From the time she started with the firm, she has done everything I have asked her to do. Hopefully, this trial will help her get some recognition. I constantly talk her up to the partners, wanting them to give her more challenging assignments. They give me lip service about how respected she is but offer an odd look when they mention how closely we work together.

I'm putting some papers in order while pondering the beginnings of my opening. Saul Hadley pokes his head into my office. His graying hair is combed to the side, and he is wearing a pressed pin-striped suit with a handkerchief neatly folded in the breast pocket.

Saul gestures to the documents strewn on the floor. "Quite untidy." He's smiling, but his narrowed eyes convey discomfort.

"I'm trying to prepare for trial. What's up?"

"You got a minute?"

"Sure, come on in." He closes my door and eases into the chair Jana vacated. He picks at some lint on his jacket, twirling it between his thumb and index finger.

"You ready for Spinelli?"

"Yes, it starts in a few weeks."

"How is Jana doing?" Saul crosses his leg and places his hands in his lap. He is the managing partner at the firm. I guess this gives him the authority to inquire about how I handle my cases.

"She's been fantastic. She took most of the depositions and is getting us organized."

Saul forces a smile. "Will she do anything at trial beyond organization?"

"Absolutely. I told her she will question at least some of the witnesses. Why?"

"You know she's never questioned a witness in court before." Saul pauses, waiting for me to respond. I don't. He leans forward. "I don't want her compromising the case."

I grab the edge of my desk. "Not an issue," I say, perhaps a little too defensively. "She's talented. She needs a chance."

He stands and walks over to the window overlooking the river. "I think you may be sticking your neck out a little."

"How?"

"We're worried about this matter. You have the trial experience, and I'm not sure this is the type of case you want a young attorney to cut her teeth on. I know Keith Carlson. He's a tricky bastard. He'll chew up Jana and spit her out."

"I will keep my eye on Carlson and make sure he toes the line. Don't worry. She knows how to do this. She will be a huge help when we get to trial."

"I hope so, for both of you." Saul stands and opens the door. "Good luck with the case." He leaves my office, and a trickle of sweat falls down my back.

CHAPTER 8

THE SMALL FOLDER FLIES onto the hallway table after I shut the door to the house. I have spent so much time on the Spinelli case, I need to put some time in on other cases. Despite every intention to be productive this evening, I realize it will probably be in the same position on the table when I leave for work in the morning.

Charley sits on his knees at the round table in the kitchen with two books propped around him and a computer in between. He jumps out of his chair and begins to gyrate his hips. He has buds in his ears, unaware of my presence.

"Nice dance," I shout to him, but he does not hear. I walk past the couch in our family area and tap him on the shoulder. He startles and yells, "Hey, Dad."

I pat him on the head. "How's the homework coming?"

"Great."

"Do you think you should sit so you have a chance of finishing it?"

"Right." He returns to the kitchen table and resumes staring at the computer screen.

Charley is a bright, articulate, energetic child who has tremendous difficulty focusing on a single task. Homework is always a chore for him. We've tried to carve out time and space for him to concentrate on it. Ordinarily it takes him twice as long as it should to do any assignment, as he continually gets distracted. We have spoken with his doctor about it, and he suggests it's normal for a kid his age.

Despite his focus issues, he's a decent student. He's developed the skill of talking with his teachers to discuss potential issues he might be having with the material and can make the teacher comfortable he understands the work. He receives solid grades and doesn't cause problems in his classes.

Two minutes later, Charley slams his textbook shut and triumphantly announces, "I've finished my homework." He switches the computer to a video game site and becomes immediately immersed. He will stare at the screen until we redirect him to a different activity.

I lean over his head. "Don't forget you have practice tomorrow."

He smacks his head and closes the laptop. "I need to work on my kicks," He jumps up from his chair and heads toward the door. Without looking for approval, he's out of the house. The thumping of the soccer ball against the brick wall soon begins.

I walk over to the window. Charley runs around the backyard wearing shorts and a T-shirt. He alternates between both of his feet generating power from each side. He's a righty but controls better on his other side. He has spent many hours developing his right foot so it is almost equal to his left. It's an advantage to have a strong left leg because defenders are used to players attacking them toward the right side. The goal is to be able to do all soccer drills equally well with both feet.

After watching for a few minutes, I head for the refrigerator and hear voices coming down the steps. Liza exclaims, drowning out Jill's high-pitched laugh, "He did not say that!"

Jill is about to respond when she enters the kitchen but realizes another adult is in the house.

"Oh hi, Honey—you're home. Liza's here."

"I heard the cackling. What are you talking about?"

"Nothing important." She changes the subject. "Anything interesting happen today?"

"No. Jana and I are starting to get ready for Arthur's trial. I can't believe how much work we have. Trial is coming quickly."

"I know. You better win. Arthur deserves it after the way his family treated him.

"You're so right. What happened in the world of research today?"

Jill shrugs. "I'm still working, and I got a paper accepted. I guess it was a positive day."

I move forward to hug her, but she walks to the other side of the kitchen with Liza. I open the refrigerator to grab a drink.

Jill's constant struggle to get grants is interrupted only by the need to publish the results from her studies. After submitting voluminous grant proposals and hopefully receiving funding, her group has to conduct the study, which generally takes years of painstaking data accumulation. She has to write up the findings and submit them to scientific journals for review and, with some luck, have the article accepted for publication. Rejection can mean years of research and huge sums of money have been wasted.

When friends get Jill talking, they get an education in the amount of effort necessary to complete a project, but also the benefits it has for society. Jill tells them every article a scientist publishes pushes forward scientific knowledge in a particular area a little, and the cumulative effect of a multitude of researchers is enormous. This process is what has made finding the cure for cancer more likely, or in Jill's case, helped thousands safely lose weight after pregnancy.

Liza walks to the far side of the island to grab an apple out of a bowl. She takes a bite and turns to me with a sly grin. "Heard soccer practice was interesting last week."

"Yes," I say, expecting a lecture. "What did you hear?"

"Sam told me there may have been a few distractions. Sounds like he was front and center in causing problems—although I thought the whole 'balls behind you' routine was kind of funny."

I'm still having trouble finding the humor in it. "It's entertaining, at the right time. There are too many of them, and they have no ability to monitor themselves."

"Do you need some help?" she asks.

"Absolutely, with someone for crowd control and supervision, I would stand a better chance."

"I'm going to tell Pete he's your assistant and to do what you tell him. I will get you somebody else as well."

"Awesome. Would love to have your husband as my servant."

Liza smiles. "You two can figure out who plays what role. It sounds like it might be rough for a little."

She gives Jill a hug and walks out of the kitchen toward the front door. Jill waves and starts to take out dinner. The thumping in the backyard continues.

The three of us have dinner in the kitchen. Charley is still sweaty from kicking the soccer ball. Despite a minor protest, he has agreed he will clear the table and wash the dishes because he missed setting the table while outside.

This is Jill's time. She insists on dinner almost every night, so we can connect as a family. Our lives have become busier each year. Charley has too many activities, plus he wants to spend more time with his friends. Even with the increased demands on his time, he knows most nights the three of us will sit down and have dinner. We may throw together a meal in five minutes, but as long as we all share in it, Jill's satisfied.

I scoop out some salad and push the bowl toward Charley. "How was your day at school?"

"Fine." He grabs lettuce out of the bowl with his hands.

I shake my head at him and reply, "I need more information."

"My day was fine and the evening is looking good, too." He turns to his mom looking for her approval of his cuteness. She ignores him.

"Thanks. I feel like I know so much more about your life," I say, trying to get his attention back. He doesn't respond.

Jill passes the water and interjects, "Did you present your science project?"

"I did. Mom, it was super awesome. The stuff we put in about Saturn's rings, everybody thought it was cool. Mrs. Woodshire had some of her own pictures of Saturn, and she showed the whole class."

Jill smiles at Charley, who continues, "Remember the rabbit, Bambi? She had babies. It's a zoo in there, literally."

"Amazing. Did you practice piano?"

Charley nods his head and swallows the food in his mouth. "I found a new piece on the internet. All I have to do is learn the left hand."

"Can you show it to me after dinner?"

"Yup—if you want me to."

I settle back into my chair and watch Jill glean bits of information from Charley, a skill I'm still working to develop. She knows each of Charley's teachers. She keeps track of his schedule and uses the data points she has at her disposal to gain more information.

Their conversation is interrupted by a knock at the front door. I tell them to keep talking and get up to see who is there. Through the small window, I see the semi-forced smile of Sally Madden, attired in her customary after-work outfit of baggy athletic pants and a T-shirt, today a bright, translucent yellow.

I suck in a huge gulp of air and plaster my own fake smile on my face while opening the door. She avoids all unnecessary pleasantries. "Just who I wanted to see. Can I come in?"

"We were eating dinner," I respond without opening the door any wider.

"I will only take a few minutes of your time. "

Sally brushes past me as she nudges her way into the house. There is a momentary silence as we stand in the entranceway looking at each other. The faint sound of the conversation from the kitchen floats by us. She takes a quick look around the living room as if to make sure everything is in its place. Satisfied, she turns to me. "I hear no soccer took place last Thursday."

"True," I confess. "What's up?"

"It's unacceptable."

"Say again?" I stare at her, having difficulty comprehending her audacity.

"You can't quit. The kids are there to play."

"And I was there to coach—but none of the kids wanted any coaching."

She takes a step back and flicks at her hair. A slight woman who enjoys being in the middle of things, She riles up all of the parents with a constant stream of accusatory emails despite having no formal role on the team. She feels entitled to know all and discuss with everyone anything related to the team.

"I think you should have more control over the boys," she starts anew.

"So do I." I'm working hard not to lose my temper. "What do you suggest?"

"I don't know. You're the coach. Plus, you can't swear at them."

"Why not? They deserved a lot worse."

"I can't imagine you can't handle the few kids who aren't listening."

"It wasn't a few. It was all of them. My Charley, your Lance—every kid. I won't coach for long if they act that way. More importantly, you and the other parents have to trust me. Practice will be cancelled, if I think it should be. If you want to second-guess me, find someone else to be in charge."

She drops her gaze and reaches into her pocket for her keys. I move to the door and open it wide to let her out.

"Is there anything else?" I ask, more slowly than necessary.

"No, I'm glad we cleared the air."

"Feel free to call if you want to discuss anything," I say, hoping she doesn't detect the sarcasm.

She steps away from the door and turns to say something. I close the door before a word comes out of her mouth. I lean back against the wall and force myself to breath slowly.

CHAPTER 9

THE PLANTS IN MY office sag toward the ground. They haven't been watered for weeks. I have a lot to do but nonetheless I grab a watering can, so I can fill it in the kitchen. The ficus, its leaves angling for the light streaming in the window, sits in the corner. In its fourth pot since I brought it here almost thirteen years ago. I can't say we are friends, but I have often talked to it about my cases and it has overheard some interesting conversations over the years.

Arthur Spinelli's file is still spread all over my desk and credenza. I think of his plight as the water sprinkles out of the can. I never would have had the opportunity to help him if we hadn't become friends, which never would have happened if not for Jill.

We were at a friend's party over seven years ago. People were beginning to go home. At most social gatherings, I am mentally prepared to leave about an hour before Jill. She loves chatting with people and will glean information from them about their families and jobs. I would rather sit and watch a baseball game and avoid any conversation.

That night, I was alone nibbling on a piece of cheese, feeling the onset of annoyance because Jill promised we could leave twenty minutes earlier. I spotted her next to a pleasant-looking man wearing a sports coat who appeared to be in his late fifties. Jill was giggling and the man obviously was enthralled with her.

My primary thought was how to get out of the party. I approached her, interrupted her conversation, and suggested it was time to make our exit. Jill ignored my plea and introduced us. She informed me he was the founder and president of Spinelli Enterprises, a well-known local business that specialized in auto parts. After semi-ironically telling him I had once purchased an oil filter at one of his stores, he gently turned the conversation around and began to question me about my work.

"So, what kind of law do you practice?" he asked.

"Litigation, I help people when they get sued,"

"Interesting. I have never been in a lawsuit."

"You should keep it that way."

"Do you get into court much?"

"I've been lucky and have tried a bunch of cases. I enjoy the give and take of questioning witnesses." I don't usually like to talk about myself or what I do, but Arthur made me comfortable and, by expressing interest, allowed me to open up.

Jill put a hand on my shoulder. "He's talented. I saw him once get this doctor caught up in a bunch of inconsistencies on cross-examination. It was fun to watch." I was a little embarrassed by the compliment but liked how she was talking me up.

Arthur, Jill, and I conversed for the next thirty minutes, with him becoming animated and providing us more details about his business. After giving us a brief history of the company, he enticed me to tell him about one of my unusual trials. He allowed me to delve into minuscule detail about the trial, and as I finished, we realized we were the last ones remaining at the party. We said our goodbyes to the host and agreed to keep talking elsewhere. He suggested we go have a drink, so we walked down the block to a neighborhood bar.

We took seats at a table in the back and ordered beers. The conversation turned to local politics and sports, and we discovered a shared love for the city's baseball and football teams. We got nostalgic reminiscing about how competitive the Pirates were when we were young and compared where we were each time the Steelers played in a Super Bowl.

By the end of the night, we had discussed subjects ordinarily left for only the closest of friends. He described his marriage to Evelyn, and their painful failure never to have kids. Beautiful and charitable, she had died a few years earlier after a brief battle with cancer. It took us about five minutes to discover she was the love of Arthur's life. Jill talked about the tribulations of being a researcher and her frustration at continually having to beg the government for money. I let Arthur in on my secret that I wanted to be an author and write legal thrillers.

We drank until the bar closed and then put our new friend in an Uber. On our walk home, I announced to Jill my intention to stay longer at parties and meet more people. She grabbed my arm and we staggered down the street.

The main portion of the Spinelli file sits on my credenza, its sheer size a reflection of the battles that have already taken place. Six folders bulging with depositions, discovery responses, business records, and a variety of correspondence hold the key to Arthur Spinelli's fate. His story and his ability to defend against the accusations made by his nephew are somewhere in this mass of papers. It will be up to Jana and me to present his claim to a jury to protect not only his financial future, but his reputation and legacy. We have six weeks to make sure we have the story straight.

Jill and I spent a lot of time with Arthur after meeting him at the party. We had him over to our house many times, and he often returned the favor. He met Charley when Charley was three and in preschool. Arthur developed an immediate fondness for him. He would clap enthusiastically at piano recitals and always brought a unique present for birthdays.

For Charley's seventh birthday, Arthur gave him a Troy Polamalu jersey. Whenever we got together, he would regale us with stories of the Steelers of the '70s and how they were the greatest football team of all time. Charley soon could name every Steeler who had won Super Bowls.

One cold winter day four years ago, Arthur invited Charley to spend an evening at his house, so they could watch videos of the championships. Charley scolded me when he came home for failing to educate him on how superior his team had been.

Arthur drove Charley when he was nine to the Pro Football Hall of Fame to check out the busts of the Steelers inducted into the Hall. Interacting with exhibits about players like Joe Greene, Franco Harris, and Jack Lambert heightened Charley's connection to the old Steelers teams and strengthened his bond with Arthur.

Arthur often invited our family to watch Steelers games at his house. Each time, he provided an orgy of food and wine. Charley with his Polamalu jersey hanging down to his knees would cheer every touchdown. The rules were different at his house than at ours, and most other places—there he could sit on the couch eating wings and watching television rather than be stuck at a table.

Last year, the three of us were invited to Arthur's house, but Charley had already scheduled time to be with Jacob, Sam, and Lance. He didn't want to miss time at Arthur's but also did not want to cancel on his buddies. Without Jill or me knowing, Charley called and finagled invitations for his friends. The boys loved the house with the huge posters of Steelers and Pirates in every room. Arthur made a feast of ribs, salad and loads of chocolate. The boys stuffed themselves and cheered while the Steelers won on a last-second field goal.

At the end of the game, Arthur suggested they go outside to play some soccer. The sheer size of the backyard impressed the boys, who quickly grabbed some garbage cans to make goals. They came inside after playing for a while to invite the adults to join. Despite being in his sixties, Arthur ran around for over an hour and astonished them with his skill. He told me he had been a soccer player in his youth. I later found out he had been named a small-college All-American after leading his team at Davidson to two league championships.

He had become a part of our family, so I was surprised almost three years ago when he called and asked to see me at my office. He had never been there before, but I was confident he had more pressing matters to discuss than the décor.

I had not seen him for a few weeks when he came downtown on a frigid December afternoon. His face was weathered and his eyes downcast as he sat in one of the client chairs in front of my desk. We made brief small talk. I asked him if he was under the weather and was surprised when he told me he wasn't. His hands fidgeted in his lap, but before I could steer the conversation to his reason for coming, he made sure to get an update about Charley and his friends.

Finally, I asked him what had brought him there. His body slumped further into the small chair, and he stared out of the window in silence. After a few moments, he turned his head in my direction. "You know about my business. I started the company when I was in my twenties because I knew about cars and not much else. Nobody gave me any help, and I learned everything I could about running a business. Still, there were lots of times we almost had to give up.

"Evelyn and I got married before we became successful. We didn't care much about money. We wanted to be together. After a while, I decided to take life more seriously. I worked hard trying to develop a customer base. She was the only other employee at the time, and there were lots of pay periods when we took nothing home."

I jotted notes on a legal pad, while listening to his story.

"We made a darn good team. I was responsible for getting the parts and dealing with our suppliers. Evelyn got to know our customers and kept them happy. Because of the relationships I was developing and our way of managing inventory, we were able to sell products for a little less than our competitors. We made sure to do whatever it took to keep their business. I remember a long time ago Evelyn driving an oil filter, a $2 item, to a small gas station across town, because they were sold out. To this day, they still buy filters from us."

Arthur glanced toward the ceiling and sighed. "I guess I should say they still buy them from…not from me—but I will get to that in a minute." He paused and fidgeted with his watch.

I offered him some water and he took a sip. He looked up at me. "Our revenues took off. We had more orders than we could handle, so we decided to open up a new location, and then another, and another. We added employees and trained them, so they understood our customer service methods. Most of our people have been with us for a long time. We treat them well."

I nodded, but said nothing.

"Two years ago, we opened our tenth store in Pittsburgh. We have had opportunities to expand, but I never wanted to lose control. We've been extremely successful, and recently hired our 200th employee.

"Like I was saying, we treat everyone who works for us well. I think everyone came to Evelyn's funeral when she died. Our people are our family. I hope they look at us the same way."

I broke into Arthur's monologue. "Your career has been amazing, but I'm sure there's another reason you're here."

Arthur shook his head and adjusted his watch. "You know Evelyn and I always wanted to have kids, but never were able to. With what doctors can do now, I'm sure we would have some, but back then, if you couldn't have them, you dealt with it. We talked about adopting, but for whatever reason never did.

"Our extended family became more important to us. Evelyn, especially, was interested in getting to know everyone. She had six brothers and sisters, so we ended up with a lot of nephews and nieces. Some of our relatives were close and some lived across country. We always had some cousin or niece working for us and never had any problem with any of them.

"About a year ago, Evelyn had already passed, but her sister who lives in Oregon called to tell me her son, our nephew, was graduating from business school and was having troubles finding a job. At the time, we had an accountant, Steve Berlin, who was getting close to retirement, so I figured it might be helpful to have someone come in and learn the books with the opportunity to become our full-time accountant.

"The nephew's name is Mike, Mike Vorat," Arthur almost spit out the name. "I knew him, just not as well as I knew the rest of Evelyn's family. He came to Pittsburgh for what I guessed would be an interview. He was family—the job was his. We never went over his resume or transcript.

"Everything was fine when he started. I checked with Steve, who had no complaints—but things got strange. A couple of months after Mike was hired, Steve quit. He walked into my office one day and said he was leaving. He was getting close to retiring, but this was sudden. Nothing I did could make him stay longer, and I was never able to find out why he left so suddenly. He moved to Costa Rica, and I have not spoken with him since."

I motioned for him to keep talking.

"We had no choice. Mike became our new accountant. He came to me after a few months and told me he needed some assistance. He wanted to hire two new accountants. It was odd because Steve had always been able to do the work by himself. It made more sense when Mike explained he was still relatively new and wanted to get some people to assist with the day-to-day activities for a short period. The business was strong, so I agreed to let him hire two bookkeepers to help.

"I didn't know it at the time, but they were his buddies. I probably should have kept a better eye on them, but I was doing my job and assumed they were doing theirs. Steve had been with the company for nearly 20 years and never caused a problem."

Arthur was getting worked up, breathing rapidly, and perspiration appeared above his lip. I told him to slow down.

"At the end of last year when our financial statements came out, the business showed a loss. I was devastated because we had had twenty-six straight profitable years.

"Last year should have been strong. Unfortunately, although I understand the statements, I don't know where the data comes from. I couldn't tell by looking at the statement if the information was valid or had been manipulated. I had no idea where to start, so I went to Mike and asked him for his input. A few weeks later when he didn't get back to me, I approached him again.

"I finally cornered him, but all he gave me was some gobbledygook about economic cycles and fiscal imbalances. So I decided to go outside of the company and hired an accountant to examine our books. I got copies of as much of our financial information as I could without letting Mike know.

"Evelyn and I incorporated the business a few years back. We did this primarily for estate planning reasons, but we had to create a board of directors. Once every year, I have to talk to them about the company's performance, but for the most part, they stay out of the way and let us operate without interference.

"Last week, Bill Paxson, the chairman, came to see me. It's the first time he's ever been in my office. He placed three letters Mike had written to him over the past year on my desk. I read them and couldn't believe what they said. They accused me of theft—imagine.

"Bill suggested my nephew had provided him with proof I had stolen money from the company, but he never showed me anything. I was fired and walked out the door with a security guard. It was humiliating. Mike was in his office. Didn't have the decency to get up and say something."

I leaned back in my chair to take in the whole story. Arthur reached forward to hand me a manila envelope. I dumped out the contents.

He shook his head. "Now, they're suing me."

It was a civil complaint filed in Pennsylvania State Court. I scanned the document quickly. There were twelve pages of neatly typed, numbered paragraphs making allegations against Arthur for stealing money and mismanagement of corporate assets, and seeking to reclaim the stock Arthur held.

I turned to the last page, where a person verifies the accuracy of the claims. It was signed by Michael Vorat, President of Spinelli Industries.

"Mike Vorat is president?" I asked incredulously.

"Dan, the little weasel says I'm a thief and gets me fired. He's trying to steal my company. Somehow he has the backing of the board of directors and I'm on the outside looking in." Arthur's eyes were open wide and unblinking. "Can you help me?"

I put the document on my desk and picked up a picture of Charley. I held the frame for a moment before handing it to Arthur.

"We've been friends for a long time now," I said. "You treated my family like it's your own. I never could imagine you stealing from your company. Your nephew sounds like a piece of trash. There's nothing more I want to do than help you."

He smiled and appeared to relax a little as he leaned forward. "What do we need to do?"

"We have to answer their complaint by going through it paragraph by paragraph and saying what is accurate and what is untrue. You need to get me every document you can to assist me in deciphering what happened. With scum like this, I think we need to get aggressive. Are you ready to fight for your company?"

Arthur inched a little closer and locked his eyes with mine. In a hoarse whisper, he calmly replied, "Absolutely—with everything I have."

MAY, TWELVE YEARS AGO

CHAPTER 10

Sue, our realtor, adjusted her hair in the rear-view mirror, her perkiness withered by our inability to find the right house. She turned to Jill in the passenger seat of her mammoth Cadillac. "Let's talk again about what you're looking for."

We had toured seven houses that day. Combined with the other twenty-two we had viewed in prior weeks, we were already through most of the backlog in Squirrel Hill.

Jill displayed little concern. "We've talked about it before. We want something old—with charm—that we can grow into. It should be sprawling so when we start having kids, it can keep up with us."

Sue smiled. The two had spent a lot of time together in the preceding weeks, and she, although tired and somewhat frustrated, had developed a fondness for Jill. Whatever her motivation, she wanted us to find the right house. We'd recently met, yet we had shared with her our vision for the future and our plan to have four kids.

"Are you sure you don't want to see anything smaller?"

I leaned forward from the back seat of the car. "We've been living in our apartment for two years since we got married. We know where we want to be, so why buy a starter home and have to trade up in three years?"

Sue pulled the car over to the curb and said, "This house isn't listed yet. I just got a call—it's about to go on the market. It's one of the old Victorians, which are hard to find. It's three floors and has eight bedrooms. I don't know anything else."

We stepped out of the car and Jill smiled as she examined the house. 'What street is this?"

"Shady Elm. Lots of trees and families—a prime location."

With her hand above her eyes shielding the sun, Jill stood on the sidewalk examining the house. A cool breeze calmly blew her hair, but she remained motionless. She appeared small compared to the sheer size of the house. Her eyes were fixed on the wooden porch running the entire width of the house. Slowly walking up the steps, she turned to me. "This is our house. This is where our kids will grow up."

I stared at her dumbfounded, not understanding how she could be so sure before she had seen the inside of the house. I wanted to match Jill's enthusiasm, but when we opened the door, I was overcome by the strong odor of cat pee.

Jill paused in the entryway in front of the wooden staircase heading upstairs. I stood behind her examining the bare quality of the green shag carpeting leading into the living room. Sue read from her phone to inform us the house had been built in 1903 and was part of a group of houses one of Pittsburgh's wealthy families had utilized as a compound. She pointed out the servant staircase right off of the kitchen.

"Unfortunately, we don't have any staff," I joked as we walked toward the back of the house.

The dilapidated kitchen smelled of rotting garbage, and we noticed the facings of the cabinets separating from the wood bases. The linoleum floor had yellowed and was peeling away from the sub-floor. Jill reached over the sink to turn on the water, and brown sludge spewed from the faucet.

"I'm sure it will clear if we leave it running," she said as we left the kitchen.

Upstairs, four bedrooms on the second floor surrounded an expansive landing, and we found the same setup on the third floor. Space would not be a problem with this house. Each room had a different vibrant color pattern with more natty carpet. Ants rummaged over a leftover sandwich on a plate of food abandoned on a desk in a bedroom. Two windows hung askew with rotten sashes dangling toward the ground. The door to the closet served no purpose, as it leaned against the wall, unattached to the door frame.

Sue placed her hand on Jill's shoulder when we got downstairs. "I'm so sorry. I hadn't seen this house before. I never would have let you see it if I knew what kind of shape it was in."

Jill put her hand on top of Sue's and smiled. "Did you see the woodwork throughout the house—can't you smell the charm?"

I stepped forward in between my wife and realtor. "All I can smell is cat pee and rotten food."

Jill shot me a look and guided us back through the dining and living rooms. "So much potential," she repeated three times.

I only saw peeling paint and damaged wood.

Sue dropped us in front of our apartment. We avoided our building, deciding to take a walk. Neither of us spoke as we walked through Shadyside holding hands while taking in the glorious spring afternoon. We passed a house where three boys were throwing a rubber ball and laughing as they fell to the ground. Jill stopped to lean on the black wrought iron fence surrounding their backyard and sighed. "This is what I want, a houseful of kids."

"We're trying." I put an arm around her back. "It will happen soon."

"I know, but it's not happening fast enough."

We walked farther in silence until she turned toward me. "I loved the house on Shady Elm the minute we pulled up to it. The way it sits on the hill and beckons, 'Kids, come here and play.' I love it."

I tried to hide my concerns, so Jill continued, "I know it's not in the best shape, but it's what we're looking for. With a little work, it will be beautiful. Those rooms can be spectacular. Think how much our children will love the house." She dropped her chin and pouted. I took a deep breath, hoping to stand my ground, but sensing it was getting shaky.

"I'm worried about how much we would have to do—the painting, hauling, demolition, even more. I know you and I can do a lot, but it would involve an extraordinary amount of time, not to mention the money."

"We could do it together."

"I don't know."

"I'm sure my parents would help out."

"Awesome." I rolled my eyes.

"Please...."

I paused. Such a project was overwhelming. Every waking minute would be consumed by ripping up carpet, sanding, and painting. I stopped and grabbed Jill's hand. She stared intently back at me.

"Okay, let's put a bid in on it," I relented.

Her face lit up. She raised her hands, screamed, and jumped into my arms. "We're getting a house."

SEPTEMBER OF THIS YEAR

CHAPTER 11

"STAND ON THE LINE," I yell. Expecting bedlam, I'm surprised to see 12 pairs of feet standing in place. I have exchanged my khakis for my coaching attire— baseball hat, U of M T-shirt, and baggy shorts. My sunglasses mask my elation that everyone is here on time, ready to practice.

"Hey, Coach." Stephen's voice pierces the quiet. "Let's scrimmage today?"

I begin to answer but think better of it. "Let's hold the questions for now and get some work in. First we warm up." I instruct them to jog in place, followed by jumping jacks. After one minute, they are tiring.

"Come on, guys, you can't be tired yet." They breathe hard and lean forward with their hands on their knees. Conditioning will be a higher priority during practices. A voice from behind interrupts my thought.

"Excuse me, Coach," a young woman with a diminutive boy trailing, walks toward me. I motion to her that I will talk to her in a minute.

I turn to the boys. “I want you to take your soccer balls and practice juggling.” Groans emit. “The ability to control the ball will help you in all facets of the game. Learn how to do it and you will become much better players.”

Andrew approaches me to tell me he didn’t bring a ball. A tall, lanky forward with athletic ability, he has yet to develop advanced skills. He gazes blankly at me. I toss him a ball from my bag and inform the group anyone not bringing a ball will have to do twenty push-ups. Being late will mean twenty-five burpees. The boys don’t respond and return to their juggling.

I head toward the new woman, who introduces herself as Jillian Hyatt. She explains that her son, Leo, is a new member of the team. I apologize for not knowing about any newcomers and ask him if he wants to join the group. He doesn’t answer and will not take his eyes off the ground beneath him. They recently moved to Pittsburgh after her divorce. She informs me Leo has played soccer for five years, but his skill level has been lower than his peers.

“All this time playing, and he hasn’t gotten close to getting a goal,” says Jillian, rolling her eyes.

“Scoring isn’t the only thing that helps teams win. He can be a vital cog even if he never takes a shot,” I say.

Leo is a small sprite of a boy with wispy blonde hair. Jillian tells me he is ten, which would make him the youngest boy on the team. Leo will also be the smallest boy, as he appears to be three inches shorter than Charley.

“You ready to play?” I put a hand on his shoulder and guide him toward the other boys. Leo nods and steps into the drill. I inform Jillian everyone is having pizza at our house on Thursday and invite her to join us. She tells me they will bring some salad. As she walks away, I think that she will enjoy hanging out with the other soccer parents.

Three boys run by me chasing errant juggling attempts. Only a few of them can keep the ball off the ground for more than two touches. Their inability to master the drill immediately frustrates them.

I talk to them while they're attempting to keep their balls in the air. "This is difficult, gentlemen. You will not get this right away, but if you keep practicing, you'll get better. If you want to improve, you will need to try the things we are teaching at home. Every day you should play with your soccer ball and if you do, you will notice results."

I blow the whistle and tell them they have a thirty-second water break before we move onto the next part of practice. After a minute, two of them are ready and I spy a social gathering off the field where the boys are getting their water. I call to them but get no response. Sam stands ready, looking impatient. Charley joins three of his teammates, but no one else comes.

Before I do anything to deal with the wayward players, Sam runs behind the goal and gets in the middle of the group. He yells at them to get on the line. He pushes Stephen to interrupt his conversation. I shoot Sam a look of appreciation when the team lines up.

Once they are paying attention, I instruct, "Ten push-ups for failing to follow directions." There are groans until Sam drops to the ground and commands everyone to join him. He counts out the push-ups and instructs his teammates to get back in line. They comply.

I put a ball in front of them. "Here are a couple of moves you can use in the games to score goals." Their eyes are on me as I demonstrate a fake inside followed by a push with the outside of the foot. It's not pretty, but they get the idea. I also instruct them on using the bottom of their shoe to pull the top of the ball away from a defender. "Practice these moves and make sure you alternate each foot."

They continue their attempts at controlling their balls as I announce, "This season is different. Everything we do is as a team. If one person fails to do something, we all fail. When one succeeds, we all succeed. Practice is for soccer and not socializing." They keep working on the moves, but I think they're listening.

"You will get here on time, or everyone will do push-ups. We will run you hard because you are going to be the fastest, strongest, and most disciplined team out there. It begins now."

Mike yells out while trying the crossover move with his left foot, "What if we don't want to run?"

"Don't come to practice."

I sense a willingness to attempt these new moves. They aren't enjoying immediate success, but the goal is for them to try. They will hopefully improve. I blow my whistle and tell them to get ready for a scrimmage. They cheer as they put on blue and yellow pinnies to differentiate the teams.

They run like maniacs and, after fifteen minutes, return to the sideline dripping with sweat and covered with mud.

Now they look like soccer players.

Their parents wander up to the field to collect them. I remind them there will be no practice Thursday because of the pizza party at our house. We walk off and Charley is close to me on my left.

This is much better.

CHAPTER 12

"How was school?" I say, entering the family room. I know the answer before Charley opens his mouth.

"Fine" is the automatic response. His face is buried in a video game.

"Where's Mom?" I ask.

"In your bedroom," he responds without looking up.

"Thanks for the conversation." I head upstairs.

"Anytime."

I walk in while Jill is changing into jeans. "Hey, Babe, how's it going?" I ask.

"Great, how about you?"

I'm not getting much information from anyone. "Good. Are we eating at your parents' house?"

"Yup, are you ready to go?"

"Yup." The end of another meaningful conversation.

Jill's parents love to cook and most Fridays make dinner for us and Jill's brother's family. The meal ends the week without fuss or hassle. Charley loves the tradition. He believes food at his grandparents' house tastes better than at our house. He also gets to spend time with his two cousins, Laine and Christopher, which allows him to act like the big brother he never got the chance to be.

When we walk in, I immediately head to the cabinet with the tablecloths to begin setting the table. It's our unspoken agreement that in exchange for them buying and preparing dinner, we set the table and wash the dishes. Charley's job is to help out, talk with his grandparents, and make them proud. Easily, we have the better side of the deal.

I place the tablecloth while Jill retrieves plates from the cabinet. Jill's brother Robert and wife Jody walk in. "Thank god the restaurant is open," Jody yells upon entering. She heads to the table and begins to place forks.

Robert approaches me and smacks me on the back of the head. "What's new, dumbass?"

"Nothing," I respond as I try to get him in a bear hug. I am taller than Robert, but he has ten years on me and deflects my advance. He moves to the side and again slaps me on the head.

"Damn, that hurts." I grab Charley and turn him toward Robert. "Attack your uncle."

He does as instructed and charges, his head lowered like a missile, again looking to get in the middle of trouble. Laine and Christopher skip over from the kitchen door wanting to join in the fray. Laine is wearing a new spring dress and a huge smile. Christopher, smaller of stature than Charley, and with a voice remarkably similar to Elmo's, follows and asks, "What's going on here?"

"Charley, can you help set the table?" Jill interjects. "Let's avoid another melee."

"I suppose," he replies. He grabs the water jug and walks it to the sink. A brief buzz of activity fills the room as the grandparents come from upstairs.

"You guys weren't in the bedroom doing anything dirty were you?" Jody asks, shimmying her shoulders slightly.

"Not now," responds Estelle, "but perhaps after you all leave." We turn away and Robert puts his finger in his mouth giving the universal "I'm nauseous" sign.

"Ew, I've lost my appetite," Jill adds, to more laughter.

Ignoring their professed disgust, I say, "I'm still hungry, when do we eat?"

We are stuffing our faces with pasta and Caesar salad when Christopher announces he has a joke. At four years old, he has a well-developed sense of humor and comic timing. He starts in his high-pitched voice, "Two hobos are sitting 'round a campfire eating a clown." He checks to make sure we're watching.

"One hobo says to the other," he continues, "does this taste funny to you?" He drops his hands to his side, waiting for our reaction.

We've heard him tell it so many times, but we all start laughing. Not the fake laughter heard after a boss' weak attempt at humor, but true laughter because for some reason we all find the ridiculous joke funny—especially when Christopher tells it.

The kids take two helpings of food. I take three. Jill shakes her head slowly back and forth, but her mom directs me, "Go ahead, dear—we have another pot on the stove."

Robert elbows me in the side. "She always liked you better." I roll my eyes.

Estelle glances at her family sitting around the table. "We love all of you."

Jody barely suppresses a burp, which marks the end to the meal. The kids bolt from the table and head upstairs to play. Jill stands to clear the table, but Russell motions for her to wait. "I have something I want to discuss."

He pushes his chair away from the table. "You know how much we love spending time with both of your families. We thought it would be fun if we could all go away together. So, as a present, your mom and I want to take everyone to Disney World, our treat."

"You're so generous." Jody places a hand on Estelle's arm. "They have amazing rides." She turns to Jill and me and asks, "You guys going to babysit?"

I shake my head and laugh. "Our kid can ride with us. You have a swell time in Kiddieland with yours."

Jody glares.

Jill interjects, "You know the grandparents will watch your kids if you ask them. You'll have more than enough time for the coasters." She turns to her dad. "When are we going?"

"We're thinking next spring. Let's check our schedules, and I will make the arrangements."

"Fantastic," I say, not quite knowing what to say in response to such generosity. Everyone else offers their thanks. We quickly scoop up the dishes and wash the pots and pans. The kids return. Jill motions them to sit. "Guys, BB has some news for you."

Laine runs to her grandfather and jumps on his lap. "What is it?" Christopher tugs on his leg, so he can also climb aboard. Charley leans over from behind. Russell smiles as he always does when his three grandchildren are so close. He informs them of the trip.

The three kids scream and begin running laps from the kitchen into the dining room. They chant, "We're going to Disney World. We're going to Disney World."

JANUARY, ELEVEN YEARS AGO

CHAPTER 13

THE CRISP LETTUCE GLISTENED in the spinner. I stood at the counter cutting carrots and celery. Small bubbles formed at the edges of the water in the pot. I was ready to add the noodles. Jill sat on the couch reading a magazine. "How's it looking, Honey?" she asked.

"The salad's in the bowl. The mac and cheese will be done soon. Have you picked out a movie yet?"

"I found one on the Cuban missile crisis starting in five minutes."

"I think I can make it," I said while bringing over the salad and dressing to her on the couch. Jill placed them on the ottoman we used as a table when we watched movies. As she leaned forward, Jill groaned and grabbed at her stomach.

"Another contraction?" I asked, almost in passing. Jill had been having contractions for weeks and the baby seemingly was no closer to arriving.

"This preterm labor is getting old."

"It's not so preterm at this point," I responded. "You're due in ten days."

"Can't wait to meet the little guy—I still say it's a boy."

"I'm betting on a girl, but you know it would have been easy to find out."

"That would have taken the fun out of it."

"True, but at least we could have finished the nursery by now."

I walked back into the kitchen and put the milk, butter, and cheese into the pot to mix with the noodles. In less than a minute, the macaroni was ready. I brought the dish to Jill, who was lying on her side on the couch. Jill's belly created a noticeable bulge in her shirt and shorts. She rolled over to get to her feet.

"My stomach hurts. I think I need to go." I helped her up and watched her waddle toward the bathroom with her hands locked together under her stomach.

She returned two minutes later to report a wasted effort. We scooped the food onto our plates and turned up the volume. Jill took a bite and remarked, "You have become such a fine cook. Mr. Kraft should thank you for keeping the company in business."

The movie began with planes hurtling toward an unknown destination. Jill groaned before we had a chance to find out where they were headed. "My stomach hurts, I think I may have eaten something bad."

"Sweetheart, do you think this might be something else?"

"No, I'm just feeling funky."

We tried to return to the movie, but Jill rolled on her side and moaned, "Oh god, another sharp pain." I stood and demanded we go to the hospital. Jill began to protest but was hit with another contraction. Her face clenched in pain, she struggled to her feet.

"Intense," she said, grabbing me for support. "We should get checked out."

We walked toward the front hall where we had placed her bag. I grabbed it, and when I turned back to her, Jill was on her knees. Her head rested on the floor in front of her.

I ran to her side. "What is it, baby?"

"I can't get up."

Stunned, I begged, "Let's get to the hospital."

Jill couldn't raise her head. "No, it's time."

Momentarily I was frozen, terrified by overwhelming feelings of impotence and dread. Jill's guttural moan snapped me back to reality. I pulled my flip phone out of my pocket and dialed 911. I said to Jill, sounding more confident than I felt, "I'm calling an ambulance and have to grab a couple of things. I'll be back in less than a minute. Don't move."

"Not an issue," Jill groaned as she writhed on carpet.

I had sheets, towels, and blankets in my hand and was talking to 911 when I returned to Jill, who was lying on the floor immediately beneath our wooden steps.

"Please get someone here as soon as possible. She's in labor. Help us."

I stood over Jill and placed sheets around her. Her face had lost all color and signaled her terror.

"Don't worry, 911's on the phone, and Jessie'll help us," I said, trying to find anything useful to say.

Sweat covered Jill's face as she raised her hips, so I could gently take off her shorts and underwear. I inspected between her legs and reported, "I need you here. We're about to have a baby." A small thatch of brown hair appeared as the baby was beginning to crown.

"Thank god we went to Lamaze," I muttered, knowing the irony because we had missed most of the classes and had not paid attention during the ones we attended.

Jill was lying on her back with her legs spread. Her eyes alternated between shut tight and wide-open staring at the ceiling. Her breath was labored but controlled.

"The baby's sliding out on its own. The whole head is out. How are you?"

"Just peachy. How the hell do you think?" Jill grunted back. I took her question as rhetorical and focused on the task at hand. We avoided more small talk.

Jill began to breathe in staccato fashion and the baby continued to ease its way out. I guided its head, but did not need to do much to assist. Within two minutes the baby was all the way out, and I was holding him. The only thing still connected was the umbilical cord.

I used the towels to wipe off the baby and gently cleaned out its nose and mouth. His brief wail told me he was breathing. I cut the cord and tied it off as Jessie instructed.

Jessie informed me to tell Jill she could deliver the placenta. After a few pushes, Jill had completed the task.

Jill, covered in sweat and exhausted, rested next to me. I cradled our new baby. "It's a boy, Babe, it's a boy." I placed him on Jill's chest, and she gently stroked him.

As we admired our son, the front door opened and two tall paramedics rushed in. They surveyed the scene, and one exclaimed, "I guess we're not delivering any babies today. Is everyone okay?" They both got on their knees. One checked out Jill, while the other examined the baby.

"This will be an amazing story to tell your friends," one of the paramedics said. "Mom and son appear to be fine, but we should get you to the hospital." Before we had a chance to agree, Jill's mother, quickly followed by her dad, burst through the front door.

Estelle glanced around the room, unable to process the scene before her. "We saw the ambulance," Jill's mom blurted out. "Is everything okay?"

I slowly walked toward them. "Estelle, Russell, are you ready for some big news?" I asked.

Jill's dad gently took the baby, now wrapped in a blue blanket. Confusion covered his face. "What happened?"

"Jill said she didn't like hospitals, so we decided to have him here," I joked. "Not the best idea."

Russell examined the baby's eyes and quickly checked his breathing and heart rate, despite having forbidden himself to play doctor with his grandchildren. Only under these unusual circumstances was he willing to make an exception; Russell allowed himself this one opportunity to check out the baby in his role as a doctor.

"He appears to be fine, but I think baby and Jill need to go to Magee to get examined properly," Jill's dad said.

"Jill deserves her night in the hospital to rest," Estelle said, beaming at her new grandson. "Does he have a name?"

Jill caught my eye. We had known what names we would give to the baby if it was a boy or a girl. Jill nodded, signaling she wanted me to tell her parents.

I handed the baby back to Russell. "I would like you to meet your grandson, Charley."

The door to the house was open. Sunlight streamed through the doorway and reflected off the floor. We stood in the entranceway as Jill held Charley. I poured over the sheath of papers in my hands.

Nick Costello, our insurance agent, waited as I concentrated. We had talked with him many times before, but this was the first time we had met.

"I wanted to bring the check over personally," Nick said, "and get a chance to congratulate you. Nothing's typical about what happened here."

I shuffled my feet and shook my head. "Next time we do it the traditional way."

"Smart idea. The floors are beautiful," he said, handing me a check.

Charley's birth by the stairs had ruined the carpet. We had known hardwood lurked underneath but hadn't gotten around to removing the carpet.

"We never liked the carpet anyway," Jill said.

"You got the insurance company to pay for the floors. Congratulations on all your good fortune. Charley's beautiful."

"Thank you so much for everything," Jill said as she closed the door behind Nick.

"I think Charley's ready to eat." She walked toward the family room and her favorite place to feed Charley.

SEPTEMBER OF THIS YEAR

CHAPTER 14

People mill around our house carrying food and drink. The smell of pizza and beer wafts into the kitchen where I'm standing with Pete and Paul. They are rebuffing my attempts to engage them in a discussion about the benefits of helping to coach the boys' soccer team. Up to this point, they have been much more concerned with analyzing the qualities of the brews they hold.

"Guys, I think we can have a strong group," I explain. "They need a little guidance."

"One more of these and I will need a little guidance," retorts Pete. He shakes his long hair and takes another sip out of his bottle. "You know Liza already commanded I help out. I'm in. It should be fun playing with the kids."

"Not looking for you to play with them. You played soccer in college. They need instruction," I interject.

"Not a problem. I expect beer in return."

"Of course," I say, relieved there will be at least some assistance. I turn to Paul, the father of Eli, our goalkeeper. "How about you? You want to help out?"

Paul genuflects in my direction. "I will also be a willing assistant. If I get to hang out with Pete, maybe some of his cool will rub off on me." Paul winks at Pete.

"Dude," Pete says back, "we will make this the coolest team, ever."

If being on this soccer team turns out to be cool, I think to myself, I should be considered for coach of the year. They were destroyed in most games last season, and no one wanted to coach them. The only reason they have one is because the coach's wife volunteered him. We are a long way from cool.

"Hey, Paul, think we should go out back and light one up?" Pete says, pointing to the back door.

"Absolutely," Paul responds as he skips toward the door. I wonder how much assistance I will be getting and what condition they will be in when we have practices.

Pete and Paul leave through the back door. My thoughts are interrupted by a tap on my shoulder. "Hey, buddy," I hear from behind me. I turn to see Vic Himmer out of his customary plaid sports coat and wide tie, and wearing a too-tight green t-shirt and baseball hat with a beer logo. Vic wishes he was twenty-five and is unwilling to make any concessions to time. A huge smile engulfs his face, and I know I will soon be asked a favor.

"So nice to see you," I say reflexively. "Did you get any pizza?"

"Only one piece, I need to make sure my belly don't lap over my belt." He chuckles, steps back and drops his hands to his side. Probably should have avoided the first piece then, I think.

"You're looking pretty good. I smile and hope he takes it as a compliment. Vic blushes but continues the conversation. "How have practices been going?"

I try not to roll my eyes. "The last practice certainly went a little smoother than the first. Hopefully we can expect to see improvement from last year."

"Hunter has been practicing a lot."

"Great," I say.

His son is tall and a natural athlete. He was the leading pitcher last season for his Little League squad and a key contributor on the school's basketball team. With soccer, he has more difficulties. He can move the ball with his right foot but has not learned any skills with his left. He revolts at the concept of playing defense and spent much of last season watching the backs of his opponents as they dribbled toward his team's goal.

"How are you going to split playing time?" Vic continues.

"What do you mean?" I answer back.

"Last year, they all played about the same amount, and I thought that was fair."

"Can't say I've thought about it much, but I would be happy to talk about it after we've had a few games," I deflect.

"It's a plan. I think I need to get some beer."

I watch as Vic saunters away. It took some nerve to suggest playing time for all the kids should be split evenly. Of course, this likely would benefit his son. His kid was the worst one on the team and didn't make up for it by hustling.

Hunter played on the same basketball team as Charley. It was coached by another father who did an excellent job of developing the kids' skills. Charley, although always hustling and improving at basketball, was not one of the more talented players on the team. Charley sat an awful lot during the games, while Hunter was on the floor for the majority of the time. Jill and I never had a problem with the breakdown of court time although on a few occasions we heard Vic mouthing off that Hunter should play more.

The playing time issue had been knocking around my head, and I was leaning toward letting those with the best attitude and aptitude play more. I want all the players to get their fair share of opportunity to improve, but I also think the team suffers when the players with positive attitudes have to sit in favor of others. I hadn't thought of how a parent might react if their kid suddenly was sitting more. Most parents were realistic about their kid's abilities, but some, like Vic, assumed their kid was a star at every sport.

Jillian Hyatt stops me before I have a chance to get outside. She thanks me for getting Leo comfortable with the team. I tell her this is a close team and to be prepared to be dragged to lots of functions. This appears to make her happy, which is quickly replaced by a hint of worry.

"Leo has played soccer before, but it's never been competitive. He's tiny, and I hope the boys don't tease him," she says.

"Not a problem. I will make sure he's fine. I don't know if you saw my son Charley, but he's not tall either. Charley's decent. I watched Leo. He has skills."

"He's always been shy because he's so small. I think playing on this team could help him."

"I agree. All I ask is the players come to practice ready to play. I think Leo will be fine."

"Thanks. That helps." Jillian is grabbed by one of the moms and taken to the corner of the kitchen where they are in a group talking. She waves as she walks away.

I walk into the backyard. It's one of those September evenings begging for playing outside. Coolness hangs in the air, which feels crisp. The leaves on the trees are starting to show the first hints of red.

"Get him!" "Stop him!" Shouts come from the open grass area in our yard. The boys have organized a pick-up soccer game. They run with enthusiasm chasing the ball. They have divided into shirts and skins. A pile of clothes is strewn haphazardly behind one of the goals.

The twelve members of the team have been joined by three of their siblings. They have assigned positions and are playing as if the game has meaning. The kids are running around with purpose and are attempting to make assaults on the other team's goal.

I enjoy watching the boys work up a lather. I wonder why they don't go outside and form their own games more often. Is there any reason why virtually every sport the kids play has to be organized by adults? They get more out of their own games and probably learn more on their own than when an adult tries to cram it down their throats.

The kids continue their game for ten minutes. I'm fascinated by their energy and enthusiasm. I also notice some players have skills that hadn't been so evident before. Yes, I knew Charley could dribble and run, but Hunter now has a strong leg and Ricardo is a bull on defense. Dylan has developed a knack for scoring and Carter was in the right place all the time.

Jacob nearly makes a goal after challenging three defenders, who offer a congratulatory rub of his head and smack on his back. Valerie Bonet interrupts the game to inform the boys cookies and brownies are in the family room. She tells them to grab some and come back quickly because there will be a surprise waiting for them.

The stampede of kids, who have decided chocolate is more alluring than scoring goals, nearly tramples me as I warn them to avoid getting crumbs on the floor.

A few minutes later, they return with handfuls of brownies and cookies. The parents straggle out of the house, followed by Valerie carrying a brown box. She places it at my feet and clears her throat as the parents make a semi-circle around the team.

Valerie cups her hands around her mouth. “We have a little announcement and something for the boys we think they will like.”

The kids murmur with excitement. I don’t know what’s in the box yet either.

“Last year,” she begins, “may not have been the kids’ best year, but we love the effort they all gave.” Light applause floats up from the group.

“You’ll remember the uniforms the kids wore last season were, how do I say, problematic.”

The parents snicker, while the boys roll their eyes. Last year, they wore plain white T-shirts with numbers made out of electrical tape on their backs. Each game there were different-colored socks and mismatched shorts as nobody ever decided what the team colors were. I’m not much of a believer in the “clothes make the man” kind of thinking, but our kids’ outfits were ridiculous. The lack of real uniforms likely contributed to their poor play and attitude. None of the boys complained, but as coach and parent, I wanted something a little better for them.

Valerie continues, “The soccer moms decided this year the boys needed a little styling.” A few hoots echo from the crowd.

“So Sally and I went out and picked up some new uniforms.”

She opens the box and pulls out the first jersey, holding it over her head. It’s black with red piping, and in white letters the team name “Pumas” is written in script. I see the number “1” on the shoulder. She flips it around and the name “Charley” appears on the back. I chuckle to myself because Charley has worn jersey number 1 on virtually every team he has ever played.

I love they have decided to put first names on the jerseys. The boys are only eleven and don’t need to be referred to by their last names quite yet.

Valerie takes the jersey and tosses it to Charley. He is beaming and puts it on immediately. Of course, it should be two sizes smaller, but he doesn't care.

The shirts start flying toward the kids. "Ricardo, Sam, Andrew, Carter, Stephen, Nate, Lance, Jacob, Leo, Dylan, Eli, and Hunter," Valerie announces as she tosses them toward their intended recipients.

The boys put on their jerseys and huddle in a group. Valerie tells the parents she will give them the socks and shorts later, so they aren't lost before the first game.

FEBRUARY, TWO YEARS AGO

CHAPTER 15

JANA AND I WERE camped on the floor of one of the bigger conference rooms in my office, surrounded by boxes Arthur had delivered after he had provided us with the complaint against him.

"What can you make out of them?" I asked as she sat cross-legged on the floor with documents encircling her.

"Nothing is clear from any of this," she said, continuing to thumb through the records. "I can say Mike Vorat is not going to win any accountant of the year awards. These are a mess." She held up one stack and reported, "Some records suggest Arthur took money from the company. The problem is," she said, reaching for another pile of documents, "there is no support for those entries anywhere else. Somehow we will have to follow the cash."

I let my eyes wander over the piles of paper, overwhelmed by the thought of distilling the information in the records and trying to understand it. I changed subjects somewhat, "How is the answer coming?" We had two more weeks to respond to the complaint, and I wanted it to punch back hard.

"It's in decent shape," Jana responded. "Arthur and I have been meeting a lot to make sure we have an understanding of the facts. I will have a draft of it on your desk by tomorrow. Given what is in these records, we need to decide if Arthur should file a counterclaim against Vorat and the company. If he didn't take any money, he has been damaged, and he should demand compensation."

"Good point," I responded. I felt lucky to have Jana around to dig into all these documents and make sure we had a complete understanding of what happened at Spinelli Enterprises. Her background in finance so far has been helpful, and her willingness to do whatever was necessary for our client was going to pay dividends. "Why don't you draft a counterclaim in addition to the answer, and I can review it in the morning to see if we can make anything stick against those slime buckets."

Jana raised her hand to her head and brought it forward in a mock salute. "I will do as you say, captain," she said, almost smiling.

SEPTEMBER OF THIS YEAR

CHAPTER 16

THE FRONT DOOR TO the house flies open. My in-laws enter. "We have news," Estelle shouts, extending the last word for emphasis.

Charley runs to them holding an apple. "Hey Momo, hey BB, what's up?" They walk to the kitchen where Jill is preparing dinner and I'm packing Charley's lunch.

Three years ago, I probably would have made a comment about their failure to give us prior warning before showing up at the house, but I say nothing. Estelle and Russell are family, and they are welcome at our house anytime. There have been so many times they have saved our butts and gotten Charley off the school bus or taken him to piano lessons, I can't count them. Letting themselves into our house with their own key is a minor breach considering there is usually something positive stemming from their visits.

Russell plops into a chair at the round kitchen table. Charley jumps on his lap, and they attack each other. Estelle approaches the stove as Jill turns chicken in a saucepan. "You probably should add some more oregano," she suggests, while shaking a little on the sautéing chicken.

"I have this under control, Mom," responds Jill, grabbing the spice jar out of her mother's hand.

"What's this news you were yelling about when you came in?" I ask.

"Let me tell you," says Russell as he scoops up Charley and places him on the floor.

"Remember the trip to Disney World? Through work, there was a deal that lets us get cheap airline tickets. We will have to book this week. Is April available for everyone?"

"It shouldn't be a problem with me," I say. "The Spinelli case is scheduled for early November. I don't have anything I can't move before next summer."

"Works for me. Fine for him, as long as it's during spring break from school" says Jill, pointing a finger at Charley.

"I'm free," adds Charley, tugging on his grandfather's shirt.

"Good," Russell responds. "I was worried your busy schedule might prevent you from traveling."

"Nope," Charley says, beaming, "I've cleared my calendar."

Everyone laughs as Jill brings over a piping platter of chicken and eggplant. She turns towards her parents. "You staying for dinner?"

"Thought you'd never ask," Estelle says as she pulls a chair out from the table.

CHAPTER 17

IT'S 7:30 IN THE morning when my sleep is again disturbed by the weight of Charley lying on my chest. My eyes slowly open trying to shake off the wooziness. Two blue eyes stare back at me. The face is smiling.

"Can I help you?" I get no response.

I push Charley off me, so he is between his mother and me. Jill rolls over and laughs.

She gasps. "You're dressed for your soccer game." Charley has on his new jersey and shorts, soccer socks over his shin guards, and is wearing his cleats. He stands on our bed and exclaims, "I am super soccer boy!" I knock him over and get on top of him. "We are five minutes into our day, and you have already violated the 'no cleats in the house rule.' I will ignore your transgression if you tell me how many goals you will get today?"

Charley squints at me and responds, "Dad, I think it will be three."

I narrow my eyes at him. "Good thing you're ready for soccer. Your game is only six hours from now."

He leaps off our bed. "I'm going to stretch now." He ducks out of the room, leaving us alone.

On the way to the game, I inform Charley he will be playing a team from Fox Chapel, the area where his mom grew up. We know nothing about how good they are, and Charley can't sit still in the backseat. "Hey, Dad, this is your first time as head coach—you excited?"

"I am," I reply. "I'm also a little nervous."

We pull up to the field. Fox Chapel is already warming up. It's a half-hour before game time, yet none of Charley's teammates have arrived. He runs to the field and steps on the well-manicured grass with the perfectly straight white lines drawn on it. He shoots me a thumbs up and begins shooting on the goal.

The field is much more impressive than the one we play on at home. The grass has no bare spots, and a small grandstand with seating for at least 500 spectators juts out from the sideline. Our field back in the city is in the middle of a public park. Before each game, we draw lines to outline the playing area. The grass is never mowed, but rather, is worn down by people who trampled it during the week. Games are often decided by crazy bounces from balls skidding off scattered potholes.

A series of banners commemorating championships won by various age-level teams for Fox Chapel hang on the surrounding fence. At our field, the only sign is one for the restroom.

Fifteen minutes before game time, the rest of our players arrive. They barely have their cleats on before the referee stops over to check them in.

On the sideline, I announce that Charley, Hunter, Sam, and Nate will start as forwards. Ricardo, Carter, and Jacob will be the defenders. Eli is the goalie. I remind the players to play their positions, not to chase, and to keep their shape. They nod, and the starting seven take their positions.

Paul and Pete, my assistant coaches, appear on the sidelines as the referee sets the ball in the middle of the field to begin. "We are here and prepared to assist, coach," Pete says briskly as he salutes. Paul giggles as he watches Pete.

"Awesome," I respond. "Can you make sure the substitutes are ready to go into the game?"

I turn my attention to the game. We have possession first. Sam touches a quick ball to Charley, who immediately makes a charge down the far sideline. Charley's ability to use his left foot is an asset, as defenders have little experience being challenged by a leftie. Charley cuts inside and powers a kick toward the middle area in front of the Fox Chapel goal. Sam is in the proper position to receive the ball, but a Fox Chapel defender extracts it by shoving Sam with a shoulder. Sam glances at the referee as he lies on the ground looking for a penalty, but the referee turns in the other direction.

Fox Chapel moves down the field with two precise passes and steers the ball across the field toward a breaking forward. The Fox Chapel player and Carter race to get it. Carter gets there first but loses possession when the other team's player yanks at his jersey. On the ground, Carter is helpless, and the Fox Chapel forward pushes the ball toward our goal. Ricardo steps up to try to cover the attack, and another Fox Chapel player moves into the area Ricardo has vacated. A deft pass across the middle of the field goes directly to the Fox Chapel player, who easily redirects the ball into the goal.

The Fox Chapel players celebrate as they run back to their side. I yell to our team to keep pressing. I wave my arms at the referee and scream, "They're fouling our guys!" The ref ignores me.

Lance goes into the game for Nate and on the ensuing play in, he trips, allowing Fox Chapel to take control. Carter steps up to kick the ball away from the Fox Chapel player, but their guy pulls it back, causing Carter to lose his balance. The player has a clear run until Ricardo again moves forward to stop the advance. Once Ricardo commits, the Fox Chapel player passes to his left and breaks to the goal. His teammate receives the ball and immediately kicks it back. The original player receives the pass and with a slight feint easily slips it past Eli.

The score is already 2-0 and the game is less than three minutes old. Ricardo screams at Carter about falling down, and Carter responds by getting in Ricardo's face and telling him to shut up. They glare at each other until the referee gets in between them and points to our side of the field, where they are supposed to be lining up.

Paul appears besides me and says, "Dude, not a great start." I thank him for his astute observation and send in Dylan to try to get something going. For most of the rest of the half, we keep them from scoring. Charley and Sam make a couple of runs but can't make a pass to any of their teammates.

With less than one minute remaining before halftime, Fox Chapel has a throw-in about ten feet down the sideline from where I stand. Our boys are in position to defend, but as their player reaches the ball over his head for a throw-in, a Fox Chapel player runs behind Ricardo. The Fox Chapel player subtly pushes Ricardo in the back, causing Ricardo to lose his balance. He drifts downfield and receives the throw-in, taking it in perfect position to run toward our goal. The player rams a hard shot under Eli, who cannot stop it as he dives to his right.

The player who scored runs to Ricardo as he is getting up. He leans over him, saying something I can't hear. Visibly enraged, Ricardo hops to his feet and races after the player. He jumps on his back, and they tumble to the ground. Ricardo reaches back to punch the other player, but the referee yanks Ricardo off and escorts him to the sideline. Ricardo's face is crimson, and he kicks a soccer bag lying near the bench.

The referee pulls a red card out of his breast pocket and waves it in the air to inform he has kicked Ricardo out of the game. The referee turns to the middle of the field and blows his whistle three times to signal halftime.

I run over to Ricardo, yelling to Paul and Pete to talk to the other boys. I put both of my hands on Ricardo's shoulders, but he stares straight down at the ground. "What happened?" Ricardo wipes at his nose and says, "He called me a 'spic.' Nobody's ever talked to me like that before."

Ricardo was born in Guatemala and had been adopted by Valerie and her husband when he was a baby. I doubt he has ever been insulted about his heritage before. In Charley's group, they are friends first and don't make an issue of someone's skin color.

I'm steaming now. "Ricardo, I understand now why you reacted the way you did. I'm going to talk to the referee about this." I approach him, reminding myself to keep my composure. "Do you realize the Fox Chapel player called my player a 'spic'?"

The ref doesn't look at me. "I didn't hear anything," he replies. "All I saw was your guy jump on his back. That's why he got a red card. "

"I get that. I take it you didn't see them pushing my players all over the field either?"

"Your boys seem to shy away from contact."

"Complete garbage, and you know it. Why don't you call the game the same for both sides?"

"I call them as I see them, Coach."

I jog down the sideline to the Fox Chapel coach, a tall, younger man with the cocky smile of a former high school athlete, who is standing next to the player who had allegedly taunted Ricardo. "Do you know what happened out there?"

"My guy tells me he didn't do anything and your player attacked him." I attempt to get the eye of the player, but he won't meet my gaze. "No, your forward called my player 'a spic.' It's crap. Take him out of the game."

The player, whose jersey identifies him as "Mahon," turns toward his coach and pleads, "I didn't say anything, really." He places his hands at his sides. "There you have it," Fox Chapel's coach says as he examines his clipboard. "He didn't do anything. We're ready to start the second half. I hope your team gets its act together."

Enraged, I turn around to head back to our bench. The last Fox Chapel player catches my eye as I pass him and whispers, "I was right next to him on the field. He called him *that name*." The player walks toward his teammates. I notice his name on the back of his jersey, and say, "Thanks, Harvin."

Our team is in a state of disarray. They're mad they are losing and apoplectic that Ricardo has been kicked out of the game. I send the starters back on the field, but it's obvious they're not ready to play. Fox Chapel drives the ball over our defense men to create a rush. Eli never leaves the goal as the ball rolls toward him. The Fox Chapel player outruns Carter to the ball. He beats Eli with a hard shot to the right side of the goal. It's now 4-0.

Our players hang their heads and kick at the dirt when they return to the center line. For the rest of the half, they barely put up a challenge, letting Fox Chapel control the ball. The score is 8-0 when the referee blows the whistle to end the game. The boys shuffle off the field dejected and beaten.

I tell the team to meet the other team at the center line to shake their hands. Pete reminds them to thank the referees. Carter responds, "But the refs sucked."

I say to the entire team, "Not the point. You shake the ref's hand no matter what."

The boys walk in a line to congratulate the Fox Chapel players. They smack hands with their opponents and mumble, "Good game." When they get to Mahon, every player stares him straight in the eyes, lowers his hand to reject contact, and withholds any congratulatory words. I admire the group's intelligent and sportsmanlike response formed so quickly.

I call the players over for a talk. They suck oranges and carry water bottles when we form in a group in a nearby section of grass.

"We got our butts kicked," volunteers Nate.

Dylan throws a cleat toward his bag in disgust. "No duh."

"Listen," I interrupt before more complaints get aired. "It's my turn to speak. I agree, we didn't play well, but there were positives. I saw some solid defensive movement when you played together. You also made a couple of strong runs at their goal. But I wanted to talk about something—you gave up in the second half and I don't like that. I don't care what the score is, you play to the final whistle. If one of you decides to take it easy, the whole team suffers." I stop for a moment. They are unhappy, but paying attention.

"By the way," I continue, "what that Mahon kid did was outrageous. I liked how you handled it after the game. You didn't say anything or cause any problems, but you let him know you have Ricardo's back. In the future, I think the best way to handle it is on the field. If anybody ever challenges one of your teammates again, what are you going to do?"

"Crush them," yells Sam.

We cheer. "Put your hands in, gentlemen." I say. "Who are we on three?—one, two three." The team screams, "Pumas!"

Our group disperses and I turn to find a mass of parents wanting an audience. They are agitated. "What happened at the end of the first half?" Vic Himmer demands.

I wave him off. "We can discuss this later." I try to move away but more questions are thrown at me. I again ignore the questions. Vic stands in front of me, essentially blocking my path of egress. He puts a hand on my shoulder. "I think we have a right to know what happened."

I shove his hand off of me and shake my head. "You don't. The boys handled it on the field. We are done."

Vic looks to the other parents for support, but they aren't finding it necessary to push me for an answer. They turn to leave.

As we are walking across the field, I catch the eye of Valerie Bonet who is walking with Ricardo. I point at an empty expanse and mouth, "We need to talk."

She nods and walks towards the grassy area.

CHAPTER 18

THE SMELL OF CHINESE food overwhelms the conference room. Jana squats on the floor sorting documents, while Arthur and I huddle at the table finishing our lunches. We have spent the past three hours in intense trial preparation and likely will be there for at least three more. Arthur sits straight in his chair with a paper napkin folded neatly on his lap. He chuckles when Jana mutters, "Everyone on the other side of this case is a buffoon."

Arthur arrived this morning with the understanding that trial, which was scheduled to commence in less than one month, was inevitable. We discussed with him his two counterclaims seeking compensation for his improper termination and for damages because Vorat had since mismanaged the company.

Carlson, Vorat's attorney, filed motions for summary judgment requesting dismissal of Arthur's claims. Carlson argued to the court there was no evidence his clients had done anything wrong. Judge Maruk almost laughed at Carlson and said, while holding up Jana's brief, "Counselor, I think Mr. Spinelli's attorneys have demonstrated that there are many possibilities as to how your clients may have acted improperly. You may disagree, but this is why we have juries. They're the ones who get to make these decisions." He denied their motion.

Judge Maruk also held a settlement conference where he ordered the parties to his chambers to try to resolve the case. It was a colossal waste of time. Carlson announced his clients would never settle for less than two million dollars. Arthur chuckled under his breath and said, "Not in my lifetime. Don't think they understand what happened here."

Now we are gearing up for trial, and it's time to prepare Arthur for his time in court.

"Let me talk to you about testifying," I begin. "You will be our first witness. The most important rule is to tell the truth. I want you to be one hundred percent forthright when you testify about what happened with Vorat. I don't want you to fill in gaps in your memory if you don't remember—this means if you don't remember, be upfront about it, and the same instruction applies if you don't know something.

"Testifying is about likability. You want the jury to like you. You don't have to be their best friend; they just have to believe what you're saying and trust it. You should embrace the jurors and speak right to them. They're the ones who'll be deciding who is right and who is wrong. Remember all the things you learned in first grade—sit up straight, dress nicely, make eye contact, don't mumble—they all apply here. Juries listen to what you have to say, but they also evaluate your appearance saying it, so keep it in mind.

"Keep your voice up and talk to them. They won't hear you if you mumble, and they'll think you're hiding something. Take your time and don't rush your answers."

I try to determine if Arthur is processing this. He sits up straight and keeps looking at me. I want Arthur to be able to demonstrate his intelligence and compassion to a jury. He's starting to understand it's not so simple to do without looking like he's pandering to them.

I change directions. "Now, you know after I question you, Carlson gets his chance to ask you more. That is cross-examination, and this is where juries really pay attention. Carlson will ask questions to you differently than I can. I have to ask you open-ended questions, and he can tell you what he thinks the answer should be."

Arthur squeezes his eyebrows together.

"Let me give you a bad example." I try to find a way to explain to Arthur how Vorat's lawyer's mode of inquiry will be different from mine. "If at trial I want to know your name, I ask you 'What is your name?' And you answer?"

"Arthur Spinelli."

"Excellent," I say. "Now, if Carlson wants the same information, he tells you, 'Your name is Arthur Spinelli, isn't it?' And you say?"

"Yes."

"See, he obtains the same information—your name—but he's telling you what the response should be. He's allowed to do this because he represents the other side. Cross-examination tries to force a witness to answer every question with a 'Yes.' But as a good witness, you may only respond 'Yes' if his question is one hundred percent accurate. If it isn't, and most of his questions likely won't be, you can't only say 'Yes,' you have to explain why. Got it?"

Arthur nods his head, and for the rest of the afternoon we pore over his testimony and practice possible cross-examination. He impresses Jana and me. He has the intelligence and demeanor to be an effective witness as he doesn't easily fluster and deals with difficult questions by offering explanations that sound reasonable. I am cautiously optimistic as we finish for the day, but remind myself that many witnesses I thought would succeed when we were getting ready melted under the intense pressure in front of a jury—one more reason why it's difficult to predict what happens at trial.

CHAPTER 19

"Gentlemen, let's get started," I instruct as the boys gather at the field for practice. The sunshine gleams off the grass, and they all have their soccer balls, water bottles, and shin guards. They move forward to get in line, but there is too much talking and touching.

"Ten push-ups for everyone," I say calmly. They get on the ground and attempt to push their bodies up and down. Most do two or three and then begin a series of fake thrusts with exaggerated grunts. They stand.

"Not bad, gentlemen. Are you now ready? If you are, I want your toes on the line." They do as instructed. "Here's how it will be. We have ideas on how we can improve. For this to happen, we need to practice. You need to listen. There will be push-ups if you don't. Understood?"

"Yes," about half respond. A hand shoots in the air and before I recognize it, Stephen asks, "What if we don't like push-ups?"

"It doesn't matter," I say. "Here's another rule, there are no questions, unless I ask for them. All you need to do is listen and pay attention so you can learn what we are teaching. Also, if you are late, it's twenty push-ups as a ticket to get into practice. If you don't bring a ball, it's thirty push-ups to borrow one of my soccer balls. Got it?"

Paul and Pete had been hanging behind the goal playing with a soccer ball. They high five each other when they hear the new rules. "There's a new sheriff in town," Paul yells.

After warming up, I have the boys do a series of sprints, followed by some strength exercises. They have trouble completing the tasks, but I don't care. "We are looking for effort." They lie on the ground breathing hard. "Other teams are practicing every day and working their butts off. We need to work harder. I want you to be the fastest and strongest team on the field each week."

Next, we work on the moves from the prior practice. Pete, our former college playing assistant, shows them how to fake one way and use the outside of the foot to push the ball in the opposite direction. Pete also demonstrates how to silhouette, or confuse the defender by swinging a leg completely around the ball without hitting it. These moves are designed to get the other player off-balance so the attacker can move into a better position. Despite their enthusiasm for the new concepts, the boys are quickly frustrated by their inability to master these skills immediately.

"Keep working on these. It's the only way to improve. Do them at home. The ball is your friend. Get to know it." I walk around as they attempt the new moves.

They practice for the next ten minutes, and then I have them gather for a quick talk. Two unrequested questions lead to twenty push-ups. After they regroup, I say. "All eyes on me." They listen. "Last game was not up to our standards. We don't care whether we won or lost but more about the effort you gave. In the second half you gave up. Fox Chapel may have been better than us, but we can never give up. Even if you are losing 7-0, you have to play hard.

"You have to make sure each one of you plays with full effort. You're responsible for yourself, and you have to make sure your teammates aren't taking it easy. We win as a team, and we lose as a team. Do you understand? What are we?" I yell.

"A team," comes the muted response.

"Again," I cajole. "What are we?"

"A team," they respond with a bit more enthusiasm.

"Excellent. Before we scrimmage, I want to practice something new. I call it the golden play." The boys lean in closer. "At some point there may be a time we absolutely need a goal. It's a long shot, but if necessary, we will try this. First, we will pull our goalie and make him an attacker. We will have all our players except one go to one side of the field. Do you know why?"

Ricardo blurts out, "Because they won't be able to cover all of us."

"Correct, but also, it will hopefully leave the other side open. We want them to commit to one side, and then we will shoot the ball to the other side of the field, where one of our guys is ready to receive it and attack the goalie. So we need someone who won't bobble his first touch and can carry the ball with speed toward their goal. Who do you think should be that player?"

The team talks for a minute about who has the greatest chance of scoring on such a play and throws out three different players as possibilities. Ultimately, they decide Charley would be the best person to try to score.

I'm glad they reach this conclusion because it was the same as mine. The problem is it is difficult to force my son into this position. The chances of such a play succeeding are minimal, and I wouldn't want Charley subject to ridicule and accusations that the reason he was chosen was because he's my son. With the backing of the team, it's easier to designate him.

For the next fifteen minutes they practice overloading one side of the field and trying to get the ball quickly to the other, where Charley is supposed to be waiting unobtrusively. I have Leo also try to be the lone person receiving the pass. Leo loves being Charley's understudy and stands near him whenever he can.

They don't have much success running the play and can't separate themselves from each other when they overload the one side. The long kick from one side to the other is more than most of them can handle. When one of them musters the power to get the ball across the field, Charley has difficulty gathering in the pass and moving quickly toward the goal. After stopping the drill, I inform them we will continue to work on this play other days.

For the rest of the practice we have a scrimmage, with half of the team donning red pinnies and the others wearing blue. Ricardo and Nate begin by allowing a ball to get by them because they were talking, so I make everyone do push-ups. "When one of you screws up," I challenge, "you all screw up. This might be a practice game, but you still need to take it seriously and work hard."

The scrimmage picks up in intensity. Ricardo and Nate get frustrated when Jacob works the ball between them and scores. "Talk to each other," I instruct as they attempt to figure out why neither player had covered the attacker.

Play ends with Charley making a crossing pass from the sideline, catching Sam in full stride on the right side, and then Sam lofting the ball into the corner of the goal. I end practice on this positive note.

Andrew's mom, Cherie, saunters over. Her huge glasses give her a bug-like appearance. "Solid effort. The boys are improving. Was Andrew playing well?"

"Everyone was working. I like that," I say as I pick up the soccer bag and begin walking with Charley to our car. Pete and Paul walk a few feet in front of us. Eli and Sam are kicking balls in the general direction of the parking lot.

I hear Pete say to Paul, "Not a bad practice. Like the push-up idea."

"Absolutely," Paul responds. "Glad we aren't the ones in charge."

In the car, Charley takes his position in the backseat. He's smiling while I try to find a song on the radio we both could listen to. "I liked practice today," he offers to no one in particular.

"Why?" I ask, looking for reinforcement.

"I don't know. I like learning new skills and playing soccer. Sam and I decided we would try to get everyone to play and not mess around. We talked at school."

"Who talked?"

"I did with Sam. Then we talked to everybody else. We said let's listen during practice."

I make a left turn out of Schenley Park. "Thanks, Charley. I think it worked."

APRIL, EIGHT YEARS AGO

CHAPTER 20

I SAT AT THE KITCHEN table alone. Nobody else was in the house. I was lost in thought staring at the window into the backyard. I knew I should be doing work or cleaning the house—something constructive—but I was stuck to the chair, where I had been for the past hour. Weariness and gloom permeated my mood, weighing me down.

Jill would be coming home with Charley any minute, and I dreaded it. Was there any way we could say what we needed to say and not start arguing again? Doubt and shame hung over me as I pondered a plan to find somewhere else to live. I was stuck because if I left, I lost everything I had, and if I stayed, Jill would resent me. Charley would be punished under either scenario.

The door slam in the front of the house did nothing to brighten my mood. I couldn't decide if this was the normal sound of the door closing or perhaps a little louder, for emphasis. I anticipated Jill's hostility as I heard her approaching footsteps.

I stood from the chair and wiped the counter to give the impression I was doing something. Jill entered the kitchen holding Charley's hand with one hand and what appeared to be a doggie bag in the other. Charley wore his standard overalls and a red T-shirt. His Velcro shoes stuck out slightly from the bottom of his pants. Ketchup remnants crusted the side of his mouth.

"Come over here, big guy," I said. Charley dawdled over to me, and I picked him up. I kept him between Jill and me. "How was everything?"

"Fine." She didn't bother to turn toward me as she placed the bag in the refrigerator. Charley rested his head on my shoulder. I wanted to be anywhere else, but I also needed to break the iciness.

"We should talk," I said.

"Go ahead, I'm listening."

"Awesome. I was hoping to actually have a conversation." Bad choice of words, and I knew it.

"Okay, let's have a conversation. You've been an ass and I don't like it."

Charley jumped out of my arms. "Mommy, can I eat something?"

"Sure, baby, I will get it for you," Jill said while walking back toward the refrigerator. I fumed—Jill got her dig in, and then used Charley to distract the conversation.

"Do you want to do this in front of him?" Jill pointed to Charley while putting some vegetables on a plate, which she placed on the table. Charley jumped into the chair and began to eat.

"Well, I don't know when we should do it. You never seem to want to talk to me," I responded once Jill returned her attention to me.

"Go ahead, say what you want."

"I don't know what to say. You're always so mad at me."

"You're always so mad at me," she retorted, not looking anywhere in my vicinity.

"I want us to be close again. Charley's now two, and we haven't talked about anything other than him for months."

"Sure, we have. I ask you about your cases all the time. You never ask me about my work."

"Yes, I do," I said meekly, knowing I had little idea what was happening to her outside of the house.

"Listen, I have to get Charley from daycare every day. I get him his meals and wash all the clothes. I'm constantly moving. You're sitting."

I paused. We were edging close to our rabbit holes.

"You never think I do anything of value. I'm so tired of this crap. You want to be recognized for everything you do, but you don't give me any credit for anything I do." My voice was getting louder.

"Can't you quiet down? Charley doesn't need to hear you yelling at me again."

"I'm not yelling. I'm trying to talk to you."

"You don't talk, you lecture. It's not just about you anymore. You have to give some."

"That's garbage," I responded. My temper was starting to get ahold of me. "You think you do everything around here and can't show appreciation for what I do. You're not so perfect."

"You suck," Jill moaned as she started to cry. "I don't want to talk to you. You're making things worse."

Charley was done eating his snack. Jill picked up his plate and placed it in the sink. She walked over to Charley and put on her best happy face. "Do you want to go for a walk to the park?"

Charley nodded, and they headed for the door. "Charley," Jill said, "your dad doesn't want to come with us now. He'll do his own thing again."

I heard the door close. My anger seethed inside of me. I picked up the book resting on the table and in a fit fired it in the direction of the window over the sink. The sound of shattering glass filled the room.

The remaining pieces dangled in the sash. I hung my head in embarrassment.

"I hope none of our neighbors saw this," Jill said standing in front of the jagged hole in the glass. "It can be fixed."

Jill had come back from the park in a conciliatory mood. My shame had not dissipated by the time she returned. Jill actually laughed when I showed her the window and became empathetic when she realized she had, at least in part, been the cause of my loss of temper.

"I should never let myself lose control," I mumbled when we were examining the damage.

"Yes, you should," Jill said. "You got to let it out if something is bothering you."

"Oh, I let it out. You should have seen how much I let it out."

Jill giggled at the image of me heaving the book through the window.

"You know what?" I grabbed her hand. "I'm not sure what's wrong with us. We don't connect, and we can't make each other realize how important we are. I love you so much, but this is killing me."

"Me too. I think we need some help. I'm willing to do anything. I mean it, anything."

"I agree. Let's make some calls on Monday and see if we can find someone to talk to. It's embarrassing, but I think it might be good for us."

"I do too. I want to find a way to get through this and make it work." Jill stepped toward me and raised her eyebrows. I motioned that it was safe to approach. She put her arms around me and hugged me fully. I welcomed the contact. Her hair smelled fresh and her skin was warm. Charley walked over and wrapped his arms around our legs. The three of us stood there motionless.

SEPTEMBER OF THIS YEAR

CHAPTER 21

THE DIN IS NEARLY overwhelming. Charley's entire soccer team, parents, and families, have decided to go out for dinner. The boys are still in their uniforms, sitting together at a long table more or less studying the menus. Adults, at an adjacent table, try to ignore the ever-increasing volume emanating from the kids.

We have secured the back room at Buffalo Blues, a local restaurant the team often frequents because they don't mind fifty people screaming while eating. Two servers attempt to get drink orders. The adults order pitchers of beer and the boys high-five when they learn they can have soft drinks.

I feel a slap on my back and turn to see Dave Barma smiling. "What's up?" I say.

"Nice work today." he says, adjusting his perfectly pressed blue oxford shirt. "The kids actually played like they cared."

A former Navy pilot whose son Carter is one of our defense men, Dave was appalled at the lack of discipline last year. At the final game, Dave stormed away when two of the boys were talking while a player from the other team dribbled by to score their team's eighth goal. "Un-freakin'-believable," He screamed as he left the field.

Dave had led the charge to get a new coach and insisted on someone who would take no guff. I assume he was disappointed I was the only candidate, but he had withheld judgment.

"Thanks," I say, "but it only was a tie."

"Don't care. The boys played with heart. I was worried when they got down 2-0, but they tightened it up and didn't let in a goal in the second half. The defense men were actually aware of each other and didn't chase after the ball."

Rumor is Dave was on the soccer team in college and apparently knew something about tactics. He smacks my back again to signal the end to our discussion.

I grab my beer. Jill faces me talking to Liza and Valerie. I make a smart remark about them not getting enough time to talk during the week. Jill ignores me and their intense conversation continues.

Pete, the assistant coach, and Tony, Andrew's dad, sit next to me at the table. Most of the men argue about what local craft brew is superior. I turn to Tony and ask him if Andrew is enjoying soccer.

"I'm not sure. He doesn't say much about it," he responds.

"It looks like he's trying," I say.

Tony angles his body more toward me. "I watched him today. He always was a step behind."

"Most of the boys are having the same issue. We're teaching them positioning—they never worried about it much before. We tell them to keep their shape and be aware of where their teammates are, so they can cover for them. It's not easy. They're thinking more than reacting, which slows them down."

"Andrew has never loved soccer. He plays because his friends are playing. I hope he's improving."

"He almost had a goal today. He needs to work on his foot skills, but so do all the players."

"The team played better. They could've won."

"Thanks. I'm glad we weren't trounced."

After we order food and more beer, the kids disperse to play the video games lining the hall outside of the room we're in. The decrease in volume allows everyone to relax.

Vic Himmer stands and raises his mug. "Here's to the goal scorers today." The parents groan because his son, Hunter, was one of the two kids who scored. Vic, a self-proclaimed soccer expert, wrote an email last season extolling Hunter's abilities while at the same time diminishing the contributions of everyone else. Hunter, a stocky redhead with a strong leg, is a quiet kid who would never want to draw any attention to himself.

Pete stands before any parent makes a comment and says, "It's not just about those who score the goals, but also about the players who assisted and those who prevented our opponent from scoring. Let's toast the team and its continued success."

A loud cheer erupts and everyone raises their glass. The boys slam open the door to the room. They have run out of quarters and the food has arrived.

AUGUST, FIVE YEARS AGO

CHAPTER 22

PETE AND LIZA STEPPED into our entranceway turning their heads from side to side. Their mouths hung open, but they emitted no sounds. Pete handed a bottle of wine to me and started to walk through the house.

"This is freaking awesome," he said, walking from the dining room into the kitchen.

Jill smiled and grabbed Liza's hand. "We decided not to let anyone into the house while we were doing the construction. I missed having you over to talk. I haven't seen you much this summer." They hugged, and Charley came bounding down the stairs.

"Who's here?" he asked in a loud voice.

"It's Liza and Pete. Sam's hanging on the porch swing," Jill said.

"Hey, Charley," Liza said while she grabbed him as he ran by. "You ready to start first grade?"

"Yup," Charley said, bolting toward the front door. Ten seconds later he and Sam stormed by to race upstairs to play, their feet banging loudly on the hardwood floor.

Pete and I joined the women near the steps. Jill said, "Can we show you what we've done?"

Liza and Pete knew most of this story already, but Jill explained that when we first moved into the house, every room needed work. Jill and I tore out the carpet upstairs and painted every room. I tried to redo the floors myself, but when the sanding machine scraped a hole in the floor of one of the bedrooms, she convinced me to hire a professional to do it right.

Other than getting new hardwood after Charley's birth, we had not done much to the downstairs. The kitchen, though functional, had peeling, yellow linoleum, and cabinets we thought were at least fifty years old. The dining room needed shelving and repairs to the plaster, while the bathroom on the first floor had a working toilet but holes in the walls and floors.

Jill and I started to do some tasks ourselves and had been able to demo part of the kitchen, but this left us with more of a mess. Jill's co-worker, whose husband was a contractor, agreed to do the work at night with our assistance. We helped him hang cabinets, redo floors, paint walls and build shelves. It had taken months, but by the time we finished, our house had been transformed.

Liza and Pete walked around the house complimenting the renovations. I uncorked their bottle of wine, and we made a toast to many happy times in our house. Jill beamed each time Liza noticed a construction detail. She put her arms around Pete and Liza and said, "We can't wait to share it with friends."

After the tour, it was time for dinner. I turned on the grill and brought the marinated salmon out to cook. When it was ready, I carried it back in to find Charley and Sam throwing a tennis ball to each other from the family room to the kitchen by banging it off the cabinets.

I put a hand on my son's shoulder and said, "What are you doing? The cabinets are less than two weeks old."

Jill shot me a glance. "Don't worry. It's your house too. Be a little careful. We want our new kitchen to be around for a long time."

Sam and Charley managed to sit and eat without getting up to run around during dinner. I loved eating in our new dining room surrounded by gleaming shelving and freshly painted walls. My feet snuggled into the soft, tan rug Jill picked out two days earlier. Pete poured more wine for the adults. He turned to Charley. "Are you excited to be playing soccer this fall?"

Charley focused his blue eyes on Pete. "You bet. Sam and I are going to be on the same team."

Last week, Liza and Jill went to the rec center to sign up Charley and Sam. Liza spoke with the parent coordinator for the league and got assurances the two could play together, which would make carpools to practices and games much easier. Jill and Liza were excited because now they would have someone to gab with during each game.

"Boys," Jill said, "maybe you can convince some of your other friends to start playing soccer. Wouldn't it be fun if you all could play together?"

"Cool," Sam answered. "Charley, let's talk to everyone when we're at school. Maybe we could all be on the same team. That would rule."

"That would be awesome," Charley said. "Mommy, can we be excused?"

"Go ahead. Clear your dishes."

The boys gathered their plates and glasses and took them to the kitchen. Soon we heard pounding on the ceiling above us and the light fixture began to sway. They were playing super hero and jumping off Charley's bed. I headed upstairs to direct them to a less intrusive activity.

OCTOBER OF THIS YEAR

CHAPTER 23

The rain smacks against the roof of the kitchen creating a light hum inside. Most times, I love sitting at the table and listening to the downpour. Today, I can't focus on the tranquility of the weather because three eleven-year-olds have taken over the downstairs.

"Can't you hang out on the third floor and play? There's so much room," I plead, but they're not taking the bait.

Charley turns his head from the couch. "Dad, we were up there, but we couldn't find anything to do," His two friends sit on either side of him.

I roll my eyes picturing the hundred games and other toys upstairs. I can't get annoyed—Jacob and Sam arrived two hours earlier and the three pals have amused themselves since without intervention. After playing football and racing around outside, the change in weather chased them inside. They played a made-up war game for the past half-hour and have taken refuge on the sofa.

I bring over some pretzels and cut-up vegetables as they display their constant need for stimulation by wrestling with each other on the couch.

"Dad, can we play a video game?" Charley asks. We usually don't want him to immerse himself in video games, especially when he has friends over at the house. Tactically, Charley is cunning in coming to me, knowing I am the softer parent.

"Charley, you guys can play for 30 minutes. Hopefully, it will have stopped raining and you can go outside. Your mothers should be back in about an hour, so I don't want them finding you deep into video games, or they will think I let you play the whole time they were gone."

Jill, Liza, and Holly, Jacob's mom, had made plans to get lunch and spend time together. Without any argument, I agreed to watch the boys.

They start playing some blow-up game on the TV, and I turn my attention to the computer screen looking to answer some emails from work. I sit no more than fifteen feet away, but as they get more involved, they forget I am around.

They lose awareness of anything outside of the zone surrounding them, which is about five feet in diameter, anytime they participate in an activity. Time has no meaning, and nothing exists beyond their inner sanctum. They speak with an unbridled honesty that they would temper if they remembered an adult was present.

Jill loves to be nearby when this happens because it's how she learns the most about Charley's life. When she drives a group of kids in the car, she keeps quiet and listens. They spill more information about events at school and what is important to them than if she sat Charley down and asked him direct questions.

"Dude, nice shot," Charley says as Sam's character destroys a slimy alien. All three boys are waving guns at the screen shooting at random images. I don't understand the purpose of their game, but I'm observing their interactions.

"Nailed him!" Jacob cries. "One less creature to bother us."

"We make a strong team," Charley says. "We might get the high score."

"Keep working together. I have your back!" Sam exclaims, squatting down to get a better shot at the predators.

After two more minutes of chaos and destruction, the last of the boys' characters is eaten by an alien. They groan because they missed their mark. They fall back on the couch and begin smacking each other. Charley picks up a pillow and bops Sam in the face.

"Dang, we were so close to success," Sam exclaims. "Next time, we kick butt and win."

"We need to work on shooting aliens. With a little practice, we will play better," Jacob adds with a broad smile framed by his straight brown hair.

Charley stops hitting his friends with the pillow to respond. "Like the soccer team. We're so much better than we were at the start of the season. We've won five games in a row."

"I know," Sam interrupts. "The way we played at the beginning, I never thought we would make the playoffs."

"My dad thinks it's because we're listening at practice," Charley says as he sticks a carrot in his mouth. "I think it's because we stopped arguing during games."

"Everyone's playing better. Even Andrew, no offense, scored a goal in the last game," Jacob adds as he jumps on Charley.

"Our first playoff game's this week," Charley notes. "Think we'll win?"

"Of course," Sam says. "Do you think we'll play Fox Chapel?"

Jacob rolls on top of Sam on the floor. "I want to kill them after what they said to Ricardo. I'm going to jump on the kid's back who called him that name if we play them, and then we will crush them."

I listen in amusement as their recollection of how the season progressed differs from mine. Either way, it's fun hearing how soccer has become a priority. I'm looking forward to their first playoff game almost as much as they are.

I watch the boys alternate between hitting each other and discussing their soccer strategy. The two significant events I have in the next few days—Arthur Spinelli's trial and Charley's playoffs—flash in my mind. I wonder if I was given a choice of winning only one, which event I would choose.

OCTOBER
OF THIS YEAR

CHAPTER 24

ARTHUR, JANA, AND I cross Grant Street dodging traffic. We head toward the statue of our former mayor that sits atop the steps of the courthouse. After the security check, we take the elevators to the seventh floor for a quick conference with the judge to determine if the parties can reach a last-minute settlement before we pick our jury.

Jana and I sit at the long wooden table in Judge Maruk's courtroom. Arthur sits in a small chair behind the counsel table. I remind him to remain impassive at all times during trial—he is in essence testifying from the moment he gets to the courthouse, because no matter where he is, a juror may be watching and evaluating him. One stupid move or one thoughtless comment could doom his case before he ever took the witness stand.

One minute before our appointed time with the judge, Keith Carlson, followed closely by Mike Vorat, slams open the door to the courtroom. Carlson lugs a box of documents, which he dumps on the counsel table. He fumbles through the materials until he pulls out a yellow pad and a pen. He plops into the wooden seat.

Jana placed binders with all our exhibits in front of our seats when we arrived. I take the binder labeled "Vorat" and hand it to Carlson. He does not raise his eyes when he grabs the papers from me. Vorat, a deep scowl etched on his face, sits immediately next to Carlson, looking forward into empty space.

The judge's tipstaff calls us into chambers and informs us to bring our clients for the conference. Judge Maruk towers over everyone in the room. His robe is opened revealing a wrinkled white shirt with two small coffee stains underneath. A half-eaten breakfast sandwich sits on his desk, which the judge grabs and throws into the garbage.

I have been before Maruk many times and respect his no-nonsense style. Despite his tendency to ask witnesses questions at inopportune moments, he will allow lawyers to try their cases, so long as they follow his idiosyncratic rules.

"Sit, please," he instructs. "I wanted to take another stab at getting this resolved. If you proceed, it will take about three days. Both parties have claims against each other, so everyone has something at risk. Counsel, I assume you have talked to your clients about there being no sure things when you go to trial."

Carlson and I nod our heads and let the judge continue. "Last time we got together, Mr. Vorat demanded two million dollars to settle. This caused Mr. Spinelli to state he would negotiate in that range. So, Mr. Carlson have you and your client reconsidered your position?"

Carlson examines his yellow pad and flips through the pages. His gut hangs over his belt, and his shirt is already sneaking out of his pants.

"Your Honor," he begins, "Mr. Vorat and I have discussed our position and recognize we were a bit aggressive at the last settlement conference. He brought claims against Mr. Spinelli because he stole from the company. The defendant tried to put pressure on us by filing a counterclaim, suggesting Mr. Vorat somehow had caused the company to lose money. We have reviewed the evidence and we believe our case is strong. We are, however, prepared to drop our claims in exchange for Mr. Spinelli dropping his claims."

Carlson smirks after completing his statement. He, apparently, believes we will jump all over his new position.

Arthur and I had discussed the possibility of such an offer. Jana and I had analyzed the evidence at length and remained confident in Arthur's case. Opposing counsel had finally done the same. Arthur understood the pros and cons of proceeding to trial, including the emotional toll any trial takes on the participants.

Arthur catches my eye and shakes his head.

"Your Honor," I begin, "I'm glad Mr. Carlson has recognized the ridiculousness of his client's previous demand; however, walking away does nothing for my client. His nephew stole his livelihood. He has lost millions, forced to watch from afar as Mr. Vorat has mismanaged and nearly destroyed his company. Our expert will testify Mr. Vorat's actions damaged Mr. Spinelli in excess of two million dollars. It will take this amount for him to forgo his day in court."

I turn toward Carlson, who has gone ghostly white. Vorat leaps from his chair and begins to whisper frantically in Carlson's ear. He listens and repeatedly shakes his head.

"Your Honor," Carlson stammers. He starts to flip through his yellow pad. "Mr. Spinelli's position is untenable. My client barely can pay my bill, so he certainly can't pay a settlement so large. After discussing with Mr. Vorat, he has agreed to pay Mr. Spinelli one hundred thousand dollars purely as a goodwill offer."

I pause for a moment. "No" is all I say.

"Your Honor, it's clear Mr. Spinelli is behaving vindictively. We're here in good faith, but Mr. Spinelli turns his nose up at what we are offering. I thought given our new position, we would be able to resolve this, but they are acting unreasonably. Under the circumstances, I would request a continuance, so we can continue this dialogue."

I'm dumbfounded—is Carlson not ready to start the trial? He must have thought we would jump at the chance to walk away from the lawsuit. I'm about to object to any delay when the judge says, "Mr. Carlson, today is the day we are scheduled to begin, and today is the day we will begin. I get the sense Mr. Spinelli feels he has been wronged by your client. I'm interested to see what evidence you both have on this issue. Next time you decide to reduce your demand by two million dollars, I would suggest you do it before the day the trial is scheduled to start. Go pick a jury."

The judge waves his hand in our direction and drops his head down toward the papers on his desk. We gather our bags to walk down the hall to select the jury that will determine the future of Arthur Spinelli.

Lawyers talk about picking a jury—it sounds like we have a range of choices. Not true. Jurors aren't picked, they are simply the ones left over after others are kicked off. In most jurisdictions, a panel starts with a certain number of people. Each side strikes a predetermined number and those remaining are the jury. For our trials, the panel is twenty people. Both sides strike four jurors. The twelve who remain form the jury.

Mostly, attorneys excuse the people they presume won't agree with their own witnesses and hope the leftovers are palatable. Lots of money is spent in bigger cases hiring consultants to help decide which potential jurors to strike. In most situations, it isn't feasible to pay a consultant and the lawyers make the decisions with some input from the client. It's more art than science because we are presented with limited information. Oftentimes, despite agonizing over final strikes, the juror whom I most wanted on the jury is the toughest on my case.

Arthur, Jana, and I had talked at length about what type of juror we would want. We thought older people would more likely empathize with our client, and women would be sympathetic to his plight. We were worried about younger, independent thinkers because they are less predictable. Ultimately, I decided anyone who appreciated honesty would be acceptable, which is usually how I feel when I believe my client is credible.

Jury selection for Arthur's case is fairly easy. A clerk interviews all the prospective jurors to see if they know anything about this matter or any of the witnesses or had any type of bias for or against any of the parties. This process usually takes a few hours and the lawyers dismiss potential jurors until they have used their strikes.

The clerk asks a series of questions about their occupations, prior litigation exposure, and any possible biases. We glean small nuggets of information to assist in our selection of the four individuals to strike.

When the interview process is complete, Jana and I discuss our suggested strikes. We reach unanimity without significant disagreement. We dismiss a middle-aged white gentleman with a felony conviction because, we presume, he didn't care much about the truth and excuse another older woman who has been sued three times because we weren't sure if she was receptive to any person suing another. For our last two strikes, we select the youngest males on the panel, only because they most closely resemble Vorat demographically.

We leave the juror room, and Jana turns to me. "Three hours of listening to those jurors and I have no idea if we have a favorable jury."

I nod my head. "We won't find out until they render their verdict."

The clerk yells down the hallway for us to get a quick lunch and return to the courtroom to begin trial.

For the next twenty minutes, I rehearse my opening while we gobble down sandwiches in the cafeteria in the basement.

Jana pats me on my back when I finish. "I believe we're ready."

CHAPTER 25

THE JUDGE IS WAITING for us in the courtroom and asks if we are prepared to begin. Carlson again asks for a continuance and when this is denied, he requests openings be delayed until tomorrow.

The judge turns his back on us, and when he slowly returns to his original position, his face is beet red. He spits out, "Mr. Carlson, we have twelve citizens of this Commonwealth who have taken time from their busy lives to hear from you. I won't make them wait. We start in five minutes."

Opening statements are an opportunity to introduce your case and client to the jury. Technically, openings should outline the evidence a lawyer expects to introduce. A lawyer is not supposed to argue or talk about what is wrong about the other side's evidence, but most experienced litigators sneak a little argument into an opening.

An important aspect of the initial presentation of the evidence is to allow the jury to witness the strength of my commitment to the case. It's also the first time the jurors begin to assess the lawyer's credibility. When a lawyer states his side will present certain evidence during the trial, he's making a promise that, if broken, might lead to the jury punishing the lawyer and, by extension, his client.

The jurors want the lawyer to feel passionate about his client's case, but also don't want to be sold a bill of goods. One of the best ways to demonstrate my conviction is to be organized and efficient. Juries hate when lawyers stumble through documents and can't find exhibits. They detest hearing the same question asked four different times. They appreciate when lawyers ask their questions without repetition and quickly get to the heart of the issues germane to witness' testimony.

I try to avoid using notes during my openings. I put a yellow pad on the lectern with a few key ideas outlined on the first page. My goal is to speak directly to the jurors without looking down. The scribbles serve as a safety net if I lose my train of thought. I want to create a little energy, so I walk from end to end of the jury box a couple of times, but I don't won't to move so much it creates distraction. I always engage each juror at some point during the opening to establish a bond.

Everyone rises as the jury enters the courtroom. Vorat attempts to make eye contact with the members, but they keep their gaze straight ahead. Judge Maruk gives his initial instructions, telling them they decide the facts in dispute, and he resolves any legal issues. He tells them how to assess credibility, which comes down to observing the witnesses and deciding if they believe the testimony.

Upon concluding his instructions, Judge Maruk invites Carlson to make an opening statement to the jury. He explains both sides have asserted causes of action against the other and are seeking money as compensation for the injuries each side alleges it has suffered. Carlson goes first because Vorat filed his claims first.

Carlson rises and struts to the lectern, placing a stack of documents on top. A couple of the papers flutter to the floor, forcing Carlson to bend over and pick them up. In an overly formal way of speaking, he says, "May it please the court." He turns his attention to the jurors, who return his gaze.

"Ladies and Gentlemen, serving on a jury is difficult, and on behalf of my client I want to thank you for taking time out of your busy days to serve as jurors. It has been said jury duty is the second-highest service one can offer to his country, and we know you will serve honorably and with the greatest attention to detail."

I lean over and scribble on Jana's pad, "Stop kissing ass and get to why we're here." Carlson apparently believes jurors like to be buttered-up.

Reading directly from his notes, he tells the jury about the case.

"Mike Vorat is a hard-working young man. He had many job offers but came to Pittsburgh to work as an accountant for his uncle, Arthur Spinelli, and his company, Spinelli Enterprises. Mike was appalled at the lack of recordkeeping when he started working there. Every time he tried to make changes, he was thwarted by the company's long-time accountant, Steven Berlin.

"Mr. Vorat was concerned something was amiss. He dug through the financial records and found evidence of criminal activity. Through diligent investigation conducted over months, Vorat uncovered systematic siphoning of cash, as well as record-keeping designed to hide profits so the owners could steal the money and avoid paying taxes.

"Mike brought what he had discovered to Mr. Berlin, but Mr. Berlin told him to keep it to himself. So, Mike threatened to bring his evidence to the board of directors. Almost immediately, Mr. Berlin left the company, never to be heard from again.

"Mr. Vorat wrote a series of memorandums to the board, outlining the instances of theft. In these memos, Mike identified his uncle, Arthur Spinelli, as the ringleader of this plan and proved in detail how Mr. Spinelli had taken money belonging to the company for himself.

Carlson fumbles with his papers and wipes his forehead with the back of his hand before continuing.

"Arthur Spinelli stole over two and one half million dollars. We are here to get it back."

I'm impressed with Carlson. He has told a coherent story and identified specifically what he wanted the jury to do. I sense a rising level of stress from Arthur, but consistent with our instructions, he remains impassive. Nothing on his face belies the turmoil roiling inside him.

Carlson finishes his opening identifying the witnesses he intends to call and offering a little taste of the testimony he expects they will hear.

He pauses and points a finger directly at Arthur, letting the moment linger. "That man sitting there is a thief. He took money that did not belong to him. We will ask you at the end of this trial to do what is right and award to the company the money Arthur Spinelli stole."

With a weak smile plastered on his face, Carlson heads back to his table and dumps the papers on it. A scowl spreads across Vorat's face as I stand.

We had worked on many versions of my opening, but I wanted to wait to hear Carlson's stated position before deciding which tack I would utilize. I walk to the jury box knowing I have no choice but to attack Vorat head on. I ordinarily won't directly call a person a liar in my opening because of the risk of alienating the jury if they don't agree with me. If a juror believes a witness is unwilling to tell the truth, I may gain little by calling him out. If a juror isn't convinced he is a liar, however, my credibility with the jury could be shot by impugning the witness. I make a calculated decision to ignore my own advice.

"Good morning, Ladies and Gentlemen," I begin. "There is a liar in this courtroom, and it's not Arthur Spinelli."

I stop talking and make eye contact with every juror. "Arthur Spinelli is the founder and owner of Spinelli Enterprises. Along with his wife, Evelyn, he built his business from nothing into a successful and respected company.

"Arthur and Evelyn never had kids. They wanted them in the worst way, so chose to be close to most of their extended family. Cousins, nieces, and nephews often worked for them and appreciated the opportunity the Spinellis provided to them.

"She died a few years ago, but Arthur continued to employ kids from Evelyn's side of the family. He loved helping out his relatives and getting them started with interesting jobs and strong recommendations.

"Mike Vorat is Arthur's nephew. His mother is Evelyn's sister. Out of the blue, Vorat's mother contacted Arthur and informed him her son needed a job. Arthur did not know his nephew well—they lived on the West Coast and did not seek out Arthur much. But a nephew is family. Mike Vorat came to Pittsburgh for what could charitably be called an interview—it was a foregone conclusion Arthur would hire him, because he was family. Arthur Spinelli hired Mike Vorat as the assistant accountant for Spinelli Enterprises.

"Soon after Mr. Vorat began working, the head accountant, Steve Berlin quit—actually he disappeared—but any mystery as to why Mr. Berlin left will be solved for you...."

"Objection," I hear Carlson bellow, as I had expected.

Other attorneys' opening statements often present opportunities to interrupt, but rarely do I stand and object. Jurors want to hear the story, and although they know we have a right to object, they resent it if they think the lawyer is trying to disrupt the flow, Carlson had said a number of potentially objectionable things during his opening, but I chose to keep my mouth shut and deal with them in my opening.

Carlson was not providing me with the same courtesy.

"Please approach," Judge Maruk says.

Carlson and I, with the court reporter between us, stand before the judge. Carlson jumps in. "Your Honor, he can't say what Mr. Berlin would think or say. He's speculating."

"Why?"

"Mr. Berlin has disappeared. He can't offer testimony."

The judge turns his head toward us and peers out over the tops of his glasses. "Mr. West, can he testify?"

"Your Honor, we have identified Mr. Berlin as a potential witness in our pretrial statement. I would never say anything in my opening I didn't think I would be able to prove."

"Well, he claims he can," Judge Maruk says, returning his gaze to Carlson, "If he doesn't, you can point it out in your closing."

I return to where I was standing and wait for the judge to rule. "Mr. Carlson's objection is overruled. Mr. West, you may proceed."

"Thank you, Your Honor." I smile to demonstrate nothing about our brief conference had worried me. "As I was saying, you will find out the real reason why Mr. Berlin left and what the financial status of the company was at that time."

Out of the corner of my eye, I notice Carlson twitch as if he were trying to avoid a punch.

I inform the jury we will prove Arthur never wrongfully took any money and didn't do anything to alter the books. "Arthur hired an accountant, Deb Creed, when he first heard the company was operating at a loss. She will take you through the financial records and prove Arthur Spinelli did not steal. In fact, she will lay out for you how Mike Vorat systematically siphoned off profits from the business and made false reports identifying his uncle as the fall guy."

I immediately sense the jurors' discomfort. They know there are two conflicting stories and it will be their responsibility to decide who they believe.

I put both hands on the edge of the jury rail and lean toward them. "You have to assess people's credibility every day. You evaluate who is honest and who is trying to sell you on something that isn't true. It's almost instinctive and it's part of your duty as jurors."

The jurors shift in their seats. I think they are ready to hear actual testimony, so I begin to wrap up. "Arthur Spinelli will make your job easy. He will give you a road map that leads to only one conclusion—Mike Vorat altered the financial records of Spinelli Enterprises. He blamed his uncle for the money he stole."

Any statement to a jury promising the evidence will prove something is fraught with danger and sets the entire case up for possible failure. I've exposed Arthur by making this promise. I understand the risk and hope we can deflect Vorat's claim that Arthur was the thief.

"Because of what Mike Vorat has done, Arthur Spinelli has lost so much. It's not merely the money, but his legacy and his company. To right this injustice, we will ask at the end of the trial that you award him two million dollars, as the evidence will prove he is entitled to receive in compensation."

I thank the jurors for their service and sit down.

The judge sighs heavily and announces, "Given it's Friday, I know you want to get home to your families. We will begin with testimony at 8:30 on Monday. Please have a nice weekend."

CHAPTER 26

"Dude, the Pumas rule." Paul raises his glass of beer. Pete, Paul, and I clank our glasses together and take healthy swigs.

"I can't believe how well we played today," Pete exclaims, genuine enthusiasm evident in his voice. "We kicked their butts 6-1 and it was never close."

Two hours earlier the boys won their semi-final match to put them into the championship game. Rain drenched the field and spectators. The three of us elected to meet for a beer to analyze the team's tactics and make plans for the next game. Jill and the other parents were happy to let us have some free time and took responsibility for putting the boys to bed.

The upstairs balcony area at Silky's offered us booths away from most patrons. We weren't subject to the din of the crowd downstairs, allowing us to talk and catch glimpses of the Penguin game. With our first beers in hand, we were getting comfortable.

"The goal Carter scored was excellent. The boys connected on three passes before he got the ball. They didn't have a defender within ten feet of him— beautiful," Pete says.

"I like when they pass and don't try to dribble past everyone," I respond. "Sam also had a spectacular shot. He booted it into the upper corner, but it was the defense that played solidly. Eli hardly had to do anything. What I liked was how much the boys were hustling. They left everything they had on the field."

Paul leans in. "They loved diving all over the mud."

We analyzed each score and picked apart how our defense responded when challenged.

"The Pumas are playing their best soccer," Pete says, smacking the table. "Every player is executing at a higher level than when the season started. I don't care who is on the field. We can win with any of them in the game."

Paul smacks Pete on the back. "Our boys are stalwarts on defense and attacking on offense. They are staying in their lanes and covering when someone's out of position."

Pete grabs a napkin and starts to draw on it with lines and arrows.

"Damn, Pete, you sound like a coach," I tease after he diagrams the goal Stephen scored.

Pete flushes and says, "When we started the year, my job was crowd control—make sure they focused on soccer and didn't mess around. They got more into it as the season progressed and I wasn't needed to keep them in line. Now the three of us have actually been coaching them. I enjoy it so much more than being a disciplinarian. The boys are looking for ways to improve. It's awesome, man."

Paul chimes in, "I agree. Once they kicked it in, it was a lot of fun." He stops for a moment. "Can I tell you guys a secret? I want to win the championship."

The three of us nod in agreement.

I pull out my phone to check the league's website. "Not surprisingly, Fox Chapel won by five goals. They're the winners of the other side of the bracket."

Pete grimaces. "They will kick our butts if we play like we did the first time."

We deconstruct when we played Fox Chapel, remembering how badly they had beaten us and how we had given up in the second half.

"It was a long time ago and the boys have improved so much," Paul says. "We shouldn't think about that game. We're a totally different team now."

"I agree," I say. "Fox Chapel is bigger and stronger than us. What do we need to do to beat them?"

"We need to get on them right from the beginning. Somehow, we have to get them worried and think we may not be as bad as they think we are. They will be ready, and we need a way to break their confidence quickly," Pete explains.

"Yes," I say. "Let's talk to the team about attacking from the opening whistle. Let's also make sure they stay in their lanes and don't get too exuberant. I think we can handle them if we play smart."

Paul and Pete nod in agreement. We pause for a minute to order more beer and to check on the score of the Penguin game. They are beating the Rangers 4-3. It's early in the season, and they're in first place.

I break the silence by saying, "Do you think what happened to Ricardo is still on their minds?"

They pause for a moment. "You know, I haven't heard a word about it from any of the kids for weeks," Pete says. "I know they haven't forgotten, but it's not front-and-center."

"We have to make sure they don't think about it. Let's talk to them about not listening to anything the other team may say."

"Agreed," Pete and Paul say simultaneously.

I feel a tap on my shoulder as we are finishing our soccer discussion. Vic Himmer and Valerie Bonet are standing next to our booths holding beers.

"We were walking by," Vic cheerfully begins, "when we saw you sitting here and thought we might join you for a beer."

"Sit right down," Pete offers as he slides to make room.

"What are you boys doing here on a Saturday and why aren't you with your wives?" Valerie inquires. For some reason, I begin to feel a little defensive but ignore it and respond, "We're trying to get our thoughts together to plan for the championship game."

"Perfect. Valerie and I were talking about soccer on the way here, and we wanted to ask you something."

I think their visit to our table may not have been coincidental. "What were you thinking?"

Vic smiles broadly and grabs my shoulder. "I was concerned you weren't being completely fair in how much the boys were playing since we got to the playoffs."

"What do you mean?" I respond, now confident in feeling defensive.

"All season you played everyone pretty much the same amount, but in the playoffs it's been different. For example, in today's game, Charley was on the field forty-two out of the fifty minutes, but Hunter only got to play eighteen minutes."

My blood begins to boil inside of me. I take a slow sip of beer and collect my thoughts to make sure I say exactly what I want to say. "All season we worked hard to make playing time as equal as possible. I wanted every player to get a chance in every conceivable circumstance, so they all had the opportunity to improve."

I stare Vic directly in the eyes. "Our goals changed when the playoffs came. We weren't looking for improvement, but for wins. To do this, I had to utilize the players who gave us the best chance to win. This means others won't play as much. None of the boys complained about this."

Not hearing an apology, Vic pouts. "How do I tell Hunter you think everyone on the team is better than he is?"

I take a deep breath and cross my arms. "I already told the kids' playing time for the playoffs would not be equal and they controlled how much they play by how hard they practice and how well they perform in games. You know if we made everything completely balanced now, other parents would complain."

"Hunter having to sit on the bench so much is rather unfair. I'm worried what he's going to think about himself."

"Ridiculous. None of the kids can be the best at every sport. Hunter is excellent at other sports. Hunter played on the same basketball team last year as Charley. Hunter played all the time and Charley was lucky he got in for five minutes a game. Jill and I never said a word because that was the coach's decisions. Charley was aware of his limitations playing basketball."

"Hopefully you'll make sure they all get an opportunity to do something in the championship game."

"I promise you this. I will put the kids in who I think give us the best chance of winning and who have the best attitude. I think Hunter will get more than enough playing time given those parameters."

"Wonderful," Vic says. He takes a last swig of his beer. "I'm glad we ran into you, but we have to be getting back to our families. Say hi to Jill."

We wave as the two friends stroll away and roll our eyes at their nerve.

"I guess this happens when you agree to help out," Paul sighs.

"We sure aren't doing it for the pay," Pete chimes in with a smile.

We down our beers and watch the Penguins finish off the Rangers. We walk out of the bar and Paul says, "One week until the big rematch."

I head to my car, surprised by how much I'm looking forward to the game. Our boys are home asleep, unaware they will be facing off against Fox Chapel and that their parents are more worried about their performance than they are.

NOVEMBER, SEVEN YEARS AGO

CHAPTER 27

"SLOW DOWN, DUDE," I said to Charley as he ran back toward the house. "Don't you ever get tired?"

He opened the door and entered the house in an instant. I carried the plastic bat and four Wiffle balls as I attempted to wedge myself back into the house. For the past hour we had been outside as he tried to learn to swing a baseball bat. Despite missing the ball on most pitches, his swing was improving. The thrilled expression on his face every time he made contact was worth the constant chasing and stooping for the balls. Charley's enthusiasm, however, didn't alter how tired I felt and my desire to sit inside.

I walked past the family room. Charley is in the front of the house building a tower out of his cardboard bricks. "Daddy, I'm going to build it really high," I stood silently admiring his engineering skills.

"I'm going to rest if you need me."

He nodded and went back to his construction. I shook my head in wonderment at the energy Charley put into everything, never stopping until he put his head on the pillow at night. I was in my mid-thirties—no chance I could keep moving all day like he did.

After grabbing some water, I collapsed on the couch and picked up a magazine. Five minutes later I heard the front door open and Jill greet Charley. Jill soon appeared in the family room holding Charley's hand. "Hey, Sweetie," she said, "thanks for picking him up from daycare."

"Not a problem. You always do it. I like seeing his classroom. Ms. Amie said he had a positive day. He's working hard on his letters. We came home, had a snack, and then we played some Wiffle ball outside. How was your work?"

"Nothing exciting. Got a paper out for review." Jill touched Charley's cheek. "Charley, can you build your tower? I will come in a few minutes to see how high it is." In a flash, he darted from the room, headed back toward the front of the house.

She took a seat next to me and placed a hand on my knee. "How was your day?"

"Same old stuff. I spent all morning answering interrogatories about the methods one of my clients utilizes to account for revenues when customers return products to the store—tedious to say the least."

Jill stared at the picture over the fireplace. She wasn't paying attention. Not surprising, given the subject matter, but unusual because Jill ordinarily remained engrossed even when I ranted about an incredibly mundane issue. "Is something wrong?" I asked.

Jill's gaze still was distant and she remained silent. Tears fell down her cheeks when she turned to me. She swiped at them with her hand. "I was at the doctor's office. I didn't tell you I had an appointment because I didn't think anything of it and I didn't want you to be concerned."

My heart beat a little faster and I grabbed her hand.

After a moment, Jill pulled her hand from mine and waved it erratically. "It's nothing to worry about. I'm fine. It's...." She couldn't get the words out. I waited anxiously for her to gather her thoughts.

She placed her hand in front of her mouth to muffle a small guttural moan. "I wanted to surprise you. I thought I might be pregnant. Really early. But I lost the baby. And...." She swiped at her nose. "The doctor thinks I'm not going to be able to get pregnant again."

"Oh god," I responded, feeling a sudden jolt in my chest. "Why?"

"I'll tell you more later. It's too much to talk about it now." Jill put her head on my shoulder.

"I guess that explains why we've been trying so hard with nothing happening. I'm so sorry."

"Me too." She buried her head in my lap and sobbed. I held her, feeling bad for me but so much worse for her. After a few minutes, she pulled away and wiped at her face. Her nose was red and her hair was messed.

"You know," she said, "I'm so devastated by this. We planned to have such a big family. I love Charley so much and we're good parents. I always imagined loud dinners and lots of birthday parties."

I nodded but could find no words to offer.

We rested our heads against our pillows in bed. Charley's light snoring floated in from his room across the hall. Books sat on our laps, but neither of us was reading.

"You know," I said as I turned to Jill, "I'm sad about what happened today, but if you want, we can still have a bigger family."

She rolled toward me, so we were face-to-face. "You mean adopt?"

"Absolutely."

"I would like that."

"So would I." I put my hand on her cheek. "You're a good mom."

"Thanks. You're pretty good yourself—as a dad, not a mom."

"I get it. I'm grateful for the family we have. Any more would be a bonus."

"Agreed."

OCTOBER OF THIS YEAR

CHAPTER 28

Jana, Arthur, and I hustle across Grant Street to get to the courthouse. For the past hour we had caucused in our conference room to review our preparation for the witnesses testifying today. A fall breeze blows in our faces warning us of winter's impending arrival. Despite the short walk and tepid temperatures, sweat drips on my back as we reach the door of the courthouse.

Judge Maruk's courtroom is empty when we arrive. Jana fusses with the documents on our table, making sure they are organized and she will be able to access each efficiently. With a loud bang, Carlson and Vorat enter carrying three boxes.

Carlson brushes by me. "Morning, Keith," I say. The grunting noise he makes informs me he is in no mood for pleasantries. I walk over to his table and ask, "What is the order of the witnesses you are calling today?"

In every trial I have ever had, even with unpleasant lawyers, they were willing to let us know who they intended to call at the beginning of each day. Nothing in the court rules obligates parties to provide this courtesy, but most do as a matter of professionalism because it makes trials move more efficiently.

"Not sure," Carlson grumbles looking down at his yellow pad.

I shake my head. "At least let me know who your first witness is."

"Nope. You'll find out when I announce it in court."

I roll my eyes, turn back to our table, and mutter, "Asshole."

I lean over Jana and whisper in her ear, "He won't tell me who his first witness will be." She shakes her head in disbelief at Carlson's lack of civility. I continue, "It has to be Vorat. Are you ready?"

"Can't wait," she says as she reaches into her document bag to gather the materials she will need for her cross-examination.

"All rise!" the bailiff yells as the judge enters the courtroom. The bailiff turns to bring in the jury before taking his seat.

Once the jurors are in place, Maruk nods at Carlson, who announces, "We will call Michael Vorat." Vorat approaches the court reporter, who administers the oath. Vorat stands, his right hand in the air, wearing a red silk shirt and gray linen pants and sporting a pinkie ring. I have significant doubts that swearing to god to tell the truth will have any effect on him.

Vorat takes his seat on the witness stand and adjusts the microphone. He smiles at the jury. Most jurors return the smile.

Carlson walks Vorat through the preliminaries. He states he's thirty-one years old and has been living in Pittsburgh for nearly four years. He has no wife or kids but expresses his dedication to Spinelli Enterprises.

Carlson leads his witness through his education and job pursuits. Vorat explains to the jury, "I received my certified public accounting degree from the University of Salem. My grades were outstanding and before graduation many offers of employment from companies on the West Coast were coming my way. My mom lives in Southern Oregon. I wanted to accept a job near to her, so I could help take care of her because of her failing health. But Uncle Arthur called and begged me to work with his company."

Carlson flips a page on his yellow pad and asks, "What did Mr. Spinelli want?"

Vorat lowers his head and glances at the jurors. "He told me the company's accountant, Steve Berlin, was causing trouble. Uncle Arthur said he wanted someone to come in and make sure everything was above board financially."

"How did you respond?"

"I tried to put him off. I didn't want to get caught up in other people's troubles, but my uncle was extremely persistent. He kept calling and emailing me. He told me family always helps out family. Finally, I relented and took the job."

I glance back at Arthur, who remains stone-faced. I sense his impatience and need to get on the stand to tell his side of the story.

Vorat sits straight in the witness box and holds his head high. He and Carlson are establishing a rhythm. This doesn't bother me. Witnesses usually retain their confidence—until they face cross-examination. Jana's calmness while taking notes on her yellow pad reassures me.

Carlson shifts into the meat of Vorat's testimony. "Please tell the jurors what happened after you began your employment."

Vorat nods his head and turns towards the jury. "From my first day with the company, Steve Berlin did nothing to help me understand my responsibilities. I was a brand-new accountant. He was in charge, but he refused to answer any questions I had."

"Did you notice anything unusual?"

"I did. Berlin was a strange guy and never let anyone examine the company's finances. I understood better what he was doing as I learned more about how the company operated."

Carlson takes a step forward. "What do you mean?"

"I kept digging. I found where Berlin hid the books buried on the computer system. It was shocking. He was keeping two sets of financial records. There was one set he used for income tax purposes and to show to the IRS. These records indicated the company was losing money. The second set, however, detailed how much the business in reality made and how profits were diverted."

Carlson smiles. "What do you mean when you say 'diverted'?"

"The records showed a substantial difference between the losses the company reported to the IRS and what it actually made. It was clear Mr. Berlin and my uncle were taking those extra profits and splitting them."

"Mr. Vorat, you uncovered this fraud, so what did you do?"

Vorat shifts again toward the jury. "I wanted to make sure I understood their scheme and that I properly documented everything. I began to send memos to the chairman of the board to keep him apprised on the ongoing investigation. He was supportive and indicated he wanted to get to the bottom of what was happening."

"Did you inform Mr. Berlin what you found?"

"I did. I confronted him with proof of the fraud. He gave a halfhearted explanation and suggested my uncle was the one who was responsible."

Vorat glances at Arthur and discreetly shakes his head.

"What happened to Mr. Berlin after you showed him the evidence?"

"I don't know. The next day he didn't show up. In fact, he never came back to work. He disappeared."

Carlson pauses for a moment to glance at his notes. "Did you ever say anything to your uncle about the fraud you uncovered?"

"I did." Vorat again turns his head in Arthur's direction. Arthur returns the stare without any detectable movement.

"I went to my uncle to get an explanation. I laid out what I found in detail. He sat behind his desk and looked sad. He told me he had no choice but to do it because he had been spending too much money since Aunt Evelyn died. I felt bad for him, especially when he begged me not to tell anyone because he didn't want to go to jail."

Three jurors watch Arthur. He doesn't twitch or release his stare of Vorat.

Carlson asks for a demonstration of how Berlin and Arthur had manipulated the books. Vorat moves to an easel, where they display blowups of three spreadsheets. He claims they detail how the fraud had occurred.

Carlson stands near Vorat in front of the jury box. "Can you explain how these identify the fraud?"

"It's extremely complex," Vorat says while pointing to the spreadsheets. "The first column demonstrates the company outlays and the second details the money taken improperly from the bank accounts. The cash removed far exceeds what the company was making. The only people in a position to do this are my uncle and Mr. Berlin."

Vorat takes the laser pointer he had been utilizing and places it in his shirt pocket. "It's clear they took the money. I understand what they did, but I have studied accounting for a long time. It's difficult to see. It's there, if you know what you are looking for."

Carlson directs Vorat back to the witness stand. After he takes his seat, Carlson asks, "How much money did they take?"

"The bottom line is through their long-standing fraud, the company is missing three-point-one million dollars."

"Thank you. The other attorneys may have some questions for you."

You can bet on it.

I shake my head as I examine the notes on my yellow pad. A tinge of regret spreads in my gut. I want to get my hands on this guy and cross-examine him. Instead, I get to watch Jana do the heavy lifting. I make a small wish she is as prepared as we thought she was last night.

Jana deliberately places her papers on the lectern in front of the witness stand. "Mr. Vorat," she begins, "you stated that before you began at Spinelli Enterprises, you received multiple offers from major companies on the West Coast."

"True, they really wanted me."

"Sir, you don't have any proof these offers in fact exist, do you?"

"Not with me. I didn't know I should bring them." He shrugs at the jury. Some members smile back.

Jana waits a moment and states, "Not my question. You don't have any documents, do you?"

"I'm not sure what you mean." Vorat says, a little less self-assured.

"Let me show you our request for production of documents." She places the document before him. "Do you remember seeing this?"

"Not really." He again shrugs his shoulders.

"Direct your attention to the last page. You see the verification you signed indicating you had searched all the company's papers and your own personal records to respond to these requests. Do you remember it now?"

"I guess."

"Turn to request number 17. It says, doesn't it, 'All documents you possess reflecting any offers of employment made to Vorat at any point before coming to Spinelli Enterprises.' And what was your answer?"

"Ah, none."

Jana walks away and returns to the lectern. "So, the answer to my original question about whether you had any documents that would prove you actually had any other job offers wouldn't be: 'I forgot to bring them.' The answer is: 'There are none'—correct?"

"I guess."

Score one point for Jana.

Jana doesn't hesitate. "Mr. Vorat, let's move on. Tell us again what degree you received?"

"I received a certified public accountant's degree from the University of Salem. It's in Oregon."

"Don't worry, we know exactly where it is." Jana says, "You never hung any diplomas in your offices, did you?"

"Not my way of doing things. I don't like bragging. I'd rather hang family pictures."

"You never showed anyone your degree, did you?"

"Nobody ever asked."

"You couldn't have shown anybody any degree, if you had been asked, because you don't have one, do you?"

Carlson is up on his feet. "Objection. That's an outrageous and unsupportable allegation."

The corners of Judge Maruk's mouth turn up. "I'm guessing we may find out how outrageous it is. Overruled for the time being. Ms. Larihall, please continue."

I think the judge may be taking a little shine to Jana.

"Mr. Vorat," Jana says deliberately, "you don't have an accounting degree, do you?"

"Of course I do." Vorat offers, looking to the jury for support. It's unclear whether any is coming.

Jana grabs a document and hands a copy to Carlson. She asks the judge for permission to approach the witness. Carlson is on his feet before the judge responds. "Your Honor, I object. I have never seen this document before. It was never produced and it's not on their exhibit list."

Jana stands calmly at the lectern. She offers, "This document is for impeachment, and under the rules we have no obligation to produce records we intend to use to impeach a witness."

Jana is correct. No party has to give documents to the other side if their purpose is solely to contradict the testimony of a witness. I wait expectantly for the ruling.

"Mr. Carlson," Judge Maruk says, "whether Mr. Vorat is a licensed accountant is a material issue—he has made it an issue. Ms. Larihall can attempt to impeach him on it if she chooses. Any document arguably establishing he is not licensed would not have to be produced, and she is free to use it during her exam."

Jana waits for a moment, knowing the jury is eagerly expecting some fireworks after the judge's ruling. She hands the document to Vorat and continues to bore in. "Mr. Vorat, this is a letter from the University of Oregon addressed to you, isn't it?"

"Yes."

"I'm going to read it. Let me know if I do it correctly: 'Dear Mr. Vorat, attached is your transcript for the prior year. Please note you failed to satisfy the requirements of Forensic Accounting II and have received a failing grade. Accordingly, you have not received sufficient credits to qualify for a certified public accountant's degree. If you wish to receive this degree, you must complete the Forensic Accounting course, as this class is a requirement for your degree.' Did I read this correctly?"

"Yes," Vorat says, not as loudly.

"You never received a degree, did you?"

"I did all the work. It was unfair they wouldn't pass me. I'd been sick."

"You never received an accounting degree, did you?" Jana slowly repeats.

"I guess not?"

"I guess you never told Arthur Spinelli or anyone else at the company you weren't actually an accountant?"

"There wasn't any need to?"

"Did you inform anyone you weren't an accountant?"

"No." Vorat avoids looking at the jury.

Jana knows she has scored a huge point. She shuffles some papers to allow more time to let the damage sink in before renewing her questioning. "Mr. Vorat, in your direct examination, you accused Mr. Spinelli of stealing money. You used three documents you claim support your allegations."

"Well, they do."

"Let's talk about them. The documents you went over before were not certified financial records of the company, were they?'

"What do you mean?" Vorat asks, avoiding the question.

"What I mean is, you accuse our client of stealing and claim these documents support your allegations, but isn't it true Mr. Spinelli never prepared those documents?"

"Yes,"

"No certified accountant prepared the documents either, correct?"

"Yes."

"In fact, Arthur Spinelli never reviewed them, did he?"

"How should I know what he did?"

"You should know because you were the one who prepared them, weren't you?"

Vorat is having troubles knowing which way is up at this point. "I did, but so what?"

"You never showed anybody any supporting evidence for the records you testified about, did you?"

"Everything is in those documents. They show clearly my uncle took the money."

"Sir, other than those three documents you put on the easel, you do not have any other support for your claim Mr. Spinelli stole from the company?"

"It's all in there. It's black and white. Arthur stole the money."

Jana is confident at this point she has damaged Vorat's credibility. She has additional potential questions to probe Vorat but has scored some major points. She chooses to end her examination without further inquiry. It's a wise decision. She sits at counsel table and I pass her a note. It reads: "Tremendous job."

I couldn't be more proud.

CHAPTER 29

After lunch, Carlson calls William Paxson, the chairman of the board of directors, to testify. A tall, lanky man in his early sixties, he appears confident, but I sense an edginess. I presume he believed sitting on the board of Spinelli Enterprises would allow him to make a little money, while avoiding having to do a significant amount of work. My goal is for the jurors to see how much responsibility he avoided while taking his paycheck.

Paxson eases into the witness stand with a nod. Carlson assumes his same spot by the rail of the jury box. After introducing himself, Paxson informs the jury that he previously had managed two companies but fails to offer any testimony about whether either achieved success. He became chairman of the Spinelli board when the company incorporated, but he didn't expect Arthur to need a lot of oversight given how well he had performed prior to incorporation.

Carlson wants to establish Paxson had no involvement in the decision to hire Vorat. "I only met the previous accountant on two occasions, so I didn't need to be involved in hiring his assistant.

We let Mr. Spinelli operate the business and left employment decisions to him."

Paxson talks about the role the board plays and how it is supposed to oversee the operations of the company. "Generally, we made sure Mr. Spinelli managed it consistent with the law, and we would review the financial records he provided." He turns to the jury and shrugs his shoulders. "Unfortunately, we can only review the information we are given. If someone decides to steal, he can often hide it by altering the records. Without a full-blow audit, we are not in a position to detect fraudulent activity. Until Mr. Vorat discovered the fraud, we were not aware of what was happening."

"Tell the jury what Mr. Vorat did and how the board responded."

"We were shocked there had been a theft. We conducted a follow-up investigation confirming Mr. Spinelli, apparently with the help of Mr. Berlin, diverted funds for their personal use."

"What did the board do once it determined Mr. Spinelli and Mr. Berlin stole money?"

"First we considered filing criminal charges. Mr. Berlin, however, had disappeared. With Mr. Spinelli's long service and in consideration of his age, we believed it was best to attempt to recover the stolen money from him."

"Did the company receive any restitution from Mr. Spinelli?"

Paxson glances down and shakes his head. He takes off his glasses, wipes them, and returns them to his face. "No, Mr. Spinelli denied taking anything and refused to return the money. We had no choice but to terminate him and confiscate his company stock."

Carlson makes a sweeping gesture in my direction. "Mr. Spinelli's attorney may have some questions for you."

I stand to cross-examine Paxson and take my time gathering my papers, so I can take a few breaths. My insides churn. I need to get my emotions under control and ask my questions slowly.

I grip the sides of the lectern. "Mr. Paxson, you are the head of the board of directors of Spinelli Enterprises, aren't you?"

"Yes, I am."

"You have a legal obligation to act in the best interests of the company, don't you?"

"Absolutely."

"If something is wrong at the company, it's your job to fix it, isn't it?"

"Of course."

"You failed at your duties. You didn't prevent the theft?"

"Well, it is unfortunate, but money was stolen from the company."

Paxson is smooth. I often tell witnesses to admit a bad fact when challenged on cross-examination. It's better than getting into a protracted discussion. If the witness doesn't appear to be admitting anything significant, the jury might miss the importance of the point. I decide to change tactics with Paxson.

"You never physically were at any of the company's locations before Mike Vorat became head accountant?"

"We had board meetings once a year, but they usually occurred at my offices downtown."

"You never actually verified Mike Vorat was a certified accountant."

"No, I guess I didn't."

I am moving quickly between subjects because I don't want Paxson to think he knows where I am going.

"Mr. Vorat wrote you three memos stating Arthur Spinelli was stealing, correct?"

"Yes."

"You were aware at the time you received the memos that Mr. Spinelli had been with the company for over thirty years?"

"Yes."

"There had never been a problem with Mr. Spinelli. His reputation was impeccable and the business had made profits for decades?"

"I guess this is true."

"Mike Vorat, when he wrote you the memos, had been employed for a few months."

"Yes."

"It turns out Mr. Vorat lied when he said he was a licensed accountant."

"Unfortunately, this now appears to be true."

"Yet despite Mr. Spinelli's years of dedicated and unblemished service, you chose to believe a person who had worked at the company for a short period over him?"

"Well, yes. He had given me strong support for his claim against Mr. Spinelli and I believed him."

"The support you are referring to is a few spreadsheets Mr. Vorat prepared?"

"Apparently."

"To be clear, you trusted a person who lied to your company over Mr. Spinelli, and you relied on a few spreadsheets he had made as support of these allegations."

"The conclusion was obvious when I studied the spreadsheets. The board's investigation supported what Mr. Vorat reported."

"So you say."

"Objection!" Carlson bellows as he pushes back his chair.

"Sustained," Judge Maruk announces to the jury. "Let's try to stick to the evidence, Mr. West."

I turn my attention back to Paxson, "You have an inexperienced accountant making accusations against a long-term trusted owner of the company, and you accept his word?"

"I believe I indicated we hired an independent auditor. It was clear Mr. Vorat's investigation was solid."

"Mr. Spinelli denied he had done what Mr. Vorat has accused him of doing, didn't he?"

"Yes."

"In fact, Mr. Spinelli told you he had retained his own auditor to review the financial records of the company."

"Yes, he told me."

"And when Mr. Spinelli tried to get you to read his auditor's findings, you refused, correct?"

"Yes, it was apparent Mr. Spinelli hired someone to make it appear like he hadn't done anything. I had no reason to trust this person and believe those results." Paxson waves his hand sideways dismissively.

I take one step closer to Paxson. "You ignored Mr. Berlin when he tried to explain what had happened."

"I didn't ignore him. His explanations were self-serving and unsupported by the documents."

"So you chose not to believe the licensed CPA with 20 years of experience and believe the unlicensed accountant who had worked for less than one year."

"That's what you think."

"It's not what I think—it's the truth, isn't it?"

"I guess so."

I pause and step back behind the lectern. "Mr. Paxson, your primary job is as a vice president with Ajax Manufacturing?"

"Yes."

"You receive a salary from Ajax every month?"

"Yes." Paxson's eyes narrow as he anticipates my next question.

"Your salary hasn't changed in the past four years."

"Unfortunately, you're correct." Paxson shrugs at the jurors and smiles. The jurors remain impassive.

"You have no other employment or sources of income other than Ajax and the pay you receive for your board service to Spinelli."

"True"

I squint at my notes. "Isn't it true that soon after Mike Vorat began to work for the company, you started putting a lot more cash in the bank?"

"What are you talking about?" he says, looking from the jurors to me and back again.

"Let me show you your account statements we have subpoenaed." I hand copies to Carlson and place the same stack on the ledge in front of Paxson. He won't touch the documents.

I continue. "Sir, two months after Mike Vorat started working at the company, you started putting ten thousand dollars extra each month into your account, didn't you?"

Jana had obtained these records recently, and although we weren't positive how Paxson had put so much more money into the bank, we had an educated guess. After some deliberation, we decided confronting Paxson with these documents on the witness stand was virtually a no-risk decision. The worst-case result was he came up with a reasonable explanation for the additional money.

"How did you get my bank statements? Those are private."

Judge Maruk interjects, "Sir, you are to answer the question."

Paxson's cool is vanishing. He stammers, "I will not respond." His options are dwindling. He turns to the judge and then to the papers in front of him. He shakes his head. Through pursed lips he blurts out, "I am taking the Fifth Amendment and not answering the question."

Music to my ears. I give Paxson the same expression I give Charley when he does something disappointing. I glance at the jury and ask the judge to instruct them how to interpret a witness' refusal to answer a question if he invokes his rights under the Fifth Amendment of the United States Constitution.

The judge tells the jury, who sit enraptured by this latest development, "A person has a right not to answer a question if he believes the response could later be used against him in a criminal action."

Maruk takes a breath before proceeding. "This right against self-incrimination is one of the hallmarks of our legal system, but in a civil case such as this, when a witness invokes his Fifth Amendment rights and doesn't respond to a question, the jury should presume the answer is one which could cause him to be held liable criminally."

I grab Jana's arm and whisper, "Does the jury understand the judge has essentially instructed them to presume the extra money in Paxson's bank account had been stolen from the company?"

Jana examines the jury and whispers back to me, "I think so. You'll hammer this home in closing."

After completing his instruction about Fifth Amendment rights, Judge Maruk nods at me to continue my cross-examination. I make no attempt to contain my smile. "I don't believe there is any need to ask any further questions of this witness."

I turn my head away as Paxson slinks off the witness stand. The jurors stare straight forward, waiting for the next witness. A slight grin appears on Arthur's face.

The judge announces there is insufficient time left in the day to hear from another witness. He instructs the jurors to return in the morning so trial can continue. He tells the lawyers to remain to discuss the jury instructions he will read at the end of the trial.

In his chambers, Judge Maruk hears argument over what should be read to the jurors after closing arguments. Jana had spent days crafting proposed instructions we had submitted at the beginning of trial. Carlson also provided the judge the points of law he wanted to be read to the jury. The court reporter spends two hours with us transcribing the arguments both sides make over the minutiae of how the judge should instruct the jury.

In many cases, but in this one in particular, I don't believe the instructions will have much influence on the outcome of the case. Here, although the judge will inform the jurors of the intricacies of the law in Pennsylvania for fraud and conversion, their primary responsibility is to decide one thing—who was telling the truth. Like many cases, this one involves two polar-opposite stories: Vorat claiming Arthur stole from the company and Arthur accusing Vorat of theft. No matter what the judge tells them, their decision ultimately will rest on which side they believe.

After finishing the arguments over the jury instructions, Jana and I gather our materials and walk out of the courtroom with Arthur.

We head back to my office. We throw our coats on hooks and hunker down for a couple of hours of work to prepare for tomorrow's testimony.

CHAPTER 30

I PULL MY CAR INTO the driveway behind our house and spot the silhouetted figures of my wife and son engaged in a discussion at the kitchen table. When I enter, I'm relieved no one else is there but my family. Charley runs over to tell me dinner is ready.

"Perfect," I say, kissing Jill. "I'm hungry and I need to finish dinner quickly, so I can work on my closing in front of the bathroom mirror."

Jill places a dish of beans and rice on the table. "It's nothing special. We kept it on the stove, so we could spend some time together. Charley's just finished his homework."

We sit to eat, and I ask Charley about math. He asks for advice on a pre-algebra problem. I'm able to offer a plan to attack the question, happy I can still offer something useful.

I'm enjoying hanging with my family but also stuffing food into my mouth, so I can get to more witness preparation. Jill notices and attempts to slow my pace. "How's the trial going?"

I reach for the jug to pour myself a glass of water. "I'm happy, I think. They finished calling witnesses. Jana handled

Vorat. Hurt him. I questioned the head of the board of directors. Amazingly, he stopped answering questions when he took the Fifth Amendment. Never saw that before. So I guess it went well. Tomorrow we will call our witnesses. We'll finish by the end of the day, if we're lucky."

Jill nods her head, but her face scrunches. "Is Arthur going to testify?"

"Yes. He'll be the first witness in the morning. I think he's ready."

Charley perks up at the mention of Arthur's name. "Why are you talking about Arthur?'

Jill and I decided months ago not to tell Charley much but to let him know I was helping Arthur, in case one of his friends heard about it. We hadn't provided him with much detail to forestall potential worry.

"You remember we told you Arthur was involved in a lawsuit." Charley nods his head. "Well, it's in the middle of trial and he's going to testify tomorrow."

Charley puts down his fork and stares at me intently. "What's it about again?"

Most of the time, Charley has little interest in the particulars of my cases, and he rarely knows when I am actually in trial. Sometimes, however, he catches a detail that piques his curiosity and wants to hear more. It's fascinating getting Charley's point of view. Often, his analysis leads to insightful discussions about right and wrong. Those conversations are much more abstract as he doesn't know any of the participants in those trials.

I'm not sure what to say to Charley but decide to be as honest as possible. "Arthur's nephew accused him of stealing and got Arthur fired from the company. He sued Arthur for the money he claims Arthur stole."

Charley's eyes widen. "He didn't steal, did he?"

I put a hand on Charley's arm. "Of course he didn't. Arthur's challenging this. He thinks the nephew may be the thief, and will say that tomorrow."

Charley smiles. "Arthur wouldn't steal. I'm glad he's fighting back. I don't think it's fair his nephew made that up," Charley states with indignation.

"I agree, and it's my job to make sure Arthur gets a chance to tell his side of the story and tell it well."

Charley turns his head to the side and then returns his gaze to me. "Can I see Arthur tell his story?"

I push out a huff of air. Charley has never seen one of my trials. Not because I wouldn't want him there, but usually because he's supposed to be in school and the logistics of having him in the courtroom are too much. I would love for him to see a trial, and I think he would learn a lot from watching.

"You know," Jill says, "it may not be such a bad idea for him to go. I think Arthur might actually appreciate the support." She smiles at Charley.

"What about school? I can't take care of him during trial," I say.

"I don't have much at work tomorrow," She adds. "I can take him to court. I would love to see Arthur testify. I think it may be more educational than some stuff he learns in class. I haven't been to one of your trials for a long time."

In the past five minutes, this has become important to Charley. I don't mind him coming to trial. Rather, I can't worry about him in the courtroom and don't want him being a distraction. I'm more concerned with whether this will bother Arthur. I'll ask him if Charley will be a nuisance.

"I don't have a problem with you going," I say. "I think you can learn something by watching. But it's up to Arthur. I know how much he cares about you, but I don't want your being there to make the trial more difficult for him. I will ask him what he thinks. If it's okay with him, it's okay with me."

"Awesome. Thanks, Dad."

Charley bounds off, not knowing what he might be getting himself into.

"It's time to get ready for bed," I announce as I enter the family room. Charley's head is buried in a book as he sits on the couch. He does not move.

I repeat, "It's time for bed."

He moves but with no urgency. "Hey," I say, "you got what you wanted."

"What are you talking about?"

"I just got off the phone with Arthur. He's fine with you coming tomorrow. He's nervous, which has nothing to do with you. Remember, this is serious. I doubt Arthur or I will be able to talk to you. You'll have to be quiet. Root for Arthur all you want, but you have to do it silently. You got it?"

Charley smiles as I push him up the stairs. "Got it, I have to be silent. Dad, you have to win for Arthur."

"We're doing the best we can. Upstairs now, and get ready for bed. Mom and I will be up in a minute to sing."

CHAPTER 31

THE WIND HOWLS ON a cold, blustery fall morning when we return to court for the third and likely last day of trial. Carlson stands to announce they have no more testimony and are resting their case. We had assumed this would be their plan but were prepared if they called the cronies Vorat had hired to assist him. Given their knowledge of accounting was less than Vorat's, it didn't make much sense for them to testify.

It's now our turn to put on evidence. I grab my yellow pad, stand, and announce Arthur as our first witness. He sits calmly in the witness chair, sporting a brown-tweed blazer and neatly pressed tan trousers. He doesn't smile but engages the jury as he awaits my questions. The jurors sit forward waiting for my first question.

My goal is for the jury to see Arthur as a person with a rich life's history. I take him through a quick tour of his significant mile-markers. He talks of growing up in McKees Rocks, a rough-and-tumble section of Pittsburgh. With a sparkle in his eye, he briefly discusses the night he met Evelyn and how they started their company. Without sounding melancholy, he conveys his love for her and the business.

I peer over at the jurors to see if they are at all captivated by his stories of the early days. It's impossible to detect their level of interest, but his ability to explain how his business operates has to impress at least some of them.

Arthur speaks briefly of Evelyn's death, but only in the context of how it affected his work at the company. We move to the evolution of the decision to employ members of both sides of their family. "We always wanted our nieces and nephews working with us. Evelyn thought it was a simple way to stay connected with people who we didn't get to see much. After she passed, I continued to put as much family onto the payroll as possible."

I shift papers in my binder before moving on to a new subject area. "How well did you know Mike Vorat before you hired him?"

A slight grimace appears on Arthur's face. "Some. I had met him probably three times at various functions on the West Coast, like when one of Evelyn's nieces was married. For whatever reason, his family did not spend a lot of time with us, so we did not know him as well as our other nieces and nephews."

"How did he end up working for Spinelli Enterprises?"

"His mother called to tell me he was getting a CPA license. She asked me if I would talk to him about employment. I said 'Yes,' of course." Arthur glances down at his hands and returns his gaze to the jurors. "We had two conversations. It wasn't an interview. We both knew the job was his. Steve Berlin had informed me he was getting close to retirement. I spoke with Mike about how he could make a career out of working for our company. He sounded excited."

"How was his performance after he began?"

"At first it was fine. I got no reports of any problems. After about two months, Steve started acted strangely. I asked him what was the matter, but he wouldn't tell me. A few days later, he left the company. He stopped me in the hallway and told me he was leaving. Nothing more. He never told me why, and he never told me where he was going." Arthur shakes his head.

"So what did you do?"

"I was worried. Mr. Berlin knew our accounting systems better than anyone. I talked to Mike about it, and he assured me he had the bookkeeping under control and could handle it. I didn't have any choice."

"Did you know Mr. Vorat never got his CPA license?"

"No, I never really thought to ask. I should have been more careful."

"What happened to Mr. Berlin?"

"Strange," Arthur begins. "Steve had been with our company for a long time. He knew his stuff and was reliable. One day he tells me he's quitting. He didn't give any notice. I talked to him once on his cell phone a few days later, but he wouldn't give me any reason why he left. I was worried about him, and I never understood why he had to leave so quickly."

"What did the company do to replace Mr. Berlin?"

"We were in a lurch. We needed an accountant and were grooming Mike to replace Steve. I decided we had no choice but to move the timetable up and have Mike assume Steve's responsibilities. He assured me it wouldn't be a problem."

"What happened after Mr. Vorat took over as the lead accountant for the company?"

"A few weeks after we put him in the position, he told me he wanted to hire two people to act as his assistants. I was confused because he had said he could handle the job responsibilities. In his defense, he said he was learning the business and needed some help for a short time. The company was doing well, so I told him to do whatever he had to do."

"What did he do?"

"He brought in two people. Turns out they were buddies of his. I'm not sure what they did. I never understood the value they added to the company."

Arthur explains that soon after he hired Vorat as lead account, the company had to do its end-of-the-year reconciliations.

"Mike came to me one day with a bunch of spreadsheets in his hand and a frown on his face. He told me the company had suffered a loss. I couldn't believe it. We hadn't had a loss for decades. I asked Mr. Vorat to walk me through the accounting, so I could understand, but he never sat down with me to help me figure out what was happening to the company financially."

"Did you obtain other assistance to help you understand the source of the loss?"

"I did," Arthur says. "At first I tried to get every financial record for the company. Mr. Vorat was not terribly forthcoming with those, so I had to search through file drawers and on our computer system to locate them. I wanted to review them myself. I have some knowledge of accounting after so many years with the company, but the documents I found were all over the place. I couldn't figure out what happened."

"So what did you do?"

"I was getting worried because the financial records didn't make sense. Mike was no help, so I retained an outside accountant to review what I had."

"Who was that?"

"Her name is Deb Creed. She's adept at figuring out these types of issues."

"What was Mr. Vorat doing while Ms. Creed was investigating the financial history of the company?"

"He had no idea at first what she was doing. At some point I think he found out someone was investigating."

"Objection!" yells Carlson as he half-stands in front of his chair.

Judge Maruk thinks for a moment. "Sustained," he rules. "Mr. Spinelli, please stick to what you know, not what you think may have happened,"

I get Arthur's attention. "Did Ms. Creed finish her investigation?"

Arthur shakes his head. "Not before I was fired. One day, Mr. Paxson came to my office and showed me the three memos Mike had sent to him. He called me a thief. They made me walk out of the place with a security guard." He almost whispers. "Like I was a criminal."

I pause to let the jury take in the impact.

"Mr. Spinelli," I ask. "Did Ms. Creed finish her investigation?"

"Yes. We had copies of the records I'd found. A few weeks later she told me her findings."

"Ms. Creed will be testifying soon, so I will let her discuss the results of her investigation, but let me ask you this: Did she find any evidence you had stolen money from the company?"

Arthur purses his lips and opens his hands toward the ceiling. "No. There is no evidence because I didn't steal anything." He glances toward the back of the courtroom. He catches a smile from Jill, and Charley gives a thumbs-up sign—until Jill pushes his hands back into his lap.

I think that Arthur has done well staying composed so far and has plausibly denied taking any money. The last area I need to get into is how these events have affected him, both financially and emotionally.

"Has your termination damaged you?"

"Financially, absolutely. I no longer have a salary. I don't receive my share of the profits. They took my stock away. My benefits are gone. But we saved a little each year, so I'll be fine."

I delay my next question, pondering whether Arthur has described sufficiently his monetary harm from being terminated.

I decide to move on. "Tell us, has your termination affected you emotionally?"

Arthur takes off his glasses and pulls out a handkerchief to clean them. He puts his glasses back on and turns to the jury. "Absolutely. I am devastated every day by the humiliation of being fired for doing nothing wrong. This is the company I started. This is the company Evelyn and I built. This is the company that trained our family to become smart business people. Now they want to steal it from me." Arthur's voice breaks slightly.

I know he's not finished, so I give him a little time to regain his composure.

Arthur turns to his nephew sitting at counsel table. Vorat attempts to keep eye contact with Arthur, who does not twitch. He speaks to Vorat as if no one else is in the room. "It's shameful what you have done. I have given my heart to this company..." He begins to say more but decides he has nothing to add.

The room is silent. I sit in my chair and motion to indicate I have completed my questioning.

Carlson rises to cross-examine Arthur. He asks him some seemingly innocuous questions about how Arthur had started the company. Arthur again displays a nearly encyclopedic knowledge of the company's history. Carlson moves to questioning about Evelyn's death, suggesting Arthur is not the same person he was since she died. I don't believe Carlson demonstrates Arthur has any limitations.

He jumps to the financial records Vorat prepared. "Mr. Spinelli," he asks, "don't these spreadsheets demonstrate how you took money from the company?"

A thin smile emerges on Arthur's face. "I don't know what those spreadsheets show. My nephew would never share them with me. I also asked Mr. Paxson for copies of them. He never allowed me to see them either. I didn't review them, so I can't say what they show."

"C'mon, Mr. Spinelli. You're trying to run from the fact you stole money and were caught red-handed."

Arthur takes a deep breath before speaking. "Not true. I have never taken a dollar I haven't earned, and I surely never took any money improperly from my own company."

It's always difficult watching my witnesses get cross-examined. They are on the stand alone and there is virtually nothing I can do to help them. I tell witnesses when they are being crossed, don't turn to me because they need to figure out how to answer the questions without looking like they need assistance. Hopefully they are prepared to give decent answers to whatever question is being posed.

Arthur deftly handle Carlson's inquiries. He takes the high road when Carlson tries to bait him into an argument. To me, he is a reasonable witness. I can only guess how he appears to the jurors, whose faces I cannot read. I am relieved he has completed his testimony without any apparent major dings to his credibility. I turn my thoughts to our next witness.

Arthur returns to his seat behind our counsel table. He again meets eyes with Jill and Charley seated in the back of the courtroom. Charley's hair is combed back and his Polamalu jersey is tucked in his pants. In the section of seats to their right, a tall, wiry man in a dark suit fidgets with his fingers. He offers me a weak smile.

CHAPTER 32

I STAND AND TURN TO the jury. "For his next witness, Arthur Spinelli calls Steven Berlin."

The tall man rises and walks to the front of the courtroom without making eye contact with anyone. He sits in the witness seat. I look down at my notes, hoping Jana's instincts were correct.

For months, we had no idea where he was living. We couldn't find any trace of him on the internet, nor did we have a way of contacting him. Jana hired a private investigator who found a possible email address, apparently in Costa Rica. Jana emailed him for weeks without a response. She had no reason to believe the email address was his. Finally, she included a personal request from Arthur in a last-ditch attempt. Berlin finally responded. At first, he said he wanted nothing to do with this case or his prior life. He adamantly claimed he would never return to Pittsburgh.

Two weeks ago, Jana contacted Berlin again and tried to figure out his hesitation about testifying. After much back-and-forth, he told her he wanted to do what was right and would come up to testify. Despite Jana's prodding, Berlin refused to provide her with any information about the nature of his testimony. He told her he would say it once, and only from the witness stand.

Jana told me she felt he would support Arthur, but it concerned me that all we had was her intuition. I talked in my opening statement about what Berlin would say, but that was more hopeful than anything else. He takes his place in the witness box, and I recognize our case could implode in the next ten minutes.

Berlin adjusts his horn-rimmed glasses. He sports a pressed gray-pinstriped suit and has the countenance of an accountant, meticulous-looking and circumspect. I presume he has never told a joke in his life.

Berlin wouldn't speak with us before testifying, so I don't know what he will say. I prepared an outline, but I know I will change course once I hear some of his answers. Mainly, I decide to let Berlin tell his story and hope it's consistent with what Arthur told us had happened.

Berlin speaks crisply, answering my early questions about his background. My initial reaction is he is playing it down the middle of the road and not wanting to shade his testimony in either direction. He tells the jury he worked for Spinelli Enterprises for seventeen years as their accountant. He loved working there because the people were easy to work with and management treated the employees well. The business made a profit every year of his employment.

Berlin takes a deep breath when I ask him what he thinks of Arthur.

"I respect Arthur Spinelli—not only as a business owner, but also as a person. Mr. Spinelli loved his company, but he also loved the people. I worked for him for a long time and feel like he treated me and everyone else there extremely well."

"Did you know Mr. Spinelli's wife, Evelyn?" I ask.

"I did. Not as well as Mr. Spinelli, but she also was a wonderful person. It was such a sad time when she died. Every employee went to her funeral—not because they had to, but because they wanted to show Arthur the respect they had for both of them."

"Tell me about when Michael Vorat came to work for Spinelli Enterprises."

Berlin glances down, and when he raises his head, his face is bright red. He spits out, "That man is manipulative, lazy, and condescending. He is an embarrassment to all accountants."

"Why do you say this?"

"He never wanted to learn how to understand the financial statements. All he wanted to know was where the money came from and where it was going. I'm not confrontational, but I had to tell him to focus on his job."

"What did Mr. Vorat do?"

"It was about four months after he began working. He approached me one day and told me I was going to show him more about how cash moved around the company. I refused and considered talking to Arthur about it but didn't. The next day he came into the office and showed me pictures of people who had been shot or stabbed and who were lying in the street. He said he had friends who took the photos and suggested they would do this to me if I didn't help him. I wasn't sure, but I believed he might.

"I have two teenage girls and my wife. I had talked about retiring and going to Florida. I decided we should move further south. We moved up the timetable. The next day, we left. I told Arthur I was quitting. I should have told him what was happening, but I was truly scared for my family."

"Mr. Berlin, did you or Mr. Spinelli ever steal money from the company?"

"Of course not. He would never do that."

I grab some financial records Vorat had submitted from a stack of documents on my counsel table and hand them to Berlin, who provides an in-depth explanation of how the records don't reflect what happened.

Berlin's testimony does not take a long time, but he accomplishes what I wanted. He has refuted Vorat's contention that he and Arthur stole the money, while painting a glowing picture of Arthur and how he treated his employees. He also had laid the foundation for the testimony of Deb Creed, our expert.

Carlson stands to cross-examine Berlin. Before he gets out his first question, Berlin scowls and grabs the edges of the witness box, looking ready to pounce.

"Mr. Berlin, you ran away to Costa Rica and tried to hide."

"I moved after Mr. Vorat threatened me."

"You have no proof he threatened you, do you?"

Berlin pauses momentarily. "I guess my proof is I relocated. There was no reason for me to move except for Mr. Vorat's threats."

"You have no letters from Mr. Vorat threatening you, do you?"

"No, I don't."

"You don't have the pictures you suggest he showed to you."

"No, I don't."

Carlson steps forward with a slight grimace. "You took money from the company and fled to Costa Rica."

"No," Berlin's voice rises. "Mr. Vorat threatened me and I decided to retire early."

"C'mon. You never went to the police. You never told anyone about his supposed threats. Did you?" Carlson points at Berlin.

"I didn't. I was too scared. I didn't want anything to happen to my family."

"You never went to the board of directors to contest the memorandums Mr. Vorat submitted detailing the fraud you had undertaken."

"I didn't know about them. He never showed them to me. How could I challenge them?"

"Well, let's put it this way, money was disappearing and you didn't do anything about it. You didn't find it, did you?"

"The financial records prepared under my direction demonstrated no fraud or cash missing from the company. If the money is gone, I suspect it left after I moved to Costa Rica."

Carlson pauses for a moment, fumbles with his notes, and says, "No further questions."

I thank Berlin as he walks by me on his way out of the courtroom. He stops briefly to whisper in my ear, "Get that slimy bastard."

Jana handles our final witness, Deb Creed, the forensic accountant. She does a marvelous job of leading Deb through the company's morass of financial records in thirty minutes. Deb demonstrates her knowledge of these documents and educates the jury on how a person with access could manipulate the entries to hide cash. Deb finishes by saying there is no evidence Arthur manipulated the books. She points out that nothing in Arthur's personal financial records indicates he had received any extra money.

She concludes by stating, "My review of the documents, the cash flow of the company, and the individual asset records of the relevant witnesses leads to one conclusion—Michael Vorat, with the assistance of the chairman of the board of directors, stole cash and manipulated the financial records to cover up his actions."

Carlson attempts to cross-examine Deb by using the documents Vorat had prepared and used in his examination. This provides Deb another opportunity to tell the jury the documents are worthless because there is nothing to indicate they are based on the company's actual financial records.

Carlson avoids taking Deb on directly about the finances, so he tries to finesse questions to her regarding the actions of Steve Berlin. He can't slip anything by her. She finishes her testimony by saying, "I have no idea why Mr. Berlin left and moved to Costa Rica. I have never spoken with him. My conclusion is Mr. Berlin did not contribute to this massive fraud at the company."

Carlson pauses for a moment and sits again.

Creed leaves the stand and Judge Maruk nods his head toward me. I rise and announce, "Arthur Spinelli rests."

CHAPTER 33

WITH A SMILE, THE judge asks if I'm ready to give my closing argument. I stand and approach the jury deliberately while maintaining eye contact. I want to give them what they need to hear, but I want to do it quickly. They know the case.

"You've heard two stories, from two very different people. Ultimately, you will have to determine which story is true, because they can't both be accurate. You may be uncomfortable and wonder how to do this. I tell you, it's not too hard. You decide credibility issues every day whenever you talk to someone.

"You size up people. You evaluate what they say. You determine if they support what they are telling you with facts.

"In this case, evaluating a witness' truthfulness is simple, and every reasonable method for determining who's honest favors Arthur Spinelli.

"First, Arthur is the real deal. You heard his story. He built a company from scratch, creating an ongoing business where nothing had existed previously. It has thrived. On the other hand,

Mike Vorat is a fraud. He held himself out as a licensed accountant when he doesn't even have an accounting degree.

"Second, Vorat can't back up his claims Arthur and Steve Berlin stole from the business. The documents he has produced provide no support. His testimony did nothing to explain them to you. You heard from Deb Creed. She took you step-by-step through the records and explained where the money went—right to the bank accounts of William Paxson and Mike Vorat.

"Third, Vorat aligns himself with the likes of Paxson, a man who came in here to testify yet left after invoking the Fifth Amendment, which as the judge will instruct you, is used by people who have committed criminal acts. Arthur, conversely, has friends like Steve Berlin and is supported by Deb Creed—solid, upstanding individuals who locked eyes with you and explained exactly what had happened.

Vorat claims Berlin stole the money and fled to Costa Rica. Mr. Berlin gave you the reason he left—Mr. Vorat threatened him and his family, providing Vorat with the opportunity to commit his crimes and giving him a scared person to be his fall guy.

"I know you can see through this. Every shred of believable testimony supports Arthur Spinelli and points to Mike Vorat as the liar."

I am confident the jury is with me so far. The evidence is overwhelming that Vorat stole from the company. Now I'm looking to generate a surge of anger and disdain directed toward Vorat and Paxson. I want them so irate that they feel comfortable awarding a significant amount of money to Arthur.

I spend a little time discussing the evidence to establish how much Arthur has lost as a result of Vorat's actions.

"Ultimately," I say, "this is about making Arthur whole again. Think about how much Mr. Vorat has taken from him." I point directly at Vorat, yet keep my gaze on the jurors. I ask them to award two million dollars, hoping I sound reasonable and they were thinking of even larger numbers. I sit and turn to Arthur. I place a hand on his arm. He nods, keeping his attention on the jury.

Judge Maruk nods at Carlson, who stands and walks to the front of the jury box.

"Ladies and Gentlemen," he begins, "Mr. West in his opening told you there is a liar in the courtroom, and he was absolutely correct."

He turns to Arthur and shakes his head. "Mr. Spinelli comes here and shamelessly blames everyone else for his bad acts. He hired his nephew, a young up-and-comer, and put him in a position where he can't succeed.

"Mr. Vorat began his employment with Spinelli and had to work under Steve Berlin, who provided him with no guidance or instruction. Spinelli had an antiquated accounting system only Mr. Berlin understood. Mr. Vorat appeared to be floundering because he was given no opportunity to succeed.

"By hiring Mr. Vorat, Mr. Berlin and Mr. Spinelli gave themselves cover for their heinous acts. He was their fall guy. They stole from the company and blamed the new hire. It's so easy to see, it's almost a cliché.

"Mr. Berlin left town without any warning after stealing the money. The fact he left town so suddenly is the proof you need that he was involved in the fraud. He only has his weak testimony that Mr. Vorat threatened him. He has no proof because he made it all up. It's only through the diligence of Mr. Vorat and his investigative work that the crime was ever discovered. I suspect Mr. Spinelli would still be taking cash he doesn't deserve, if Mr. Vorat had not come along and exposed his malfeasance.

"Mr. Vorat found the fraud, reported the stealing and now comes to you to get the money back for the company. Don't let Mr. Spinelli and Mr. Berlin's systematic withdrawal of the profits and their coordinated attack on the finances of Spinelli Enterprises go unpunished. We are looking for you to force them to return what they took and ask that you find in favor of the company and against Mr. Spinelli for the amount we have proven he stole. It's the only fair justice in this matter."

Carlson returns to his chair and sits with a thud.

Judge Maruk announces, "Let's take a ten-minute break before I instruct you as to the law you will consider before you begin your deliberations."

CHAPTER 34

Judge Maruk strides back to his seat on the bench with a sheaf of papers in his hand. Without looking up, he begins to instruct the jury how they are to conduct their deliberations. He tells them that when they are discussing the case to allow each person the opportunity to express his or her views but reminds them to stick to their own beliefs. He instructs them on Pennsylvania's law on fraud and the burden of proof either side must demonstrate to prevail. The members listen attentively, and when the Judge finishes, they leave the courtroom to begin their deliberations.

The judge's tipstaff informs us we can go back to our offices, but should be prepared to return quickly. This is never a problem.

Among the most excruciating ordeals is waiting for juries to arrive at their verdicts. Certain unwritten guidelines exist predicting what a jury may be thinking while they are deliberating. Lawyers who are defending personal injury cases want juries to return quickly, believing juries need a decent amount of time if they intend to award substantial damages. Conversely, we presume the juries that deliberate for a long period are more likely to be discussing the money they are about to award. Neither of these concepts is universally correct. Juries can award significant compensation even if they are out for a limited time, and sometimes they deliberate for hours and return no damages.

As long as deliberations continue, I will fret. Whenever I'm waiting for a jury to decide, the trial plays in my head, causing me to focus on questions I didn't ask or objections I failed to make. People in the office know to stay away from me while a jury is deliberating because I am cranky and susceptible to unpredictable verbal outbursts. Nothing anybody says is helpful and I'd much rather wait to hear the news alone. I stare at the phone willing it to ring. When it does and it's not the court telling me they have a verdict, I lash out for no reason at the person calling.

We arrive at my office across the street from the courthouse. Arthur and I head for a conference room. I will only be able to stay with him for a short time before I will have to leave and be by myself, but I want to quickly debrief with him. Two take-out lunches await on the table.

He begins talking before we sit. "Dan, I don't know what the verdict will be, but I wanted to make sure you know how happy I am with what you and Jana did for me. Not only do I think I had the superior lawyers, but you did it with class. No matter the result, I'm glad I decided to fight."

I chuckle. "You say that now, but you'll feel a lot better if you win."

"True."

Arthur and I talk about some highlights of the trial and discuss our perceptions of how the jurors reacted during closings, but I leave him with the thought that it is impossible to predict what a jury will do. I remind him of some of my trials where I felt the evidence on our side couldn't have been stronger, but I still ended up losing. "Juries are strange beasts," I say. "I would never try to make money betting on how they might decide a case."

I leave the conference room and head down the hall to bounce off the walls.

Four hours later, after everyone else in my office has left for the day, I get the call telling me the jury has reached a verdict. I tell Jana to find Arthur, and we trek back across the street to the courthouse.

A buzz of activity greets us when we return. Vorat and Carlson wait at their table. The court reporter sits in front of the witness stand and the tipstaff is standing by the door expecting our arrival, so he can get the judge back on the bench.

We take our places and rise when Judge Maruk enters the courtroom. "I hear we have a verdict. Should we see what they have to say?" Nobody responds as we all assume the question is rhetorical. He signals to his tipstaff to bring in the jury.

Two minutes later the jurors walk directly to their seats. They don't make eye contact. Juror number 1 holds the form with their decision.

The tipstaff takes the paper and, without looking at it, hands it to the judge. Judges usually like to take their time reading the verdict to make sure there are no inherent problems in it. Judge Maruk also knows he can add a little unneeded drama if he delays while everyone nervously waits for him.

Holding up the slip, the judge states, "With respect to the claims brought by Michael Vorat and Spinelli Enterprises against Arthur Spinelli, the jury finds in favor of Arthur Spinelli and against Michael Vorat and Spinelli Enterprises."

I hear Arthur chuckle to himself as the judge prepares to read the portion containing the jury's verdict for Arthur's claims.

"With respect to the claims brought by Arthur Spinelli against Michael Vorat and Spinelli Enterprises, the jury finds in favor of Arthur Spinelli and against Michael Vorat and Spinelli Enterprises in the amount of six million two hundred thousand dollars."

A small, yet audible moan escapes from Carlson.

Jana smacks me on my back as I attempt to digest the jury's decision. I turn to congratulate Arthur and see him with his head bowed. I wait a moment, and when he is ready, I put out my hand to shake his. He stands, puts both arms around me in a bear hug and whispers, "Thank you. You are a true friend—and a fine lawyer."

Jana leans into Arthur and kisses him on the cheek. "Nobody deserves this more than you," she says.

After delivering a verdict, juries are free to leave and get on with their lives. Judges often encourage them to talk to the parties and give them insight as to what they thought about their case. Some jurors love to gab—some don't. We mill around the courtroom and the jury foreman informs us they decided to keep their thoughts private and wouldn't disclose them to either side. Despite this, each juror when walking out comes over to shake Arthur's hand. Two of the women give him a brief hug. Vorat is left standing by himself.

After a trial, I will usually shake the opposing lawyer's hand to tell him he tried a good case or to wish him well. After some thought, I decide not to touch Carlson, and under no circumstances would I approach Vorat.

Carlson selects his coat from the rack in the back of the courtroom and walks over to me. He grabs my arm to say, "The verdict is crap. We will file our appeal tomorrow."

As he leaves, I yell back, "Can't wait to read it, Keith."

It's well past dinner time, and I can feel the adrenaline coursing through my body. I'm ready to get home and see my family. Jana volunteers to get our papers back to the office. After thanking her, Arthur and I walk out of the courthouse—happy men.

CHAPTER 35

JANA AND I SIT in my office the morning following the jury verdict reviewing every detail of the trial. We both have other work needing our attention, but we want to spend some time debriefing. She tries to relax in the chair in front of my desk but can't keep still. The ice in my Diet Coke clanks quietly against the side of the glass.

"This is wonderful," I say, raising my hand in a mock toast.

Jana's smile widens as she leans back. "I can't imagine how poorly we'd be doing if the jury had found against us. I don't think I can remember ever feeling more nervous than I did when they were deliberating," Jana responds.

"It wasn't really about having them find against Vorat and the company," I respond.

We knew we had a decent shot with our liability evidence. We were more concerned with shaping the trial to get them to award a significant verdict in Arthur's favor.

"It is rare," I say, "you will ever get testimony like Vorat lying about his accounting degree or finding direct evidence of somebody padding his bank account. With those facts, we better win. For me, it was mainly about how much money they would award."

"Were you expecting to get more than the two million dollars you asked for in your closing?" Jana asks.

"I knew the two million was justified and hoped they saw we were being reasonable. I was hoping they would award more because of how nasty the other side came across. I thought we had a better chance of getting it if we didn't appear greedy and directly ask for it."

Jana nods and says, "It worked out well, didn't it?"

"Yes, it did."

We keep talking and try to find words to describe our euphoria, but neither of us can express it. Victory at trial always feels rewarding. This time, it's so much more satisfying. Never had I represented a friend in a case that went to trial. I am always upset when I receive an adverse jury decision. Many of my clients are corporations, and when they lose, they have to pay money. Not something they want to do but usually a cost of business. Today, had we lost—had Arthur not been vindicated—Arthur would have lost his business and his dignity. My devastation would have been massive. I would have failed him, and I'm not sure how it might have affected my friendship with him.

"Do you think Arthur will get paid?" Jana asks, raising a question I had pondered.

"I can't imagine Vorat has a lot of money. So, to the extent Arthur gets any, it will have to come from the company. First, we have to win any appeal."

"I was already thinking of any potential issues they could raise," she says. "I think we made a record at trial that will help us, but let's see what we think when we review the transcript."

"Think about how much fun it will be to read the testimony. I can't wait to see if Carlson's muttering ended up in the record. Let them file their post-trial motions before we worry."

"This is definitely the better position to be in." My telephone rings, interrupting Jana's thought. I point to the phone and push the speaker button.

"Arthur, how are you? I have Jana right here in the office."

"Hi, Dan. Hi, Jana. How's everyone doing?" He sounds understandably chipper.

"We're great," I say. "What can we do for you?"

"I wanted to tell you how happy I am today. I thought all last night about the trial and wanted to tell you this before, but win or lose, you guys did an unbelievable job. There was so much information and you had it all distilled and at your fingertips."

I give Jana a thumbs up.

Arthur continues, "But more importantly, I wanted to let you know how much I appreciate everything you both did for me. Dan, when I was let go and they filed a lawsuit against me, it shook me to my core. You allowed me to walk out of the courthouse with some dignity."

"That's wonderful to hear, and you know it was a pleasure representing you. I wish all our clients were so appreciative."

"You're being way too kind, but thank you anyway. I wanted to let you know I just got off the phone with Stan Adkins. He's one of the other members of the company's board of directors. From what he tells me, the rest of them knew nothing about what Paxson and Mike were doing. They had a special meeting last night. They fired Mike and accepted Paxson's resignation. I think there is a reasonable chance the district attorney will press charges."

Jana and I smile at each other. "Wonderful. I was thinking of contacting the DA myself to see if he would be interested in what happened."

"Also, I didn't tell you, the new board offered me my old position. I'll be back to the company next week."

"That's the best possible result," I say. "It's yours and nobody but you should be running it."

"I know," he continues. "I'm looking forward to getting back. One more thing, I was ecstatic to see Charley at the trial. He's such an amazing kid and having him there when I was testifying helped. Whenever I was worried about a question during Carlson's cross-examination, I would catch a glimpse of him in his Polamalu jersey. I'm not sure why, but it made me smile."

"Arthur, I have to tell you Charley also got something out of watching the trial. He looks up to you so much, and he was so happy you won. I'm not sure if I could have explained it to him if the jury came back for Vorat."

"That would have been difficult," Jana interjects.

"So, make sure you tell Charley to get ready for his soccer game," Arthur says, "because I'm going to be there to root as hard for him as he did for me. Hopefully with the same success."

"You coming will mean a lot to him. I bet he tries to score a goal for you."

We all laugh and say our goodbyes.

I hang up, but Jana and I make no move to begin working on other files. We probably won't get much work done today.

NOVEMBER OF THIS YEAR

CHAPTER 36

CHARLEY STRETCHES OUT HIS legs in the corner portion of the sectional couch in the family room. He says in our direction, while resting his hands behind his head, "Hey, can we get some popcorn here?" A huge smile covers his face. He knows it's time for one of his favorite activities—family movie night.

Jill stands at the island pouring her concoction of butter, salt, and garlic in the bowl. I'm not sure there is anything she would rather be doing than sitting on the couch with her family and watching a movie.

I yell over to Charley to get out of my seat. He groans, but he knows the corner is reserved for me. This is one of the few accommodations to age he makes for me.

Jill brings over two bowls and puts them on the ottoman in front of the couch. Charley grabs a handful.

"Let's all try to keep the popcorn in our mouths and not on the floor," she says. At some point we will get out the sweeper and find a trove of uneaten kernels under the pillows. It is a small price to pay for an evening's entertainment.

"What are we watching, Charley?" Jill has allowed him to make the choice tonight after he reminded us at dinner how dreadful my last selection had been.

Charley beams. "*Star Wars*—the original."

"Again?" I groan. "How many times have we watched that?"

Jill interrupts, "It's his decision."

I don't care because most likely I will be dozing on the couch long before the Death Star explodes.

"Are we ready?" Charley points the remote control in the direction of the television.

"Fire away," I say, as I wedge into the corner, Charley to my right and Jill on his other side. He will alternate between lying right on top of me and leaning against Jill. We recognize the days of snuggling with our son are waning and soon he will want to spend more time out with his friends and less time watching a light saber battle with his parents.

The screen brightens and the familiar block letters scroll to the top. The room is filled with the *Star Wars* theme. We shovel popcorn into our mouths. Charley watches like it's all brand new and he has no idea who Luke's father is.

I soak in the scene—the fire in the fireplace, the pictures of our family scattered throughout the room, and Jill alternating her attention between what's on the screen and Charley's face. Occasionally, she reaches around Charley and grabs my hand. She glances at me to let me know how much these moments mean to her. The couch is our oasis from the rest of the world and tonight we aren't sharing it with anyone.

The popcorn is gone quickly. Jill denies Charley's request for more, so he leans back to take in the battle scenes. We all shout at the same time, "There's no kissing in *Star Wars*!" when we get to the scene where Han kisses Leia, paying homage to Charley's indignation the first time he watched the movie.

The Death Star is finally blown up and the Jedi Knights triumph. Charley lightly protests but heads upstairs.

"Get your pajamas on, brush your teeth, and get into bed," Jill instructs. "We will sing to you in a few minutes."

She sighs, "The end of another exciting evening."

"Would you rather have gone out somewhere?" I ask.

"Not at all. I can't think of anything else which would have been more fun." She steps toward me and reaches around me, resting her head on my chest. I smell her hair and have an immediate flashback to our first date. She kisses me and says, "Do you want to go first?" I nod, return her kiss, and walk up the stairs.

Charley brushes his teeth in the bathroom while I sit on his bed. Posters cover the walls of his room. A *Star Wars* print hangs on his closet door and one of Messi is tacked behind his bed. His bookcase is packed with his favorite books. The three he's reading rest on his nightstand. Sports trophies have their own separate shelves, their gleam reflective of his teams' success at soccer, baseball, and basketball. His clothes, of course, are strewn at the foot of his bed.

Charley bounces out of his bathroom and announces, "I am ready for bed." He is wearing his sleep pants, but also his soccer jersey.

"Are you sure you want to wear that to bed tonight?"

"Absolutely," he replies. "It will bring me luck."

He climbs onto the bed and begins to get under his covers. "I can't believe you are playing in the championship game tomorrow," I say.

"I know. I bet you didn't think we would make it after our first practice."

I smile, thinking back. These kids had come a long way.

"I was looking at some of your trophies. It's an impressive collection."

"Dad, most of them everybody got just for showing up."

"Perhaps, but take this one, for example," I say, holding up his trophy for his all-star team winning a baseball tournament.

"I barely played. You forced me to play baseball."

Charley was the eighteenth best out of the eighteen eager boys who tried out for the all-star team. He could have quit when he was told he would never play, but he went to every practice just to be part of the team. His desire to work hard, likely without ever getting an at-bat, made us proud.

He smiles but scrunches his nose. "Dad, you know I don't like baseball. Why'd you make me play?"

"I didn't make you play—I expressed my strong desire for you to give it a try. I love baseball and knew if you didn't play when you were young, you never would."

I sit on his bed and put my hand on the blanket and feel his leg.

"It's also more complicated. Your mom and I think playing sports is important—the getting outside and running around—but also it lets you learn how to win and how to lose. Sports often forms the basis for friendships. How many people are your friends because you played sports with them?"

"Most of them, I guess."

"So yeah, I knew soccer was what you liked best, but I wanted to make sure you were exposed to as many sports as possible, even if you aren't the greatest at a sport." I lock eyes with him. "You know what? It's not easy helping your children make those kinds of decisions. I didn't want you to resent me for pushing you to play baseball, but every decision we make involves trying to decide what's best for you. The problem is, we never know if what we're doing is the best thing for you."

"Then I don't get it. Why do you make me play baseball, if you know I don't like baseball?"

"It's because in the long run, we think you may learn to like baseball or at least get some positive experiences playing it." I smile. "I find being a parent isn't easy."

"Dad, you're doing good," Charley says, patting my leg.

"Thanks." I pause. "You know, I wrote a little essay about your baseball experience."

"Really—why haven't I ever seen it?"

"I wasn't sure you would like reading about yourself. I sent it to Mom and Momo to read. They loved it and called me teary-faced. They passed it along to some of their friends. It was *a bit* of an internet sensation for about a day," I add with a touch of sarcasm.

"People were reading about me?" Charley exclaims. "Can you show it to me now?"

"I don't know, it's not what you think."

"Please. I want to hear it." I hesitate, knowing how personal the essay was. I'm not sure if Charley would understand the feelings parents have and how this story, at least the way I had written it, was more about me than him.

Sensing my ambivalence, he puts on the charm. "Dad, I can handle it. I'm sure it's awesome. Please."

I relent. "Okay, let me see if I can find it."

A few minutes later I return with a wrinkled piece of paper. "Are you sure you want to hear this?"

Charley sits up on his pillow and pats his bed for me to sit. "Absolutely," he says.

I begin to read:

> For nearly every decision my wife and I make about our child, we over analyze and evaluate rather than trust our instincts. We often go round-and-round

about the significance they may have and usually revisit our thought process long after I believed we had made a final judgment.

It's rare we're given objective evidence our choices are correct. This summer, however, it took one smile— one ear-to-ear grin— to let us know a decision we had pondered for weeks was absolutely, positively the best one we could have made.

Our son Charley is like many nine-year-old boys. He runs around from morning to evening only stopping to eat and sleep. He has trouble focusing on homework, often doesn't know what day it is, yet manages to do well in school and has a tight group of friends.

He loves sports, but is the smallest kid on every team on which he plays. So far it hasn't been much of a problem, but the boys are now six or eight inches taller than he is and are learning how to use size to their advantage.

Charley started playing baseball two years ago and was always passable. Last year, he played for his league's eight-year-old all-star team and got his first taste of the rigors of post-season ball. This spring, baseball became much more serious as private coaches were hired and the boys developed new sets of skills.

Charley was invited along with 17 other aspiring players to try out for the all-star team. He was one of few kids at the tryout not to have his own bat and it was evident from my evaluation Charley was the eighteenth best player on the field. He had some skills—but Charley was just learning to catch a fly ball, while the others were figuring out the complexities of an outfield relay to home. Some of his teammates were smoking line drives into the gap, yet he was happy to make contact.

The nine-year-olds were coached by a friend of ours whose son is one of the better players in the league. Many of Charley's friends were clearly in the upper echelon of those who had tried out so there was no doubt they would make the cut.

I got a call from Coach Rich before the roster was announced, who told me instead of picking the best twelve to make the team, the coaches decided not to cut anyone. Rather, they planned to utilize certain kids every game, others most games, while three boys, including Charley, would be on the team, but probably would never play.

This was the beginning of our parenting dilemma. My wife Jill and I were ambivalent about having our son commit to eight weeks of practice without ever getting the opportunity to get in a game. We analyzed the pros and cons of committing to the team, versus quitting and possibly saving Charley the embarrassment of never playing.

Ultimately, we decided to give him the choice. We discussed with him how going to practice was a reward in and of itself, how he could get better and how, if he showed the coaches he was willing to work hard and was always prepared to play, he might get into a game.

Charley, when presented with the decision, of course, picked playing over quitting. He wanted to be with his friends and I don't think he thought there were any options.

He went to every practice and worked at improving his skills. He started catching fly balls and learned the nuances of stealing bases. Although still the least skilled player on the team, he had moved up to number sixteen as the other two who were told they would likely not play decided to drop out.

Jill and I for the next six weeks constantly questioned whether it was right to have him continue. Was he embarrassed about his status? Was it worth the effort of trudging to practice and not getting to play?

Charley was thrilled when he received his uniform with his red T-shirt with blue vest on top. He felt a part of the squad and most of the kids treated him as an equal. Once, one of the kids suggested Charley wasn't a true member of the team. He stood up for himself and said he was as much a part as anyone. One of the coaches strongly supported him. No one challenged Charley's legitimacy again.

They entered three tournaments. The coach announced the rosters for each game. When the email arrived, we would eagerly read it hoping, unrealistically, he would be in the lineup. Without fail, we were disappointed when Charley's name did not appear on the roster. Jill would break the news to him, and he would get upset and say, "I just want to get in once."

Every time, however, he would cheerfully put on his uniform and go to the games. He would sit on the bench and root on his teammates. He also developed an appreciation for the art of spitting sunflower seeds.

Last Sunday, the team was in the middle of its third tournament. A doubleheader was scheduled due to a rain-out. We had a family reunion that weekend so everyone was busy.

I asked Charley if we were going to the games. His answer was unequivocally affirmative. For me, I didn't feel like sitting through two more games with temperatures in the nineties and Charley again occupying the bench spitting seeds.

For Charley, his boys were playing, so he wanted to be there.

When we got to the field, Charley ran off and joined in the warm-ups. The game started, and he was riding the pine, as expected, while I was on the metal bleachers with some fathers, feeling like an extra appendage.

In the second inning, I peered into the dugout and saw Charley wearing a batting helmet. Then I saw him pick up a bat. I had no idea what he was doing. It turns out one of the boys had gotten sick and went home. The team was down 2-0 and Charley was about to go in.

Jill was still at the family reunion, so I called her. I told her Charley was at the plate. She exclaimed, "You're kidding."

I could hear Charley's grandparents in the background yell, "Go Charley." Through the cell phone, I started to announce the game. "Runners are on first and second, no outs. Ball one. Next pitch, fouled back."

All the parents are enthusiastic supporters of the other players while they bat, but it was a little louder while Charley was batting. "Get a hit," came from behind home plate. "You can do it," was yelled from the group of mothers.

The count was 2 and 2, when Charley hit a bouncer to the mound. "He hit it to the pitcher," I shouted to Jill. She relayed, "He got a hit," to her parents. I told her the pitcher threw the runner out at second and Charley was standing on first.

While waiting for the next batter, Charley gave his coach a smile that was broader than his entire face. He got a high-five in return and then turned his attention back to the game. He ended up stealing a base and scoring the tying run. This was the start of a huge rally as Charley later walked and scored again in the same inning.

At the end of the inning, the first-base coach sauntered over to the stands and said Charley's smile had brightened his whole summer. Jill hopped into her car and made it to the game by the time Charley was playing in the outfield. The mothers came over to Jill to share in her happiness and Charley's success.

The boys won in four innings as they mercy-ruled the other team. After the game, Charley came over and said with another huge smile on his face, "Mom, I played. I PLAYED!" We congratulated him and I gave Jill a look to suggest we had made the right decision.

I'm not sure what message Charley will take from this season. Will it be one of perseverance, teamwork, or practice as its own reward? Who knows? I do know that when we talk about this game twenty years from now Charley will remember it and I will recall his smile that, for once, let me know at least one decision we had made for our kid was the right one.

I stop and put the paper down. Charley is subdued. “I don’t get it, Dad. Why is it such a big deal I played?”

“I think it’s because it was so unexpected, and I think because you deserved it. You were promised nothing—in fact you were told you weren’t going to play—but you went to every practice. You worked hard and because of your perseverance; you ended up being rewarded.”

He and I exchange glances. I say, “This is why I love sports so much, especially for kids. There are so many lessons to be learned. Competition can be healthy, but learning to get better, learning to be a good teammate and how to deal with losing will help you for the rest of your life.”

“Cool, Dad.”

“I think your soccer team is a prime example of this stuff. You all have worked hard, dedicated yourselves to improving, and now you are rewarded by playing in a championship game. All of you have become so much tighter. You’re better friends because of what you have gone through together. You and your buddies are going to talk about this season for the rest of your lives.”

“What if we lose?”

“It doesn’t matter. Just go out and play the best you can and have fun.”

“I can’t wait for the game tomorrow.”

“Neither can I, Charley.”

“Dad,” Charley says, “thanks for being the coach. I think you did an awesome job.”

He has no idea how much his words mean to me. “I think you also did an awesome job. I love coaching you and your friends.”

I put my hand on his back and let it sit. The warmth of his skin is soothing. “It’s late and you need to be rested for tomorrow. Are you ready for me to sing?”

“Yup.”

I start my special song for Charley. Jill and I have been singing to him before he goes to bed since he was a baby. I have my song, she has hers. It's always been a part of Charley's bedtime, and he doesn't think about it. At this point, I think we do it more for ourselves than for him.

I finish and kiss Charley on his forehead. "I love you, Big Guy," I whisper.

"I love you, Coach."

I walk out of his room and Jill enters to take her turn. I hear their whispers from the bedroom before she starts her song.

When she is done saying goodnight, Jill comes into our bedroom. She lays next to me and rests her head on my chest.

"He's such a good boy," she says. She rolls toward me. My arm tightens across her back. She gently kisses my neck. She smiles. "You're a good boy, too."

CHAPTER 37

AFTER A LONG MORNING trying to calm Charley and get him to save some of his energy for the game, it's finally time to get into the car. He and I will travel together. Jill will follow with Liza and Valerie. It's their custom to get coffee and arrive minutes before the game begins.

The team has developed a routine for game days. We try to be the first at the site, scoping it out and setting out balls for when the others arrive.

Charley likes to shoot on a goal by himself. I watch as he sets a ball about twenty feet from the goal. He takes four shots with his left foot, trying to place the ball in each corner of the goal. He uses his right foot to repeat the process. He runs at nearly full speed after kicking the ball, retrieving it from the net and returning to his original spot. At first, I worried he should save some energy for the game, but I soon learned his reservoirs are seemingly limitless and trying to rein him in is a fruitless endeavor.

I stand on the hill above our field. I couldn't be happier. Sunlight is spreading warmth and the smell of autumn hangs in the air. Trees on the far side of the grass sway in the light breeze.

The leaves have turned brown and make a slight rustle that floats on the wind. The only other sound I hear is the thump of the ball whenever Charley strikes it.

A feeling of pride begins to rise in me. The strength Charley generates reminds me of all the times we implored the boys to power through their kicks. I realize every kid on the team has improved dramatically since our early practices. Each boy is more adept with the ball and able to make better decisions on the field.

The whole team's confidence is so much higher now. More than ever, they are playing as a unit. At the start of the season, they were individuals, unaware of where teammates were or what they were doing. Now, every player has more awareness of what is transpiring on the field and making proper responses to game conditions.

Passes now have a purpose. The boys are thinking ahead and anticipating, rather than reacting. Before, their defense was a group of kids chasing after an opponent who had the ball. Now they operate as a coordinated blanket spread over the defensive zone that makes shooting difficult and passing problematic.

Offensively, instead of running straight lines down the field and merely hoping to get the ball, they zigzag and overlap each other, confusing the opposing defenses and opening up areas to exploit.

Charley continues to bang shots on the goal while I stand on the hill feeling proud of him and his team's accomplishments. I admit readily that I enjoy when the team wins much more than when we lose—not because victory itself is so important but because it's a reflection of the work the kids have put in all season.

We have stressed to them practices are not social gatherings but are a chance to hone skills and improve. This, we promised them, would lead to better results during the games. They started to win and their confidence surged. They played stronger. The winning became self-sustaining and validated what we had been teaching.

Charley continues his warm-ups, and his teammates begin to arrive. Eli takes his place in goal and the boys pepper him with shots. I notice they are not saying anything, simply concentrating on getting loose. There is no high-squeaked laughter coming from Stephen, and Sam is not telling people where to go. I watch them practicing. They appear nervous but focused.

On the other side of the field, the Fox Chapel team begins its preparations diligently. Their matching warm-ups sit in a pile. One of the parents neatly folds the jackets and pants.

Their players walk with confidence. They have played for championships before, and it's evident from watching them they expect to win. My boys have never competed for any type of championship in soccer. I wonder how much pressure they're feeling.

I yell to the team to gather around me. There are still twenty minutes until start time and I want to minimize their nervousness. The boys, already breathing hard, encircle me under a massive oak tree.

"Save some of your energy," I instruct. They nod and gulp their water. The group waits for instructions. Pete and Paul stand to the side.

"We have about twenty minutes," I begin. "Sam, Jacob, Lance. and Charley will start up front. Hunter, Ricardo, and Carter, you play back. I want you to be aggressive. Defense men, if the opportunity is there, make a rush and get a goal. Mid-fielders, you need to help out on D and not let them have free runs up the field."

They are listening attentively. "Anyone who gets tired, let me know. I will get you back in as soon as you get a quick breather. Any questions?"

It's the same stuff I have said to them every game, but it feels necessary to say it again. They appear anxious to get back on the field.

"Boys, I know you're ready to play, but I want to say one more thing to you." I still have their attention. "This has been a tremendous season. I can't tell you how wonderful it's been coaching you." Pete and Paul nod and high-five each other. "Your soccer has improved so much, and it's because you've dedicated yourselves to getting better. Let me tell you, it shows.

"You know if you win today, you are the champions. It's also true that if you lose, you will still have had an amazing season. It will be no shame, because this Fox Chapel team is talented and you know it.

"Here's the thing—you guys are just as strong. You have improved so much and those boys over there don't know it. They still think you are the same weak bunch they trampled in the first game. Is that you?"

"No!" they respond together.

"I didn't think so. You're all different than you were at the beginning of the year. You all have reasons for wanting to win," I say, looking at Ricardo. Everyone pats him on the back.

"I said it would be no shame to lose. Which is true, but it would be sweet if you won. You need to take it to them from the first play. Get in their faces and do not give them any room. They think you can be bullied, and I think you're going to show them who's tougher. Gather closer."

The boys huddle around and put their arms on each other's backs. They are now a swarming mass of humanity. They begin to sway together. Sam yells, "Who's going to win this game?"

"Pumas!" they respond in unison.

"Who's going to win this game?"

"Pumas!" they yell even louder.

"I said, who's going to win this game?" Sam is never bashful and loves leading cheers.

"Pumas!!!" they yell, their voices loud and strong.

I lean over the group. "Go finish your warm-ups. Sam, get them ready."

Pete, Paul, and I walk away as Sam stands in the middle. They sway back and forth. They rhythmically chant "Pumas, Pumas, Pumas" until they reach a crescendo. The boys yell and run across the field.

The parents are gathering on the sideline placing their folding chairs. Coolers sit open while some people spread blankets. Nate's dad yells for the team to get excited. They take their final shots to complete their warm-ups and return to the bench area eager for the game to begin.

Paul says to Pete, "This is going to be a lot of fun."

I smile at the two coaches. *I really hope he's right.*

I call for the team to come to the sideline. I point to the fence running around our field and tell them that inside it's our territory. I glance at each player. "It's your responsibility to protect our turf."

The boys glisten with sweat. They listen.

I love these guys. They are an amazing group of kids on their worst day. They don't cause problems at school, are loyal to their friends, and most, if not all of them, are going to be successful when they grow up.

If they had lost every game this year, there would still be so many reasons to be proud of them. But they have drawn together and dedicated themselves to getting better. Now they have a chance to win a championship no one ever thought was possible.

"Guys, right from the first ball I want you to challenge them. I want you to attack on offense and be aggressive on defense. Give them no room. Any questions?"

I see thirteen sets of eyes looking at me. They are ready. Sam raises his hand. "I have something to say." I signal for him to speak.

"Nobody believed in us," he begins in his husky voice, "but we are here. I really want to win this game. I think we can beat these guys. Don't you think we can do it?" All eyes are on Sam. The boys begin to nod their heads. All at once they announce, "YES!!"

The boys take the field and go to their positions. Fox Chapel slowly does the same. They walk with an air of cockiness and sneer disdainfully at our players. The Fox Chapel team is stout, but our guys stare back at them, and each leans into his Fox Chapel counterpart as if to show there will be no backing down.

Stephen stands ready to begin the game and makes a short tap to Jacob who immediately drives the ball down the right sideline. Sam streaks past a Fox Chapel defender and takes control in stride. At the same time, Charley sprints down the other side and is left alone as the Fox Chapel defense men shift their attention to Sam.

Two defenders converge on Sam. He sends a pass flying across the field to the area in front of Charley. With a quick flick, Charley takes the ball and moves it past the last Fox Chapel defender. The goalie shifts to his right expecting a shot. Charley strikes the ball solidly and it elevates from his foot.

From my vantage point on the sideline, it's apparent the goalie has no chance to stop the shot. I raise my arms expecting the ball to hit the net at the back of the goal. It rises a little too much and slams into the crossbar. With a solid clang, the ball ricochets wildly and heads out of bounds.

Charley lowers his head when he realizes he missed. I shout, "Good try!" and instruct the team to get ready for the goalie kick.

"Get possession!" I yell.

Fox Chapel appears a little disorganized. Charley's shot, although not a goal, has rattled them. "Move up on them!" I scream.

Our defense men, sensing we have an advantage, creep up. Their goalie lifts his head when attempting the free kick and tops the ball without much force. Ricardo moves forward, gathers it in, and jukes twice to get past two opponent players.

He makes a short pass to Nate, who waits while the Fox Chapel defenders approach. Again, at the last moment, he flicks a pass toward Stephen, who crushes a shot toward the goal. The kick is hard but aimed down the middle. Their goalie snatches the ball.

The boys move as a unit as they anticipate the play. Fox Chapel has not had possession yet and appears frustrated.

"Don't give them room," I say as I scan the field.

They aren't actively listening but are doing what I want. Each one steps in front of a Fox Chapel player to prevent the goalie from having a simple pass. They attempt to get free but can't find open space.

With the ball in his hands, the goalie is yelling at his teammates, but there is no one ready to receive it. He sees a lone defense man just outside of the box and sidearms the ball in his direction. The defense man, not expecting the throw, lunges to stop the ball, but it awkwardly deflects a few feet away.

Sam sprints toward the loose ball and gets to it a split-second before the defense man recovers. He pushes it ahead into the right corner while scanning the field to see where his teammates are positioned.

Jacob sprints in the opposite direction. Two Fox Chapel defense men re-position to stop Sam but leave a huge opening in front of the goal.

Sam gets control, with the two defenders converging on him. Jacob moves into open territory. Sam pokes the ball like a golfer hitting out of a sand trap. It arcs over the defenders' heads, landing in the area where Jacob has taken position.

I tense. The ball is going to bounce near Jacob, and I'm unsure whether he'll be able to quickly get control of it. Jacob raises his right leg and brings it down on top of the ball to stop it from bouncing.

He has possession immediately in front of the Fox Chapel goalie.

I think to myself, "Pick a side, Jacob, pick a side"—all he has to do is avoid shooting right at the goalie.

Jacob draws his leg back and strikes the ball firmly. It's clear from my vantage point he has avoided aiming at the middle of the goal, and it's headed toward the right side of the net. The only question is whether he has shot it too far right.

The netting flickers. *It's a goal.*

Our sideline erupts and the boys jump up and down celebrating our quick lead. Andrew and Nate hug each other. I grab Leo and tell him to go into the game.

I yell, "Awesome, guys. Strong passing. Now focus and keep being aggressive!"

The boys line up at the center line. They instruct each other, not needing input from the sideline. They prepare for the inevitable Fox Chapel onslaught.

I glance over to the other sideline and see the folding chairs lining the edge of the field. None of the parents are in their seats as they cheer passionately. Arthur is next to Jill wearing a Steelers tassel cap and waving his arms excitedly. Russell has a huge grin on his face. Estelle jumps up and down next to him.

Paul and Pete stand next to me, and the remaining boys wait expectantly wanting to be called to enter the game. Pete puts his arm on my shoulder and exclaims, "Now that was some serious passing. Our boys are finally getting the hang of this soccer stuff." I laugh and turn my attention back to the field hoping we continue to press the Fox Chapel team.

For the rest of the half, Fox Chapel attempts to mount attacks by using its sheer physical strength to force its way toward our goal. Although they control the ball in our end for most of the rest of the half, each time they try to get the ball in scoring position, one of our defense men is able to thwart the attack. Eli has to make a few saves, but they are routine.

The half ends, and I'm pleased we have the lead, but I'm concerned because the majority of the play has been near our goal. The boys jog to the sideline for halftime dripping with sweat but looking confident. I don't want to shake their confidence by pointing out how dominant Fox Chapel has been, but I want them to realize there are areas where they can improve.

"I liked what was happening on the field," I begin. "Defense, stop them from taking shots in front of the goal. Forwards, I need you to come back more and help on D. This will also help get the ball out of the zone and allow you to attack. Keep pressuring them and do not give them room to move. Keep attacking."

The boys are tired, but they have enough in reserve to get them through the game.

I pause and watch them drink their water. I decide to raise a point I hadn't talked to them about before. "Listen up. There's something I want to talk about if we are tied near the end of the second half." I see the boys lift their heads.

"If the score is even at the end of the game, we go immediately to a shootout. There's no overtime, just a three-person shootout. Those are the rules."

I make sure they continue to listen. "I watched Fox Chapel practice their penalty kicks, and they are solid. I don't want to get into a penalty kick contest with them. So, if the game is tied near the end of the half, Eli will leave the goal and join the attack. You got that—if we are tied, I will pull the goalie."

Their faces register surprise but no overt rebellion. "To avoid this, keep the lead—or better, go get another goal. Same starting lineup. Hands in."

Everyone puts their hands in together. Sam says, "One more half. Play hard and we can beat these guys." They scream "Pumas!!" and the players take their positions.

Fox Chapel comes on the field. They don't say a word and are ready to play. One boy, Harvin, stands next to Carter and extends his hand. Each of our players, except one, reaches his hand to his opponent next to him, and it is quickly shaken.

Sam rests with his hands on his knees next to Mahon, the player who had taunted Ricardo in our first game, unsure what to do. Sam decides to extend his hand. Ignoring the sportsmanship gesture, Mahon drops his head toward the ground and spits. Sam shrugs his shoulders and glares at Mahon as if to say the issue will be settled on the field.

The play at the beginning of the second half is ragged. Fox Chapel tries to muscle the ball up the field each time, but our boys continue to out-maneuver them. We are unable to get any chances to score because the stout Fox Chapel defenders use their size advantage to shield our players from taking the ball to the goal.

During a brief lull when Jacob had kicked the ball out of bounds and the Fox Chapel player is chasing after it, I glance across the field and catch Jill's eye. She is next to Arthur; worry etched on her face.

Usually after games when I talk to Jill about what had occurred, she is unable to give me any meaningful detail about the game. Early on, I realized most times she and her friends paid less attention to what was happening on the field and more to their sideline chats.

Jill had never expressed much concern over how well the team performed or if it won or lost. She cared how Charley played, but more about whether he was having fun doing it. Jill's fundamental issue is fairness, and to her, fairness on the soccer field meant everyone had an equal chance to succeed.

Her usual analysis of the team's performance didn't focus on if the team won or lost.

But now I realize she and the other parents are paying complete attention. They have been yelling encouragement and are aware our lead is tenuous. Jill forces a smile at me, but her concern overwhelms her attempt to cover it up.

I shake my head in amazement—Jill is invested in the outcome. She will feel the sting of the loss almost as much as Charley if the boys don't hold this lead.

As the referee gets ready for the action to start again, time appears to freeze. The boys stand tall, reflecting the strength and innocence of youth. The spectators stare on, emotionally invested in a game of eleven-year-olds. The referees, one adult and two college students, are entranced, wanting to do their jobs competently, so they don't interfere in the outcome.

For this brief period, this is the most important thing in our lives. We are all joined by the efforts of these boys and will be touched by the emotion they invest. We revel in the competition unfolding in front of us.

Jacob throws the ball in to Charley, who dances with it as a Fox Chapel player desperately tries to take it away. Trapped next to the sideline, Charley shoots the ball around the defender. Our players position themselves to play defense, instead of chasing the ball.

"We're playing too conservatively," I say to Paul and Pete. "Get them to attack."

Pete steps forward to tell the team to keep being aggressive and try to get shots, but they're playing not to lose. We're losing the field position battle as most of the action is now occurring in our defensive zone.

"How much time's left?" I ask Paul.

"About twelve minutes," he responds.

"Way too much to play like this."

Lance elects to pooch a shot toward their goalie, rather than attempting to beat the defender. He immediately drops back to help out on defense. I groan as I see the Fox Chapel team organizing an attack near the center line.

Fox Chapel has possession while none of our players are anywhere close because everyone has dropped back. This allows Fox Chapel to move up field without any opposition. A pass is made to the outside of our goal box. Three of our players chase the ball.

"Stay in position," we all yell as we notice our entire team shifting too much. The Fox Chapel player with possession sees we have lost our shape and crosses a pass to the other side of the field where a teammate awaits. Again, our defense moves toward the one player and it's clear we're leaving too many players uncovered.

Fox Chapel quickly passes to the top of the goalie box. Harvin gets the ball without any of our defenders positioned to oppose his shot. He has too much time. Two of our defense men run at him, but Harvin lines up his kick without resistance.

He places his shot low toward the right goalpost. Eli is in position and dives, extending his body, but the shot is too well-placed. He cannot get there in time. The ball rolls unimpeded to the back of the goal.

Fox Chapel celebrates.

"Dammit," I swear.

I bow my head momentarily. I'm picturing their players shooting before the game. We can't beat them in a shootout.

After the referee starts play again, our boys try to muster some offense, but Fox Chapel is too strong. Each time, they thwart the progress of our attack and boot the ball down toward our goal to kill more of the clock.

"Seven minutes left," Paul says in my direction.

Not a lot of time.

I pull Nate from the bench and tell him to get into the game. I instruct him to get the team shooting. Nate enters the field and runs to his teammates to offer encouragement.

Our boys get the ball and continue to attack. It's futile as Fox Chapel is content to keep kicking the ball away from their goal without trying to organize any offense. They are willing to take the tie, confident of their ability to win in the shootout.

Charley runs by me on the left wing as our defense gains control of the ball. I tell him to stop, so I can instruct him. His eyes flash toward the ball rolling in our defensive zone. He doesn't want to listen because he's ready to help out, but he pauses. My face is flushed as I lean over to talk to him.

"You have to score. It's time to try our secret play."

He nods as he turns back to the action. Almost immediately he's running at full speed, his skinny legs carrying him to the defensive side of the field as Ricardo is trying to out-maneuver two Fox Chapel players.

Charley scampers back and yells out, "Golden Play!"

Ricardo takes the ball toward the right side of the field. Eli runs out of his goal and assumes an attacking position. Fox Chapel adjusts, thinking we are trying to overload the far side.

"They pulled their goalie. Watch, they're attacking on the right side," one Fox Chapel player yells as he motions for the rest of his team to shift.

Ricardo maintains control, allowing Charley to drift to the far-left side, near the sideline. The Fox Chapel defense men ignore Charley and move toward Ricardo. The wave of Fox Chapel players attempts to swarm our team. Ricardo boots the ball to where Charley waits.

My throat tightens as the ball sails across the grass. This is our last chance to score in regulation.

The pass is on the mark and Charley receives the ball alone on the left side. All the Fox Chapel players, except one, are stranded on the other side.

Charley crosses the center line. The only person with a hope to stop him before he gets to the goal is Mahon, Ricardo's nemesis.

With the patience of a man twenty years his senior, Charley entices Mahon to commit and challenge him. Charley surveys the field and slides the ball behind him, toward his left heel.

Mahon moves forward to secure the ball, thinking Charley has bobbled his dribble. With a deft move of his foot, the ball is on Charley's heel, allowing him to flick it in an arc over his head and in the direction of the goal.

Mahon immediately realizes the ball is going over his head, and he has over-committed. Stunned horror flashes on Mahon's face as Charley, and the ball, pass by him.

The play seemingly slows for an instant as the spectators on the sideline stand. Paul and Pete place their hands on each other's shoulders in a communal effort to will Charley along. Everyone leans out over the field, straining to view the play.

I watch Charley's silhouetted body gather in the ball and move toward the goal uncontested.

How many times had we practiced free kicks? Often, we would end practice by breaking the boys into two teams and have each one attempt one unopposed kick, with the losing team having to clean up the field. We were lucky if the players scored on a quarter of their shots and were happy if the majority were actually directed at the goal. Those free kicks had no pressure and no one cared if they missed.

This is different.

I force myself to think positively and watch Charley get set to shoot.

With Mahon trailing him by ten yards, Charley has time. The Fox Chapel goalie takes a step toward him, wanting to challenge him, but he thinks better of it and retreats to the middle of the goal.

Charley gets to the top of the box and feints as if he plans to aim at the right-side of the goal. The net minder begins to lean in anticipation. Charley quickly pivots and pushes the ball firmly and accurately toward the left side.

The goalie switches direction trying to recover. His momentum is too much to overcome. He stumbles to the ground as Charley's shot sneaks past him and moves the net.

Charley leaps into the air once his shot has beaten the goaltender and sprints to the sideline. He stops and extends his arms in the air. A smile takes over his face. His teammates chase him and finally catch up to him. They mob him. The celebration is the first time when I actually get to witness the kids experience unbridled joy.

The parents jump up and down and reach for the nearest person to hug. Jill has one arm around Arthur and her other straight up in the air in celebration of her son's unbelievable goal. Russell and Estelle, with their mouths open, high-five each other.

I yell at the boys on the bench to calm down because the game isn't over yet.

The referee, with his bright-yellow shirt and high black socks, blows his whistle to get the play started again.

"There is less than a minute left," Paul informs as he leans over my shoulder. I breathe deeply, trying to maintain control.

"Oh god, let this be over," I exclaim as Fox Chapel tries to quickly mount an attack. Their first pass is errant, allowing Carter to gather in the ball and move it toward the sideline. The shrill sound of the referee's whistle pierces the air to signal the end of the game.

The boys look around not convinced the game is over. Fox Chapel players head off the field, dejected. They had lost the championship to a supposedly inferior team.

The realization of victory sinks in, and bedlam breaks out. Our boys scream and run across the grass. Then, as if pulled together by an unseen force, they gather at midfield and jump in unison.

I watch from the sideline as they mob each other and, ultimately, form a tight circle, clinging to the next person and leaving an invisible imprint of their hard-fought victory on their teammates.

While they gather in their scrum, Paul walks over to the group to remind them to congratulate the other team, which is now waiting in a line on the sideline.

I take a few steps on the field and Charley comes running toward me. "Dad, we did it. You said we could and we did." I smile and catch Charley as he leaps into my arms and hugs me with his entire body. I savor the moment and say, "Charley, you are awesome. What a tremendous goal."

I clutch at Charley for a moment before letting him go.

After shaking hands with the other team, the boys mill around and receive congratulations from the spectators. They have already begun to retell the story of the game. It's clear today will achieve legendary status within hours.

I stand back and revel at how much the boys have grown this past year—not only physically, but emotionally. My reward is being a part of this group and sharing in their experience.

The parents come over to share in the glow of victory. Congratulations are spread to everyone on the team and to all family members. I receive many pats on my back and deflect the compliments to the kids.

I have a hand on Leo's shoulder, and he is beaming as his mother explains this is the first championship team Leo had ever been on. Vic Himmer edges through the crowd to approach and gets my attention with a wave and a smile.

"Awesome victory," he says. "They played tremendously."

"Thanks, it was a fantastic game."

He continues, "I wanted to apologize. I shouldn't have said anything to you about playing time for the boys. You all did such a fine job of coaching and today proves it. Truth be told, I was glad Stan was on the bench at the end because I was so worried he would do something to screw up and let a goal in."

I laugh. "I doubt that would have happened."

"Charley's score was amazing. Nobody else on the team could have done what he did. You should be proud."

"Thanks, I am." Vic walks away. Andrew and Lance toss a ball to each other while leaving with their parents.

The sun retreats behind some clouds and the families head to their cars. I'm ready to go home and relax.

Jill approaches me to remind me she has to take Charley to his piano lesson. I nod my head, pretending like I had remembered. I tell her I will see her when she gets home. Folded in her hand is a clean shirt for Charley to change into.

Arthur walks excitedly towards the group. Charley sees him and runs over to thank him for coming. A little misty-eyed, Arthur pats Charley on his head and whispers something in his ear. He waves as he turns to leave.

I yell, "Charley, amazing game. Enjoy your piano lesson."

Jill hands him the clean shirt and instructs him to put it on. Slightly embarrassed, he pulls off his dirty jersey and tosses it to me. I feign disgust as I catch it.

He laughs and walks away with his mom toward the parking lot. Absentmindedly, I place the shirt on my shoulder. After picking up the balls and making sure the field is in proper shape, I walk to my car feeling a subdued euphoria.

Charley's goal replays in my mind. I question whether he could ever make the play again.

The radio blasts as I leave the parking lot. Up ahead I see Jill make the right-hand turn to take Charley to his piano lesson. I push the lever down to signal my left turn. Home awaits. I'm ready for a beer and my couch.

CHAPTER 38

THE GARAGE DOOR SLOWLY falls and covers the opening. I'm exhausted, spent from the emotional ups-and-downs of soccer. Pictures of the kids on the field swirl in my head. I see their near-misses, the effort they put in on their runs, and the wild celebration.

Again, I'm struck by the level of involvement we have all shared with this team and how important this game had been not only to the kids, but to their families and friends. I remind myself this is a bunch of eleven-year-olds and wonder how significant can it truly be.

Real significant.

The age of the players doesn't matter. We cared because the kids were invested, and we were rewarded almost as much as they were.

I open the door to get out of the car and see Charley's jersey thrown on the seat of the car with the name, "Charley," and the number "1" visible. I can't make the effort to reach over and pick it up. I leave it there, promising myself to get it the next time I get out of my car.

The house is quiet. No lights are on. Jill had straightened everything before she left for the game. The pillows rest intentionally on the couch, not strewn on the floor. The dishes have been rinsed and put into the dishwasher. The counters have been wiped off. Jill has taken Charley's toys and action figures upstairs. I can walk a straight line into the kitchen without having to dance around the stuff he often leaves randomly on the floor.

As I head to grab a beer, I stop to examine the series of photographs we have of Charley on the bookshelf. On the top sit seven pictures depicting a growing Charley in every soccer uniform he had worn since starting to play.

I love looking at these photos because they capture how he has changed throughout the years. They trigger memories of seemingly distant places and events. I remember many of his games. I don't recall the specific outcomes; I just have a recognition of how much fun he has playing.

Some funnier incidents, like when he tripped over the ball and landed in a mud puddle, jump into my mind. I think of all the coaches who instructed him and friends who helped get him to remote games. These communal events are at the core of our family and form the backbone of who Charley is growing into.

I'm happy no one will be home for a while. I walk into the kitchen to get dinner started. Charley has earned a celebratory meal and I want to make him something he will enjoy. The refrigerator is stuffed with food, but nothing inspires me. I move items around and find a steak marinating on the top shelf. Apparently, Jill had already decided Charley was going to want meat.

With this decision out of the way, I elect to pull out some beans and bake them the way his grandfather does. I throw them in water and get out the ingredients necessary to give them the proper flavor. Charley won't care if I strictly follow any recipe, as long as I put in enough brown sugar. I get another beer when I complete my preparations.

I return to the family room and plop on the couch. The novel I'm presently reading sits on the table, but guiltily I pick up the remote control. I switch aimlessly between channels, unable to settle on one show, until I come to a golf tournament heading to its final holes. Leaning back in the couch, I know the soft tones of the announcer will induce a well-deserved nap. I do not fight it as I drift off to sleep.

My slumber is interrupted by the blare of the phone ringing. I grab at it and mumble hello. I hear a deep, officious voice on the other end begin, "Sir, this is Sergeant Mulvoy from Precinct 12. Is this Dan West?"

"It is." I bolt upright.

"Sir, there has been an accident involving your wife and son. They are being taken to Presby."

"Oh my god. Are they okay?"

"I don't have information regarding their status. Are you able to get to the hospital?"

"Yes, Officer. I'm on my way."

I slam the phone back into the base. I grab my shoes and fly down the steps to get into the car.

My mind is a blur as I drive. I can't imagine what's happened. Charley's piano teacher lives only a mile from our house. Horrific pictures run through my head and I will them away, praying they were involved in a minor accident and taken to the emergency room only out of an abundance of caution.

I leave my car with an attendant and sprint into the hospital. The door is locked and I bang on it just wanting to gain access.

An overhead camera points down at me and I wave and gesture at the door in a burst of frustration. A loud buzz signals the doors' release. I yank it open and am stopped by a security guard who gently asks if he can help. I spit out that my wife and son had been in a car accident. He pats my back and points at a passing nurse..

I approach her and ask about Jill and Charley.

"They were brought in a little while ago," she says. "Their car was broadsided by a truck. They're both in surgery now."

"Surgery?" My heart pounds so hard. "How serious is it?"

"I don't know." She reaches out to touch my arm. "When the doctor is available, I will make sure he talks to you."

I express my thanks and collapse into a chair. I am overwhelmed and unable to comprehend what I need to do. An inky blackness surrounds me. Perspiration has soaked through my shirt. I pick up a magazine and heave it against the table.

Images dance through my head—some happy as I visualize Charley as a baby and Jill and I when we were young and single. Some are scary—I see Charley and Jill horribly injured. I picture Charley with his grandparents, which jolts me to call Jill's parents and let them know what had happened.

I mumble into the phone something about the accident. Russell and Estelle are as stunned as I am. They say they will get to the hospital immediately.

After minutes of pacing around the waiting area, a young doctor in scrubs approaches and introduces himself. He is covered in sweat and I see stubble on his face when he lowers his mask.

"Your wife and son were injured in the accident," he says. "They each have suffered significant internal wounds. We are doing everything we can do to stabilize them, but we are having difficulties." He looks me straight in the eyes. "Both have a first-rate team in the operating room. I wanted to give you an update, but I have to get back. I will let you know when we have more information.

The doctor rushes back down the hallway. I slump against the wall, needing to scream at the unfairness.

They're both in surgery and can't be stabilized?

I claw the wall, wanting to dig a hole for myself. The pain I feel when I rip my fingernail is no relief.

I walk the hall without purpose and turn into the bathroom. At the nurses' station I again ask for an update. They have nothing to offer.

I try to watch television in the waiting room, but I need more information. Without anyone to give me any, I am directed to a different room, where I can't sit.

I walk out of the room and see the doctor who had spoken to me previously approaching. A young nurse walks next to him. Defeat is etched on their faces. He makes eye contact with me, but is shaking his head. He points to a family meeting room and guides me inside. He slowly closes the door once everyone has entered.

Before he says anything, I am crushed. Tears flow down my cheeks, and he puts a hand on my shoulder as I slouch forward.

"We tried, please believe me we did everything possible, but there was nothing we could do to save them."

"Both of them?" I weakly respond.

"The accident was significant. They were critically injured and losing a lot of blood before they got here. I am so sorry." He holds out his hands and shakes his head. "Nurse Karp will stay with you as long as you need."

The doctor walks away and I'm left alone with the young nurse. She looks at me wanting to offer something, but can only place a hand on my shoulder. I suck in breath in short bursts and feel a wrenching tightness gripping my chest. The room spins as the world has flown out of control. I fall to my knees and place my head on the white tile floor. Its coolness offers no relief to the burning pain I am feeling in my entire body.

I lift my eyes to see Estelle and Russell rushing into the meeting room. From my knees, I raise my hands to the side as a gesture of complete futility. They run over and kneel with me on the floor.

"They're gone," I moan. "I have no idea what happened, but they're gone."

Estelle and Russell hold tight to me, and I feel them heaving as sobbing takes control of their bodies. I am unable to move.

"I'm so sorry. I couldn't do anything," I say.

I couldn't do anything.

CHAPTER 39

I'M IN THE LEATHER chair in the entranceway without knowing how long I've been here. Light streams through the window and reflects off the piano. Books line the shelves. The red rug in front of the door is slightly askew. I'm unable to process what I see because nothing has any meaning.

The same clothes I wore to the funeral, wrinkled and disheveled, hang from my body. I am not sure how I came to be in the chair, but I haven't been upstairs. The thought of climbing the stairs and encountering Charley and Jill's belongings is too much.

Nothing has changed in the house, but nothing is right.

I'm breathing, but my chest has an unbearable weight crushing it. Keeping my eyes open is burdensome. To stand from the chair feels impossible. I have known loss, loneliness, and grief before, but nothing has prepared me for this.

Pain consumes me and drives into my soul.

Vague images from earlier dance in my head, but I cannot focus as they are distorted by the hazy fog enveloping me. The only memories I have of the funeral are blurry pictures of two caskets, one big and one small; tears on the faces of the hordes of people; and two open holes, which swallow the people who gave my life meaning.

I try to recall more intimate details of the funeral, but I can't. So many people offered words of comfort, but I can't remember anyone who was there or anything that was said. I lean my head back against the chair and wallow in the emptiness. The house feels huge and imposing,

What the hell am I supposed to do?

My stupor is interrupted by a light knock at the front door. Every impulse in me wants to ignore the intrusion, yet through the glass I see Liza standing outside. She carries a bag and looks washed-out and haggard. She sees me and waves.

Using all my reserves to get out of the chair, I stand and shuffle to the door. I run my hand through my hair. Liza forces a smile when the door opens. We stare at each other for a moment before she offers, "I wanted to see how you were doing and say 'Hi.' Can I come in?"

"Sure," I mumble as I open up the screen door.

Liza walks in and engulfs me in a hug. I melt, allowing the contact.

"I have no idea what I'm supposed to do," she says, leaving her hand on my shoulder. "I didn't want to bother you, but I am so worried about you, I had to make sure you were okay."

I take a ragged breath. "Thanks. My family felt the same way. They said they were coming over. I'm not sure if I want any people here, but I also don't want to be alone for too long. We're all supposed to go to Jill's parents later."

"I brought some of her stuff from the hospital. Do you want it?"

"Oh god, Liza, I can't deal with it now. Can you hold it for a while?"

"Of course. Whatever you want."

We stand in silence.

Liza clutches at the bag. "Okay, I guess I should go," she says. "If there's anything you need, please...." Her voice trails off.

I gaze at the bookcase and then at the piano. I sigh and say, "Liza, I can't picture the funeral. I know I was there, but I can't really remember it."

Liza stares uncomprehendingly at me.

"Liza," I start again, "I need to know what happened. Please."

Liza takes a breath. She contemplates where to begin as her eyes dart back and forth. "It was beautiful. And painful. So painful." She turns her head away.

I purse my lips. "Thanks, but can you give me details? I need to know."

A tear falls down Liza's cheek. She nods her head. "I don't know if I have the strength. Can we have something to drink first?"

We walk into the kitchen. Liza goes right to the drawer where Jill kept essentials and measures some coffee grounds for the machine. She's had coffee here so many times she knows how to operate our appliances better than I do. She opens the refrigerator and picks out the milk. She moves slowly to the cabinet for two mugs.

When the coffee has brewed, Liza carries everything over to the kitchen table. She pours two cups. She adds milk to hers and takes a sip. The table is clear and the house is silent except for a chirping bird outside.

Liza begins: "I'm not sure how the funeral service came together. You took care of the arrangements, but we knew you were in no position to decide the details. Jill's parents couldn't handle being involved.

"All the moms from school wanted involvement, but so did so many others. We decided it would be best to let different groups choose who should speak. There was a group of Jill's close friends, some work friends, Charley's buddies, the people from school who all wanted to express their feelings. Your family and Jill's family needed to be part of the service. There were so many people who wanted to say something."

"I couldn't deal with making any of those decisions," I mumble.

"Dan, there were so many people there. The receiving line took an extra hour and a half. It didn't matter."

I offer a weak smile. "I recall a lot of people tried to say words of consolation."

"You thought it was best there be nobody official in charge," Liza begins again. "Somehow I was chosen to speak first and I remember getting up and looking over all the people. I was overwhelmed by the outpouring of sympathy and the number of people there."

"I remember you up there and feeling comforted, but tell me what you said again."

She fights her emotions. "I probably should have written down what I wanted to say, but I didn't. I started talking about my anger and general unfairness. This was so sudden and I hadn't any chance to process what had happened. My reaction when I saw the kids and the palpable pain in everyone's eyes was to lash out. I talked of my loss and guilt and the hurt everyone was feeling."

Liza pauses to assess if I am hearing what she is telling me. "I realized this wasn't the proper tone. I thought of Jill and Charley and what they meant to the people there. I started talking about Charley and his life. I mentioned the friendship Sam and Charley had and how strong the bond was between them."

She places her hand on my arm. "I told some stories from camping trips, like when Sam and Charley disappeared only to be found carrying 15 frogs from the lake. Mostly, I talked about how important Charley was to Sam. What an amazing group of friends they have and how supportive they are of each other.

I lost it when I spoke of the hole that's been torn in their group and how it would never be repaired."

I look Liza in the eye. "I was thinking then about what an amazing group of boys they are."

Liza pauses again. I hand her a tissue and keep two for myself. Tears stream down her cheek. "I made sure I captured my friendship with Jill right—about what a genuine person she was. I wanted everyone to understand how much I loved hanging out with her because she had such amazing insight. She made me feel better about myself. Of course, I mentioned how Jill and I would talk on the corner every morning after the school bus came. It was so painful."

"You and Jill were always laughing together."

Liza turns away from the table and groans with the pain the realization causes. I put a hand on hers, and she starts again. "I think the hardest part for me was when I saw you. I can't imagine what you're going through.

"I saw Jill's family sitting next to you. Jill's dad appeared so frail, like this had aged him 15 years in a day. Jill's mom had her head on your shoulder. I always thought the worst thing that could happen to someone would be burying a child, but what about a grandchild? I realized Jill's parents had to deal with the loss of their daughter and grandson. It's unimaginable.

"I gathered inspiration from the people there. I spoke of the unfathomable pain this has caused you and the hole ripped in your life—what a true friend you are and how your family has had such a huge influence on everyone in the room. I talked about how Pete, Sam, and I were all better people for knowing Jill and Charley, but I lost it. I had to sit down."

I know now Liza was the best person to capture the spirit of Jill and Charley.

Liza stands and pours both of us more coffee. She's spent. I say, "That was perfect. If you don't want to go on, please stop. I have a better picture in my mind now."

"No," she protests. "I think this is important for you to understand how beautiful the funeral was."

I take a breath. "Please tell me more."

"After I spoke," she resumes, "a group of Charley's friends spoke. To tell you the truth, I was a little worried whether they would handle this appropriately, but it was amazing."

"I can picture the boys up there. They were spread out in a semi-circle. They looked so sad."

"There were probably thirty-five boys. Jacob pulled out a sheet of paper from his pocket. They stood motionless in their suits and combed hair. Jacob started to speak but was overcome by emotion. Sam went over and put his arm around him. Jacob then talked about Charley and, I think, got to his essence.

"Jacob said Charley was the funniest boy in the fifth grade. He made school more fun for them. Charley was short but was a tremendous soccer player. He spoke about the winning goal Charley scored in the championship game. He told everyone how important Charley was to their group of friends and how he was the glue that kept them together because he always had something kind to say."

"Charley is funny. He was right."

"Jacob started crying when he talked about how much they all were going to miss him and how school would be meaningless without him, but he continued. He finally said the soccer team was dedicating next season to him.

"The boys all had a little token of expression for Charley. They each placed a stuffed animal, jersey, or ball next to the coffin. I think Charley will be comforted by those things. Without saying another word, they took their seats. It was beautiful."

"They are all such good boys."

I can picture their faces from the funeral now. So sad. This is so painful for me to hear, but so necessary.

"Jill's work colleagues got up next. They spoke in such glowing terms about her—how she had become a leader but also ran her lab with kindness. She was recognized for her teaching, not only of students, but also of the people she mentored. They summarized her research accomplishments and finished by noting how the scientific community had lost such a huge asset."

"Jill really knows her stuff."

"There was a group of Charley's teachers who spoke. I think there were thirteen of them and included at least one from every grade he had been in. There were pictures of Jill and Charley all over the place. Mrs. McMaster from third grade talked about how unique Charley was in her class—how his wit and charm helped him with his teachers and how much he was liked by everyone. You know they closed school. They had to because so many kids were at the funeral."

I nod my head. "I saw a lot of the kids there."

"Some of your family and Jill's family told stories of vacations and sporting events. Mainly, they painted a picture of how beautiful your family is and what a treasure it was to be around them. I think your brother may have summed it best when he said this is a tragedy no one can find a way to justify. He also spoke of his anger but said he had known Jill for sixteen years and Charley for eleven. The pain of their deaths was palpable, but having been a part of their lives and the love they spread was worth it.

"Jill's brother was the last one to speak and I can't imagine anyone saying anything more fitting. Robert had troubles getting words out as he kept choking up but told everyone what a supportive older sister Jill had been growing up. Jill had always been a dedicated student and, apparently, he wasn't. For two years Jill helped him with his homework and made sure he kept his grades up. When they were in college, three hundred miles apart, Jill once drove to Robert's school to help him when he was sick and had to study for finals.

"He talked about when they were adults and how happy he was they both lived in the same city. He loved being the best man at your wedding and told everyone what a positive influence Jill has been on Laine and Christopher, and how much they love her.

"Robert ended by promising he would somehow keep Charley and Jill's spirit alive and instill in his kids their positive traits."

As Liza recounts the events of the funeral, I'm amazed I barely have any recollection of the details.

"The most beautiful part of the service was the end. Everyone sang your songs to Charley. I know this is so personal, but it was the saddest and most beautiful thing I had ever heard. Can you imagine a thousand people singing 'Stay awake' and "Kumbaya'? I really think he could feel the love of these people and was comforted."

I stand and walk over to the sink, sobbing. I needed to hear this—to remember the funeral, but the wound is so open. An overwhelming need to hear what happened courses through me. I turn to Liza and ask her to finish.

"Well, after the songs there was a silence that was spiritual. Nobody moved. The only sounds were of people crying. Everybody wanted to go to the cemetery. The funeral procession cut off traffic for miles. I was told cars arrived before some even got a chance to join the line.

"The graveside service was short. People were respectfully quiet. The holes in the ground was devastating. My knees buckled when the two coffins were lowered. You threw the first dirt on both graves and walked away. The kids shoveled dirt next. Each one was crying, but they were so strong. They formed a group and held on to each other. Everybody was holding someone.

"I remember how strong they were."

"Dan, losing Jill and Charley is killing me. There are so many other people who feel the same. I can't imagine what you are feeling, but we all will be here for you and will do anything to help you."

Liza stands and approaches me. She has no idea how much I appreciate what she has done. She wraps her arms around my head and engulfs me. I try to express something, but nothing comes out except a pitiful wail.

MAY, FIFTEEN YEARS AGO

CHAPTER 40

My two best friends from college, Scott and Ben, sat with me at the table on the sidewalk. Spring was in the air and everyone was out looking for fun. Every year since we had graduated from Michigan, we had agreed to meet somewhere and spend at least a few days together. This time we met in Pittsburgh for a weekend of drinking and reminiscing. Both had come in on Friday and we spent the evening going bar to bar in Shadyside until about three in the morning. We woke up on Saturday to massive headaches.

After spending most the day Saturday recuperating, we went at it again Saturday night. This time we were hanging out on the South Side. It was a cool June evening, and we were outside of Dingo's bar drinking beer. Scott, blond, tan, and always with a smile, was retelling the story of how we had met in college. It was our first weekend there, and we latched onto each other. We had been best friends ever since. We had met Ben sophomore year and the three of us lived in a house with three women friends our last two years. Ben was tall and had lost the awkwardness that had marked his college years.

We were in our late twenties, starting our careers, and felt invincible. Each of us was single and none of us was looking for any attachments.

The conversation morphed into a discussion of our relative abilities to meet women when we were in college.

"Ben, I don't remember you actually talking to a woman back then," I said while taking a chug of beer.

"Not true," Scott interrupted. "You can't forget Melissa from East Quad. She was hammered at some party and came up to Ben and started making out with him. You could see her tongue all the way down his throat."

"My exact point," I interjected. "Ben never actually said a word to her. Even when we saw her leave the next morning, Ben kind of waved as she left the house."

"Well, you were not much better," Ben directed at me. "You thought you were so smooth, but when the chips were down, we could always count on you to embarrass yourself. Junior year, you saw a girl at the bar who you said you could hook up with. We bet a case of beer. You said you would go right up to her and find out what her name was."

Ben paused for effect, but we all knew where the story was going. Ben continued, his eyes locked with mine. "You stood there for about ten minutes nervously sizing up the situation, and you saw the girl was about to get up and leave. You mustered up every ounce of courage and rushed toward her saying, 'Excuse me, but I have a delivery for you.' Nice line. She gawked at you while you charged her and you slipped on something on the floor. You ended up knocking her down while spilling her beer over both of you."

Scott and Ben laughed at the memory of me on top of the girl, covered in suds.

"What you leave out," I said, when they stopped laughing, "is she found the whole scene hilarious, and we went out for dinner the next night. I won the bet and you gave me the case."

I sat back in my chair with my hands behind my head to mark my triumph.

"I'm sure you're much smoother now, aren't you?" Ben asked with a wink.

"Absolutely," I boasted, knowing it probably wasn't true.

"Let's find out how accurate it is. How about another little contest? The next woman we select, you must get her phone number. If you fail, you lose. Agreed?"

"It's a bet," I said, understanding my chances of winning were small. It had been a while since I had been out with a woman. Work was eating into my free time and I hadn't felt motivated after a nasty breakup two months before.

They examined the crowd milling around outside. There was a lot of action with groups bunched at metal tables. More people were walking down the sidewalk deciding where to drink.

"How about that one?" Ben said pointing to a short woman in a pink dress.

"No. No women in bright colors," Scott responded.

After a few minutes of disagreement, Scott nudged Ben and exclaimed, "There she is. She's perfect," nodding his head at a petite, slender woman with incredible legs. "She's way out of his league," Ben said after seeing three men approach her and then walk away rejected after brief conversations.

"She's the one. The bet is on."

Her back faced me, and her long, brown hair fell gently down her neck. The small waves in her hair bounced as she laughed while talking to her friends. She clutched a drink with one hand and gestured with her other hand as she spoke. I agreed with my buddies; this woman was clearly out of my league.

I stood next to our table gathering resolve. I figured to get the rejection done quickly so it would be less painful. I promised myself not to wait awkwardly for five minutes before making my approach. I took a swig of beer for courage and began to walk toward her.

The ten feet separating us felt like a chasm. I had a near slip but this time did not lose my balance. This is not going badly, I thought as I stood behind her. I tapped her lightly on her shoulder, and she whipped around, her face evidencing weariness of the constant onslaught of bad opening lines.

"I'm sorry to do this, but I wanted to introduce myself. My name is Dan," I said with a smile. She turned and locked her brown eyes on mine. Despite her lack of immediate warmth, I detected a glint of connection. She lowered her head to check me out from head to toe. She appeared unconcerned with my discomfort standing motionless in my jeans and blue button-down shirt.

"Dan—a rather plain name, isn't it?" she said, returning her gaze to my eyes.

"I didn't have much choice, unfortunately. Do I get to find out if you have an interesting name?"

"You're going to have to guess," she said as she touched my arm.

Her intoxicating brown eyes briefly caused me to lose my focus. She's engaging with me, I thought. I needed to continue the conversation.

"This won't be easy; let's eliminate some first. I'm confident you're not a Selma, Harriet, Evelyn, Lucille, or Maxine."

"You are correct," she said, smiling.

"You're also not a Wanda, Tricia, Morgana, Anita, or Pat. Probably not a Joan, Ricarda, Millie, or Destiny, either." The names were coming quickly and she began to laugh.

"You're not Alicia, Meredith, Tanya, Gretchen, Beth, Carla, Louise, or Gail."

"You're talented," she said. "Can you do this all day?"

"I think I'm getting to the end. At some point you will have to let me know your name."

"It's Jill," she said, holding her hand out to shake mine.

We talked for a few more minutes and I offered to buy her a drink. She refused, saying she was leaving. I asked her for her phone number. She immediately reached into her purse and grabbed a pen to write her information. Her friends were already walking out the door, so she quickly followed. She turned back toward me and mouthed, "Call me." There was no doubt I would follow her instruction.

Ben and Scott pretended to faint when I showed them the napkin with Jill's number on it. "I thought I had this sealed in the bag," Ben said, recognizing he owed me another case. To me the beer was secondary—the best-looking woman in the bar had told me to call her.

A few days later I was standing in the waiting area of Clark's, a remote bistro near the North Side. My nerves were askew as I waited for Jill to arrive. The new sports coat I had purchased the day before was thrown over my arm in a futile attempt at coolness. To my chagrin, my reflection in the mirror had sweat stains under his arms. I quickly put the jacket back on.

I had been on many first dates before—probably too many—but I'd never been this nervous before.

I kept pacing, trying to find a place to stand where I felt comfortable. I moved from sitting in a chair, to leaning against the wall, to resting on a couch. Nothing felt right.

I had called Jill the next day after our bar encounter, and we had a terrific conversation. She quickly made me feel at ease and after laughing about how we met, our talk turned in different directions. In our thirty-minute call, I found out that after graduating from college, she took various jobs having no connection to her ultimate goals. She now was at the University of Pittsburgh completing her Ph.D. Within the first ten minutes of our call, I learned she was an avid reader, watched any type of movie, had a varied music collection, and was close with her family, all of whom lived in town. Even before we had gone on our first date, I knew more about her than many of the women I dated previously

Jill also tried to squeeze information out of me. She found out I was a lawyer, also loved to run, rented in Shadyside, and had always wanted a dog.

I ran my hand through my hair as I glanced in the mirror for probably the tenth time.

I had asked Jill if she wanted to go to dinner over the weekend, but she elected a midweek meeting. She insisted we go for a drink and was adamant she had plans later in the evening. She refused my offer to drive her, despite living only three blocks away from me.

A tap on my shoulder interrupted my pathetic inner monologue. I turned to find Jill, who warmly returned my smile. She wore jeans and a pullover top but made the casual outfit appear like it had been taken from a fashion magazine.

We were shown to a small table in the bar area and given menus.

"I had a long day today and got into a heated discussion with a colleague. I'm not going to mess around with a frozen drink; can we just order bourbon?" she asked as she tossed the menu to the side.

"What happened with your colleague?" I asked.

"Oh, it's nothing; it's sometimes men think they're so smart."

"Seriously?"

"I'm working on this grant with another doc. He knows nothing about this area of research and all he's offering is his title. He doesn't want to do any work, but he wants most of the credit." She threw her hands up in the air.

I leaned forward slightly and rested my hands on the table. "Is it possible it's an issue with his profession, rather than something to do with his gender?" I open my hands up to the ceiling.

Jill paused for a second, glanced up to the ceiling and then mimicked me by leaning in toward me. "You know, you may be right. This guy is an ass, but it may be because he's a doctor and not because he's a man. Some of the nicest people I know are men."

I laughed and grabbed my bourbon from the waiter. I raised the glass. "To men, some of the nicest people I know." Jill took her drink and clanked it against mine, looking me directly in the eyes.

We ordered a second round of drinks after Jill explained her area of research and how she and her colleagues were trying to find ways to help pregnant mothers who smoked to quit smoking and to lose weight after giving birth. I was given a tour of the grant process and how researchers like Jill must request funding from the government and utilize the money by conducting research and publishing the findings in peer-reviewed journals for other scientists to study.

As we sipped our drinks, she began to lob questions at me. I told her I was an associate lawyer at a medium-sized law firm who was working hard to become a partner. She asked what I like about my job. I responded with a long story about how being in court felt so natural to me.

"I'm lucky; many lawyers my age don't get a chance to try any cases. I've tried a bunch."

"Tell me about your most unusual trial."

"Easily the most interesting case I had was representing a grocery store in Ohio. A shoplifter bolted with about two hundred dollars in unpaid groceries. Two of the employees chased him into the parking lot. They caught him and tackled him. The thief was strong, and he started punching everyone. It took four people to hold him down before the police arrived."

"Let me guess," Jill said. "He sued because the employees broke his arm when they tackled him.

"Not quite," I responded. "His estate sued the company because when the police showed up, they got off him, but he had suffocated and was dead."

"Wow," exclaimed Jill, "that's a difficult one. Should he die just because he was caught stealing?"

"Exactly. The problem was the store had a shoplifting policy where workers shouldn't chase shoplifters outside because it was dangerous. Also, it wasn't clear if any of the employees had been trained."

"So what happened?"

"Well, the guy's family wanted millions of dollars to settle and the company didn't think they deserved anything. We tried the case for two weeks. It was terrifying. The company's officers were grilled on the witness stand about supposedly killing people on their property. They handled it well and explained that this guy would still be alive if he hadn't decided to steal. The case got some publicity and was in the newspapers and people were offering their opinions on the radio. Ultimately, the jury deliberated for three days but came back in favor of the company. It was nerve-racking waiting for them to render their decision."

"I bet. Trying cases sounds stressful."

"Sometimes it is. A lot of time is spent behind a desk reading through documents and legal papers to get a case ready for trial. It can get tedious, and there's nothing worse than when a jury deliberates. Nothing."

Jill peered at her watch as she took the last swig from her drink. I sensed our time together was coming to an end. "You know what," Jill said, "I'm getting kind of hungry. How's the food here?'

I stared at her blankly. "Don't you have to be somewhere?"

"I think I can cancel. Do you want to get some dinner?"

"Absolutely," I smiled and signaled to the waiter to bring back our menus.

After eating, we walked out of the restaurant into the cool night air. It was nearly midnight and the streets were empty. We ambled side-by-side in the direction of the parking lot. Only a few cars remained.

"Where's your car?" I asked

"Over there," she said, pointing to the lone car in the far corner.

"I enjoyed my pasta and liked talking with you."

"Me too. I loved the stories about your eccentric stepmother."

"Your family sounds too good to be true. Your parents might be the nicest people in the world," I said.

"Might be," Jill mumbled as we reached the driver's side of her car.

I turned to face her and again was struck by her intense brown eyes. I froze before I could do anything. She leaned into me and kissed me deeply. I relished her touch and the softness of her lips. The kiss did not last too long. Momentarily, she rested her head against my chest. The fresh scent of her hair wafted up to my nose.

Briefly, we lingered close, and I said, "I want to see you again."

"You will. How about Saturday? I will cook dinner. Do you like artichokes?"

"Absolutely. I can't wait."

She eased into her car and waved as she drove out of the lot. I stood there paralyzed, her scent imprinted on my brain.

FEBRUARY, PRESENT DAY

CHAPTER 41

I WATCH THE FLY ON the living room ceiling with detached interest. It jumps from one spot to another with no apparent purpose, which amuses me momentarily. The leather chair by the window envelopes me as I lean back. What has brought this insect into my life at this moment, and why does it find our piano area so inviting? Consistent with most of my thoughts these days, I have no answers. The question swirls in my head until it disappears without resolution.

Four months since the funeral and each day is a collection of minutes that pass monotonously. I spend an inordinate amount of time sitting in the chair and gazing out the window.

For so long, I tried to make sense of where destiny had left me, but the emptiness inside pervades every thought and moment. My conscious evaluation and reconstruction of our lives is horrifically painful, but I need to catalog every memory of Charley and Jill. I will myself not to allow any piece of them to fade from my consciousness and evaporate into oblivion.

I try to come up with a reason why they were killed. Always expecting them to walk into the house, I stare at the door begging them to return. I know logically they are never coming back, but emotionally I am unable to accept the finality of their deaths.

At some point every day, I come downstairs and sit in the chair to think about them. I have relived finding Jill and falling in love so many times. At times, it feels like she is nearby but never actually close enough to touch. As for Charley, I have willed myself to remember every moment of his life. I'm five feet away from where he was born, and sometimes I think I can feel him. I use the moments of our lives as a prism and have attempted to make sense out of their deaths. Despite constant reflection, I am unable to fathom any justification for what has happened.

Never having been too religious, I find no refuge and no comfort in the alleged existence of a god. After a while, thinking about the good times causes too much pain. The realization they are never coming back, that I will never touch them again or share in their thoughts or laughter, is too much.

Friends and family have called to check in and I try to sound like I'm mending, despite every contrary feeling in my body. People invite me to dinner, but my primary reaction is to avoid human interaction and the emotional turmoil I know it will cause.

Take-out food arrives periodically at the house and I eat portions before throwing the rest away. I take the trash out and pay some bills, but there is not much to fill my days and no reason for me to try.

The fly circling transfixes me. My phone ringing startles me. I have no desire to have small talk with a friend, so I intend to let it go to voicemail. It sits near my head as I slouch in the chair and after the third ring, I pick it up reflexively.

"Hello."

"Yeah, hi," responds the caller in a soft voice. "Is this Dan West?"

"Yes, it is," I say, assuming this is a solicitation and wanting to cut it short.

"Ah, my name is Bill Dwyer and I wanted to talk to you," he says, fumbling for words.

"I'm listening."

"I was told not to call you, but I felt like I had to."

I don't recognize the voice, but something in his tone makes the hairs on my neck stand up.

"Go ahead," I say, regretting answering the call and dreading where this might go.

"I'm not sure how to say this, but I'm so sorry for your loss. I wanted to come to the funeral, but...." His voice trails off.

"Sir," I interrupt, "I appreciate that, but I don't know who you are." I'm suspecting he's some type of reporter looking to do a human-interest story. I have no interest in participating.

He continues. "I don't know how to say this, but I'm the driver of the truck that was involved in the accident with your wife.

I stop cold, feeling like the air in the room has been sucked out. I put the phone in my lap. Never had I expected him to be on the other side of this call. I spoke with the police a few times about the crash and had a vague sense of what happened. The truck came down the steep hill near our house and didn't stop at the red light at the bottom. The investigation continued, but at this point, I had no idea why the truck went through the intersection.

There had been talk about improper speeds, poorly maintained brakes, and other possible causes, but I don't care. Did it matter if it was the driver's fault or a slippery road or plain bad luck? It happened and took away my family. I'm unable to muster enough energy to concern myself about the details.

Jana and some other lawyer friends spoke to me to gauge my interest in pursuing a lawsuit. The truck company's insurance company called to see how I was doing and probed about whether I was willing to come to a settlement. I wasn't offended, but I also was non-committal. I knew I would never file a lawsuit because I would have to relive their deaths at every stage in the litigation. The representative reminded me I had two years to decide. I laughed and told the man I understood how long the statute of limitations was. The thought of getting money for their deaths was unfathomable. I didn't want to talk to him or anyone else about the accident.

I put the phone back to my ear and say, "Go ahead."

"Like I said, I was told not to speak to you, but I haven't slept since that day."

"Neither have I," I say without any empathy.

"I know. I wanted to tell you I don't really know what happened. The truck wouldn't stop going down the hill. I think the brakes were bad. It was so horrible. I'm so sorry."

He sounds like a nice-enough man and I guess he's sincere. I'm sure he's troubled by the accident. Perhaps he talks to a shrink, but his pain is nothing compared to what I've dealt with. I'm not going to get my sleep back by talking this out with a professional.

"I understand, sir," I respond. "There's not much I have to say."

I don't care what this man has to say. If he has excuses, they won't make a difference—the accident happened and I never want to talk with this man again. Up to this moment, the truck had been an inanimate object that had indiscriminately plowed through Jill's car. A human driver makes this so much more personal and infinitely more painful.

"Like I was saying," he continues, "I'm sorry. If there's anything I can do...." His voice trails off and I let the silence hover over us. I understand this man might be suffering, but I can't make it easier on him if it only increases my pain.

"Well," I say, "I appreciate the call."

"I hope you're doing okay, and I'm so sorry."

The line goes dead. I put the phone in my pocket and lean my head back on the chair. I don't know if the driver feels better now, but I have a new pounding in my head. Rubbing my temples does little to alleviate the throbbing.

The fly drops from the ceiling and lands on the armrest. It twitches and flies away.

MARCH, PRESENT DAY

CHAPTER 42

I pull into Arthur's driveway dreading the next three hours. Arthur called last week suggesting we get together for steak and wine. I can't remember the last time I've been out of the house. It's been weeks since my last face-to-face conversation with anyone.

It's a beautiful pre-spring evening. Temperatures had been near seventy this afternoon and the warmth remained as the sun was setting. I approach the front door of Arthur's house and take a deep breath. Every impulse implores me to turn and jump back in my car.

He must have sensed my trepidation. He opens the door before I have a chance to knock.

He offers a gentle hug and turns me, so we can go inside. We pass through the heavy wooden front door and by the sports posters and memorabilia hanging on the walls. He leads me to the outside deck and hands me a glass of wine.

I lean on the wood railing and stare out over the trees lining the backyard. Two squirrels run crazy patterns on the grass chasing the other. Everything reminds me of games boys play.

I picture Charley and Sam running after each other, scurrying back and forth, until falling over laughing. A sense of melancholy fills me. I try to avoid thinking of all that has changed since the last time I was here.

"Dan, sit, please," Arthur says, pointing to one of the chairs scattered on the deck. I comply and sigh as I lower myself into the seat.

He pulls his seat close to mine. "I hate to ask this, but how are you doing?"

I turn my head away. "Fine, I guess. All things considered."

He draws back a little and gazes over the railing to the trees swaying in the breeze.

"I remember when Evelyn died," he says wistfully. "We were so close. We were together so many years. I had no idea what I was going to do. I spent months sitting in my bedroom staring at the walls. I don't think there was anything I was capable of doing."

I smile ironically. "I know what you mean."

"After a while, I started getting back to the stores. At first, I forced myself, but I realized it felt less bad to be out of the house than in it. It helped and after a while, I was able to function."

I get it, Arthur; it hurts when someone close to you dies.

"I still have pain. Evelyn's in my thoughts every day. I miss her so much. At some point, I realized sitting home alone, wallowing in my grief, didn't help. Now, I'm not trying to compare my situation with what happened to you. Jill was so young, and I can't imagine ever losing a child." He puts a hand on my knee and continues, "But there will come a time when you will be able, for short spurts, to put your pain aside, and see people. It won't be easy and if you're like me, you'll feel guilty for not being consumed by your pain."

I shake my head a little. I say quietly, "I appreciate what you're saying and it might happen, but I'm not there yet. Seeing people or talking to people is impossible. All I can do is sit in my house with the lights off. Everything I see, *everything*, in some way reminds me of them. It's just so painful."

He lets my words sink in. He exudes an aura of dignity and reasonableness. I understand he is still in pain over Evelyn's death years ago. Yet, like most people who lose someone close to them, he eventually pulled his life back together.

I start again, "Thanks for what you're doing, but I don't know if I have it in me. Just when I thought I had life figured out and things were going well, it's all taken from me."

He waits for me to continue.

"Jill and I had some rough times after Charley was born. We didn't realize how much a baby would change our life. We fought about stupid stuff and I thought we wouldn't make it. We got some counseling and figured out a few things. The past few years had been great with us. Then it gets taken away."

I stop because I'm beginning to yell. I take a sip of wine. Arthur says nothing, I feel the swirl of raw emotion inside of me.

My anger boils up and forces me to start talking again, "I don't know if I ever told you, but we always wanted to have lots of kids. At some point after Charley was born, we found out we couldn't have any more. Turns out we were lucky we had him. We decided to adopt. We spent months filling out papers with adoption agencies. After a long time, we received a call about twins from Russia. We were so excited on the way to pick up the babies in this small town outside of Moscow. We met with people from the agency, but the babies were no longer available. We came back home empty-handed after three years of waiting."

Arthur takes a deep breath. He wants me to talk.

"We were shocked and devastated. It was like Jill had been pregnant and we lost the baby. We kept our names active with the agencies, but we didn't push things. We wanted a lot of children, but Charley was such a special kid."

Knowing there's nothing he can say to ease my pain, he lets the story sink in. I wonder, like I have a thousand times in the past few months, whether having other kids would have lessened some of the anguish from the loss of Jill and Charley.

I feel a need to keep talking. "Nothing is right with my life. I wake up every morning and can't think of one reason to keep going. I don't do anything. I'm hounded by thoughts of them.

"I never sleep. At first, I started in our bed, but it wasn't right. For a while I tried sleeping in Charley's bed. I felt closer to him, but the little sleep I got was haunted by nightmares of the accident. I now try sleeping on the couch downstairs but can't say I'm doing too well there either."

Arthur makes no attempt to interject.

"I realized a while ago I can't stay in the house—too many memories. I want to move, but the thought of dealing with getting a new place and trying to sort out their stuff is overwhelming. Every day I try to get out of the house for a little. I stand on the porch, but I can't go anywhere. I end up back in the house, sitting in silence."

I stop. A surge of emotion roils inside of me, and I'm unable to control it. I slump forward to get a breath. Arthur places a hand on my shoulder.

We sit without talking for a few minutes and watch the squirrels run around the yard.

Finally, he says, "I see how much pain you're in. Anybody can see it. I know you haven't reached the point where you can get your life back together and that is part of the reason I wanted to talk. You know my appeal is supposed to be argued in two weeks."

"Yes," I say, "Jana has been keeping me updated with what's happening." She has been calling me at home periodically to inform me about what's going on with all my cases. She took them over because I have been unable to get to the office and am incapable of handling my workload. Even with her updates, I have no real sense of their status. I don't care much about them at this point either.

"She's been keeping me updated also," Arthur informs. "I want to tell you again how much I appreciated everything you and she did at trial. Winning is great and I thank you, but it was more important that we won with class. You and Jana were able to make our case and still let me retain my dignity. I will be forever thankful."

Arthur smiles at me paternally. "I think this appeal is garbage, but obviously it's significant. I have so much trust in you and Jana, but I wanted to let you know I don't want you to worry about the appeal. She's so on top of things and I know she can handle the appeal herself."

This is something I had been thinking of but hadn't wanted to deal with. I'm in no position to argue the case. Ordinarily this would feel like a kick in the teeth, but I can't muster the energy to prepare for the appeal. Arthur recognized this and was letting me out gracefully.

"You're right. I'm not the right person to handle this. Jana is. She'll be excellent. "

"Of course she will. But I want you to know the next time I get sued I'm walking right back into your office and dumping my problems on your desk. So you better get back to work soon."

"We'll see—try not to get involved in litigation again."

Arthur smiles and gestures toward the grill, "Let's eat some steak and watch the game."

DECEMBER, FOURTEEN YEARS AGO

CHAPTER 43

I WAS AWAKENED BY THE sound of muffled noises down the hall. Jill stirred and I rubbed my eyes, feeling comfortably rested. The sheets lightly lay on top of us with Jill's body nestling closely to mine. Slowly she started rubbing my leg and kissing my neck. The warmth of her skin was intoxicating.

Hearing voices outside our door, I rolled away, causing her to groan. "There are too many people in the house," I said. Jill's small features, accented by her hair falling gently on her neck, made it difficult to refuse her advance.

"Those damn Wests," Jill said. "I love your family, but there are a lot of them."

"What do you mean, a lot?" I roll my eyes. "There are only eighteen people in the house."

My dad's house in Florida was the center of activity for this family week. He had built it five years before so some or all of us could visit whenever we wanted. Every Christmas, his five children, plus spouses and six grandchildren, traveled to spend time together. Jill, after a period of thoughtful hesitation, agreed to join for the first time.

Jill had already met the entire clan separately at some point during the eleven months we had dated but never with everyone at the same time. Since we arrived, she had competed in monster games of Boggle, led book discussions, and put on a strong showing at the swimming races.

The grandkids, my nieces and nephews, already loved her and had taken to calling her Aunt Jill. She had begun exerting influence over dinners by introducing a more varied and interesting menu into the lives of a group used to grilling meat and eating cereal. By the end of her third day, she was a member of the family, subject to heckling by my dad and unannounced lap dives by the grandkids.

I turned to her and whispered, "Let's get out of here." She leaped out of bed and threw on some clothes. We walked down the staircase at the front of the house and were met by my dad and Ellen sitting in the kitchen. "Hey, you two finally get out of bed? What do you want to eat?" Dad asked, pointing to fruit and bagels on the counter.

"Nothing now," I said. "We're off for a walk on the beach."

We scampered down the small path leading to the beach. The sand was cool as the sun was just above the horizon and hadn't warmed the sand yet. I took Jill's hand, and we moved along the shore as the waves broke beside us, picking up seashells and watching little birds forage for food.

"Your family is awesome," Jill said. "A few idiosyncrasies, but they're so much fun. I have to say they didn't like it when I beat them in Boggle last night."

"I know, they're not used to losing. Next time, you should take it easy on them—let them win."

"They wouldn't like that."

Except for an occasional shell collector and jogger, we had the beach to ourselves. "I was hoping to get away. The day is beautiful," I say.

"I love how it smells in the morning. We should make sure to get up early every day."

"I was thinking..." I said as we slowly ambled.

"Are you worried about something?"

"Not worried, only thinking. We've been going out for almost a year now. It's been fun, but I was thinking about making a change."

"Oh my god, you want to break up?"

"No, nothing like that. Let me try this again." We stopped and I turned to face her. "I've been thinking about how wonderful you are and how you make me a better person. I love every minute we spend together. I love how excited you get when you start a new book or find a new recipe. I love how you get worked up about solving issues at work. I love everything about you."

Jill stared me in my eyes while bouncing on her toes ever so slightly.

"There is nothing I want to do other than be with you. I was lying in bed last night thinking we have to spend the rest of our lives together. I don't want to wait any longer."

I stop because I'm not saying what I want to say. "I'm doing this all wrong. I realized I needed to make it happen now. I don't have anything to offer you other than my total devotion and love. But, will you please, please marry me?"

She was now bouncing up and down quickly, holding both of my hands and impatiently waiting for me to finish. She put her arms around me and engulfed me, kissing me with everything she had. "Oh my god, yes, yes—there's nothing more I want."

She relaxed as the birds circled overhead. Time wasn't an issue as we were going to be together forever.

"Let's go tell everyone." Jill led me back toward the path. "By the way, you're supposed to have a ring when you do this. My mom's going to kill you."

We got back to the house and were greeted by my family eating breakfast in the kitchen and family room.

"Did you have a nice walk?" someone asked as we encountered the swarm of people. Jill smiled broadly and squeezed my hand, enjoying the last moments of our secret, yet wanting to share it.

She began to say something. Even though she was smiling, her eyes welled up at the same time. My oldest brother's wife Elaine, stepped forward and put an arm around her. "What is it, Sweetie—you can tell us."

Jill tried to speak again, but emotion overwhelmed her. Tears were pouring from her eyes. She took a deep breath to regain her composure. "Well, this is Dan's news, no it's ours, but he should say it."

There were now sixteen sets of excited eyes on us.

"Let me try." I stepped forward and began to talk, knowing I would have to speak quickly or suffer the same fate as Jill. "Jill and I went for a walk, and we decided we should spend our lives together. We're going to get married. We..."

Loud cheers and whistling interrupted what I was about to say. The mass of people stepped forward and showered us with hugs and kind wishes. After the kisses, we were forced to recount the story of our walk and engagement. We instinctively knew whatever we said at this point would become part of our lore that we would repeat to our kids for years.

Without malicious intent to deceive, we embellished on the details. My family questioned us about what happened, so we created a newer, slightly revised version of our engagement.

In our retold story, instead of me just asking Jill to marry me, I had gallantly dropped to one knee and grabbed Jill's hand and placed it next to my heart. Instead of this being a private moment, now when she had said "Yes," a group of passersby had clapped.

Everyone gathered around Jill requesting to see her engagement ring. I flushed when I recounted how I had proposed without first buying a ring, although they seemed to accept when I explained how I had been overcome by love and confused by Jill's prior pronouncements that engagement rings were promoted by the same companies who profited from Valentine's Day.

Jill pulled a seashell out of her pocket and explained we had felt an engagement ring was so typical, and we wanted something more reflective of who we were to commemorate the moment. We had decided to exchange seashells as a token of our love and as we were walking back from the beach, we saw two beautiful, slightly irregular, seashells in the sand. They symbolically represented what we wanted from our marriage even more than what a ring could.

They "oohed" and "aahed" when they heard about the seashells, and I saw two sisters-in-law wiping away tears after the "story" of our engagement and seashell exchange.

One of my brothers asked me to show my seashell, which momentarily knocked me dumbstruck. Jill yanked my arm. "Honey, let them see it."

I reached into the pocket of my shorts and felt a bump inside. I grabbed the seashell and took it out. I smiled at Jill as it was passed around, and when it was returned, I put it safely back in my pants.

I pulled her aside and pressed her up against the wall in the hallway when the celebration died down. I leaned in closely and kissed her. I said, "Where did you come up with stuff about the seashells? How did you get the seashell in my pocket?"

She glanced at me with triumph etched on her face. "I saw them on the sand as we were walking back. I knew your family would ask about a ring and thought this would make a compelling story. I slipped it in when I put my arm around you. I hope you don't mind."

I shook my head. "Absolutely not. Our kids are going to love that."

"I know. Speaking of kids," she said looking at me expectantly, "how many do you think we should have?"

"If you keep looking as hot as you do now," I said, checking out her tanned legs, "we will have a lot."

"I hope so. You're going to be such a great dad."

"You will be a great everything."

We leaned into each other, hugging. I couldn't imagine feeling anything better than I did at that moment.

MARCH, PRESENT DAY

CHAPTER 44

ESTELLE PLACES THE TUREEN of gazpacho on the table and asks me to ladle out the soup. Christopher is seated to my right, but he doesn't want any. Laine, who always loves her grandmother's food, says "Thanks" when I give her some and immediately starts to lap some into her mouth. After the rest of us have some in our bowls, we quietly begin to eat. The coolness of the soup is refreshing.

"Anybody thinks the Pirates are going to do well this season?" Russell asks to no one in particular.

"I do," Jody responds. "They finally have enough pitching to make a run this year."

Nobody else offers any insight about the Pirates' chances.

After finishing our soup in near-silence, I begin to clear the bowls. The clanging of the dishes as I set them next to the sink is the only sound in the house.

I return to the table and Laine gets out of her chair. She comes to my side and stands next to me, unaware how compelling her brown eyes are. "Is Aunt Jill coming for dinner?" she asks me.

"Oh, honey, Jill's not coming," I say, knowing Laine and Christopher haven't comprehended what had happened.

"What about Charley?" she asks earnestly.

"I'm sorry Laine, Charley's not coming either," I glance around the table for help.

"I miss them," Laine says.

"Me too," Christopher adds.

"Laine and Christopher," Jody says, "Jill and Charley aren't coming back." She tilts her head at me and turns to Estelle and Russell, "Is it okay to talk to them now?"

"Of course," Estelle says. I nod my assent.

"You know Aunt Jill and Charley were in a bad car accident. They were hurt. They went to the hospital, but the doctors couldn't save them."

The kids listen impassively.

"Are we ever going to see them again?" Laine asks.

"No, honey," Jody answers, "we're not."

Laine turns to me, "Uncle Dan, do you miss them?"

I bite the inside of my mouth and gaze directly at Laine's penetrating, innocent eyes.

"So much, Laine. I miss them very much."

Laine grabs Christopher's hand. "Let's go build some blocks," she says as they run away from the table.

The five adults sit around the table after having cleared the dishes. Jill's parents eventually restarted having Friday night dinner. It's probably beneficial for me to get out of the house, but getting together has been remarkably painful. Jill's parents try to maintain a daily routine, but their anguish hasn't dissipated. Laine and Christopher are only reminders of the potential of youth and how Charley will never fulfill his.

Photos of Jill and Charley still sit on shelves and tables around their house. I know they are reminded of them every time they enter a room. I have little to say when I'm with Jill's family as my thoughts are constantly consumed with my internal turmoil.

Robert and Jody, of course, have suffered significantly. They have lost a sister and a nephew, which is a huge burden for anyone. But as jaded as this sounds, their loss pales in comparison to mine, and they quickly resumed their lives soon after the funeral. Two young kids prevent them from wallowing too much in their grief. They're lucky compared to their parents and me.

We poke at our desserts, making futile attempts at small talk. Russell returns from the kitchen, taking a seat at the head of the table. He says, "Dan, I wanted to discuss the Disneyland trip."

"Sure," I say, not in any way wanting to engage in the conversation.

"It's supposed to be in three weeks, so we need to make a decision whether we should go. I spoke with the travel agent last week, and she said if we wanted to, we could reschedule and not have to pay any penalty.

"Estelle and I thought we should still on go on the trip. It's never going to be the same, but I think we need to get away. We want to spend time with Laine and Christopher. We still want you to go...."

I sigh. "Thanks," I say, "but I don't think I could do it. Not without them, I couldn't."

Russell turns and places his hand on my arm. Estelle leans over and touches my other arm. "I know," he says. "We completely understand and expected that is what you would say." His eyes well. "I just want to say how much a part of the family you are. It was difficult for us to decide, but we thought it was best for us if we went," he says, his voice trailing off. He turns to Estelle.

"Oh god, I understand. I know you're suffering as much as anybody. If you think you should go on the trip, I absolutely want you to go. I would be heartbroken if you didn't because you were worried about me."

Estelle wants to say something, but her words stumble out of her mouth. She leans over to quickly hug me and says, "We miss them so much every day."

She grabs a dish from the table and takes it into the kitchen.

APRIL,
PRESENT DAY

CHAPTER 45

Breakfast is bringing me little satisfaction. The Cheerios have the same oaty taste they had yesterday and the day before that. It's almost lunchtime, but at least I've made it out of bed and downstairs. I thumb through the news looking for anything of interest. The mayor has been indicted for misuse of public funds. The stock market has risen. The Pirates started the season on a winning streak.

None of it means anything. I don't care.

I shovel the cereal into my mouth absentmindedly.

I have no plans for the day. Yesterday I promised I would start running again. I used to run a lot. I had no talent, but I loved getting up early before Jill and Charley got out of bed to go for a run. It allowed me to organize my day and seemingly daunting tasks felt manageable by the time I got back.

After we met, Jill and I began to train for a marathon, a goal I had long held, but one I had little chance of reaching without significant help. She was a strong runner and insisted if we trained properly, we could handle running twenty-six miles.

We would go for runs early in the morning. It started as a way for us to spend time together and to get to know each other better. She pushed me to increase my mileage.

As the training intensified, Jill's natural competitive instincts took over and she would lose patience because her pace was naturally faster than mine. She would end up way ahead of me and have to wait at our destination.

We decided to finish our preparations separately. She trained with some friends and I ran by myself. I found running alone for three hours almost spiritual—Jill's training with her friends was instead communal.

On marathon day, we lined up at the start line together. By the first-mile mark, Jill was out of sight in front of me. I ran by myself and loved it. She chatted up other runners along the route and ran the last ten miles with two college buddies. She finished in less than three and a half hours. I didn't meet my timed goal, but it still was amazing.

I want to get outside and experience the high of running. The thought of putting shoes on, however, and being seen by the neighbors is too much. I put my bowl in the sink and return the milk to the refrigerator.

I feel the vibration of my cell phone in my pocket. I pull it out.

"Hey, Jana. What's up?"

Her voice is tinged with excitement. "We just got out of oral argument on the Spinelli appeal."

"How did it go?"

"Amazing. The judges thought Carlson's arguments were garbage. You know what they were claiming. First, Judge Maruk at trial was biased against them and made prejudicial comments to the jury. Their second claim was the award was not based on the evidence, so the judges should, at a minimum, reduce the amount they owe."

"I remember. Go ahead."

"I haven't done a lot of appellate arguments, but I can't imagine a panel ever demonstrating they thought a lawyer's position was such crap any stronger than they did here."

"You're right. It's unusual for judges to give much of an indication of their rulings during the argument. Tell me what happened. Give me the details. I have nothing but time."

"We got there early to sign in for the argument. Carlson started giving me crap about how compelling his presentation was. He said the judges wouldn't like that you weren't there to argue. Ridiculous, right? I think he thought I was a newbie and I could be intimidated."

"I'm sure you weren't."

"The courtroom was packed, and we were the first called. I can't tell you how many people came up to me to ask about you and when you're getting back to work. I told everybody I would relay their best wishes to you."

"Consider it done. Keep going."

"Carlson argued first. He started with his argument that Judge Maruk had made comments to the jury demonstrating a dislike of Vorat. Judge Peters was the senior judge on the panel, and he literally snickered when Carlson spoke. He interrupted to ask what he was relying on to make the claim the trial judge was biased."

"Seriously? I love Judge Peters."

"Yes. Carlson said the judge had commented on Vorat's testimony and had indicated through his gestures that he didn't like Vorat."

"Nobody liked Vorat. He's a thief."

"I know. Judge Peters didn't like casting aspersions on the trial judge. He told them he knew Judge Maruk and doubted the judge would in any way show his bias if he happened to have one. Peters suggested it wouldn't be hard to have a bias against their client, given some things he had done and how we proved he had deceived."

"Plus, there's nothing in the record...."

"Exactly what Peters said—they failed to demonstrate Maruk said anything or made any gestures to influence the jury. If they believed the trial judge had done something improper, they hadn't preserved it on the record."

"Wow," I say, "those are some strong words coming from an appellate judge."

"Agreed. The judges told him to move to other arguments. He argued the verdict of six million dollars was not supported by the evidence. They claimed even the two million dollars you asked for in your closing was outrageous. This panel was hot—they had read the entire transcript and kept directing Carlson to portions evidencing how much Vorat had taken from the company. The judges displayed no indication they supported any of the arguments he made."

"What did you say when you got to argue?"

"Here's the funny part," Jana responds excitedly. "Judge Peters asked me if I thought it was necessary to go into detail as they were intimately familiar with the record. I took his comment to mean they were on our side and I shouldn't say too much or risk hurting our argument. I spoke for under three minutes and sat down."

"Smart move. The less said the better."

"I hate to say this," Jana says, "but I almost guarantee we win the appeal."

I smile, remembering some guarantees I've made that had blown up in my face. "Have you talked to Arthur yet?"

"No, I wanted to tell you first. I am literally walking out of the courtroom. Dan, it couldn't have gone better."

"I know. I'm glad we have you on our side. Thanks for covering this."

"I'm going to call Arthur and let him know the argument went well."

"Thanks. Don't guarantee anything when you talk to him."

"I won't." She pauses. "How are you doing?"

"I'm fine, Jana. I'll see you soon."

"Goodbye, Dan."

With the conversation ended, I'm left alone to decide what to do with the rest of my day.

CHAPTER 46

FOR WEEKS, I'VE BEEN meaning to clean behind the refrigerator. The dust bunnies have been accumulating for months. Originally, I assumed Jill would get to them, because she took care of those kinds of chores. That was how things worked with us.

Years ago, we had some old sheets and somehow ripped two sets in the same week. We were down to our last pair. Jill asked me to pick up a new set on my way home from work.

Each day she would glance at my hands when I came home and her eyes would flash disapproval when she saw I didn't buy the sheets. Despite the silences, I knew I was disappointing her. This went on for nearly a week.

On the sixth night, Jill took me by my hand when I returned from work. Leading me upstairs, she told me she wanted me to see something. We got to our bedroom, and she said Charley was playing at a friend's house.

She flopped on the bed and asked me if I noticed anything different. My eyes wandered over her body, but I only shook my head. Jill rubbed her hand on the bed and beckoned me to join her.

She pulled down the edge of the comforter to reveal new sheets. I sat next to her while she explained how she bought the nicer, more expensive ones. With one arm around me, she pointed to the closet and informed me there were three more sets.

A feeling of melancholy overtakes me while I reach behind the refrigerator. I remember how Jill showed her displeasure with me for neglecting to purchase the sheets but somehow did it in a funny, almost seductive way, which made me laugh at my own failings, rather than cause us to argue.

Now it was me, and only me, who would ever capture the dust bunnies. If she were here, she would ask me to move the refrigerator, so she could clean behind it. I would object at first but would relent. She would squeeze behind and do something funny like make a mustache or earrings out of the clumps of dirt. In the short time it would take to complete the task, she would make sure we did it correctly and laughed while doing it.

I slide the refrigerator forward after grabbing some rags and cleaning solution. I get down on my knees to begin the process. In my new typical uniform of T-shirt and shorts, I'm dressed perfectly for the task.

I haven't been outside for a while. The last time, a few days ago, I wanted to go for a walk to get out of the house. Two houses down the sidewalk, I ran into one of neighbors.

I hadn't seen Mr. Gregg in months and our conversations, under the best circumstances, are stilted. He tried to make some small talk commenting about the weather. I was unable to respond with anything coherent. Given the limited number of encounters I've had recently, I may have lost the ability to converse. Even after a few seconds with Mr. Gregg, the thought of continuing to interact became physically painful. In the middle of a question, I mumbled goodbye and left. I walked around the block and retreated into the house, fearing any more personal contact. I hadn't ventured outside since.

It takes about five minutes to clean behind the refrigerator. I can't decide if I feel any sort of accomplishment. Looking around the kitchen, I am overwhelmed by the number of potential tasks lurking: Throwing away moldy food, changing the two burned-out lights in the ceiling, getting some oil to fix the squeaky chair, emptying the dishwasher. Too much to think about now. I leave the room knowing I had accomplished what I could for now.

I walk into the living room and scan the shelves hoping something jumps out at me. I have tried to start many books in the past few weeks, but I can't sit and read. Each one, no matter what subject, sends my mind racing. Novels about lawyers stress me out thinking about what I've been avoiding at work. Sports stories make me think of all the activities we used to do as a family. Any mention of a child causes me to slam the pages shut.

Jill was a voracious reader. Most of the paperbacks on the shelves are ones she had read. She also had tons of e-books loaded on her Kindle. Spotting it on the shelf creates images in my head of the times I saw her curled on the couch or nestled in bed reading.

I never could compete with Jill when it came to reading. For me, books were a way to kill time, and I never had Jill's passion for them. I always chose a spy novel or lawyer thriller over any book focusing on relationships or feelings. She wanted us to read the same books, so we could discuss them. It turned out, she liked hers—I liked mine.

The bookshelves loom over me and the titles run together. A picture of Charley in his Little League uniform in a small wooden frame captures my attention. I guess the photo is about three years old. Charley is smiling and carefree as any eight-year-old should be.

My focus shifts to the framed pictures placed all over the shelves. Jill and I didn't like choosing art. Around the house, there are only three pieces of what could charitably be called art—all given to us as presents. Instead of lithographs or stencils covering our walls, throughout the house is an array of photographs we had taken over the years.

For every Mother's Day, I would take Charley to the park and snap pictures as he played. On the holiday, he and I would make Jill breakfast and while she ate, we would present her with the photos.

Jill's face would glow as she reviewed every picture. To her, this was art. After she picked her favorites, I got them framed, and we placed them throughout the house. Every year I also made sure to get photographs of them together. Focusing on close-ups of their faces, I wanted to capture a glimpse of their closeness.

The photos of Charley and Jill, and what had been our life, stare back at me. Pictures of them in the park, at picnics, at school events remind me there would never be new ones. My urge is to take every one and throw them against the wall to crush this constant reminder of what would never be. At the same time, the beauty of their faces and the memories the pictures evoke stop me from doing anything. Paralyzed, I stare, swaying back and forth.

A knock on the door releases me from my trance. A group of kids gathers on the porch in front of the window. They clearly are excited, or agitated, and vibrate like bees around a hive. I have no idea why they are here.

I open the door and am greeted by the swarm of boys. I'm curious and annoyed at once. My annoyance level increases when I hear twelve voices speaking on top of each other.

There stands Charley's soccer team. They were all at the funeral, but I haven't interacted with them as a group since they won the championship.

They are a mass of energy, pulsating and humming in randomness. Words are being thrown toward me, but I comprehend nothing. I take a step onto the porch, and they encircle me. Momentarily, I feel like cornered prey. Their sounds reach me, but I don't understand what they're trying to tell me. I'm only aware of their sense of injustice and unfairness.

I raise one hand above my head to signal for quiet and put the fingers of my other hand to my mouth. I whistle as loudly and as shrilly as I can. I yell, "What is going on?"

The boys stop momentarily but only to catch their breath. They all begin again at the same time.

"I can't believe it."

"It's so unfair."

"It's not what we want."

"Nobody cares."

I hear their words now but still am having difficulty understanding the context.

Again, I raise my hand. "Slow down. One at a time. Take a breath."

The group is agitated. Indignation is a familiar response from eleven-year-olds. They believe things are never fair and someone else is always getting an advantage.

I heard this refrain many times from Charley. Jill and I often discussed with him his perceived injustices, trying to get him to view a situation from any perspective other than his own. When we were successful, he recognized fairness was relative and even if it didn't resolve the way he anticipated, it may have resulted from many factors, not just a lack of fairness. We tried to teach him results were usually the product of effort and equality balanced out in the long run. Most of the time, these concepts were lost on him.

The boys quiet and glance at each other to formulate a plan of action. Through silent consensus, Sam steps forward and begins to spout, "There's a meeting and everything is wrong. They all think they know best. But they don't. Nobody cares what's best for us."

Inwardly I smile. I love this about the boys. When they feel something, truly feel something, it consumes them and makes them incapable of doing anything other than focusing on what they feel. This happens when they play board games or video shootouts. I think this is what overtakes them when they start to notice girls, and the power is overwhelming. It can interfere with normal conversation, but when channeled properly, it can propel them to do amazing things.

I'm momentarily taken back to our championship game when this energy was focused solely on playing as a team and took these boys to a level they had never seen before.

"Slow down, Sam," I interrupt. "Let me get some water. Talk among yourselves and think about what you want to say."

I return a few minutes later with a pitcher of water and plastic cups. I slowly pour some for everyone. They are scattered to the four corners of the porch. Three boys sway on the swing.

Sam takes a step forward. He stares at me and then drops his gaze to his feet. He still has the mass of freckles on his face. His red hair, uncombed, frames his face. He has gotten taller and has an air of maturity that wasn't there previously.

He says. "They're having a meeting at the rec center. They're trying to decide who should coach the soccer team. Nobody is listening to what we want."

"I am," I say quietly.

"Anyway," he starts again, "there are people who want to coach the team. Some teachers, some fathers who want their kids on our team, and some guy who owns a store down the street all say they should be in charge. I guess because we won last year, they think it would be cool or it might be good for their business. None of those people ever believed in us before. They don't even know us."

I hadn't thought about the team or the kids for weeks. I didn't realize spring soccer was about to start.

"What about Pete and Paul?" I question.

"They said they never would take your place. We asked them before, but they said they couldn't do it. They all were talking, but nobody cared what we had to say or what we wanted."

"Is this meeting still going on?" Everyone's head nods affirmatively.

"We just left." Sam continues. "They think we're playing in the field. They don't know we're gone. Jacob and Eli thought we should come and talk to you."

"Why?"

"Because you're the coach."

I turn away. This is heading in a direction I was not prepared for and not one I think I can handle. "Guys, I'm not the coach anymore."

"Why not?" Eli asks defiantly, as he sits with his back to the porch railing.

"Because I don't have a son on the team."

The boys are frustrated. Sam stands in front of me, looking at me. He's trying to get his thoughts organized. Our eyes meet, but I can't hold his gaze.

"You're still our coach," says Sam. "You taught us about soccer and how to win as a team. You're part of our team."

"Sam," I start. My words get stuck in my throat.

He continues, "You can't just quit. We need you. None of those other people could coach us like you did. "

"Sam, Charley isn't on the team anymore."

"I know. We miss him, a lot. The team won't be the same without him. We need you to help us. Please." Sam won't break his stare even with a tear rolling down his check.

"Sam, I can't. It's too much."

"Yes, you can. You have to. We need you."

Everyone is silent but gazing directly at me. Each in his own way is willing me to say 'Yes.'

Before this moment, I hadn't thought of myself as their coach since walking off the field after the championship game. Charley wasn't here. The team didn't exist as far as I was concerned. The pain of dealing with these kids and not getting to see him was too much. I couldn't find any reason to consider their request.

"You told us we were a team." Sam was talking again. "You told us 'team' is what mattered, and we would be a team for the rest of our lives."

"I was referring to you guys, not me," I say feebly.

"That's crap. We're still a team and it's because of what you taught us. You're our coach."

I hesitate and they sense it. The kids offer their view on being part of a team. They throw back everything I said to them the last season and remind me how well we did when we stuck together. They tell me if I quit on them, I would be teaching them the wrong lesson.

They stop. I glance around the porch at each set of eyes staring at me.

"I don't know if I can do this," I say. "I miss Charley so much and you are all a reminder of him. I don't know if I have the energy."

Jacob stands and starts to speak, "We all have talked about quitting because Charley isn't here anymore. We know things aren't the same, but we also know he loved soccer more than anything, and he would want us to keep playing. We all decided we want to play. It wouldn't be right if you weren't with us."

I stand dumbfounded, struck by the unexpected force of the emotions running through me. The thought of being with this group of kids overwhelms me. Without having Charley there, it seems impossible. Their plea, however, does have some validity. We had been a team and had accomplished more than we ever had reason to expect. Every one of these boys had matured. They also made me better.

I gaze over the railing and up to the sky to avoid their eyes. I sigh. "Boys, what you did last year I will remember for the rest of my life. I have so many memories of each of you and what you did to help the team. It's what makes being a father so special."

I realize that without Charley being here, my first reaction is to push them all away. To be done with them, because they're a reminder of him and it hurts so much to think of him. Yet, I know every one of them is hurting also—that they miss him as much as I do.

"I hadn't thought about how this has affected you. I hadn't thought about the team at all. You're right, I said those things—and I meant them. We are a team. Being a team helps us climb the mountain together, but it also helps us when life doesn't go as well as we hoped.

"Things haven't been going really well for me. I've been hurting a lot. Maybe you're here today to help me. I might need you guys more than I thought."

I pause, not sure what to say next. Sam stands in front of me and locks eyes with me. He says, "Please, Dan, please be our coach."

Not having the energy to fight them anymore, I say, "Maybe I should give it a try."

The boys rush and encircle me. They slap me on my back. I welcome the contact, and the first real smile in a long time comes to my face.

CHAPTER 47

We enter the rec center as a group. Banners and trophies line the hallways. We walk up the stairs toward the gymnasium where the soccer meeting is being held. Sam and Jacob slam open the doors to the gym. The kids' parents, teachers, and other interested bystanders fill the first three rows of seats.

Mr. Edelstein, the gym teacher who runs the rec center, stands behind a podium at the front. He is saying how he appreciates how many people are interested in becoming coach of the team, but they need to make a decision. I can tell immediately there has been a lot of debate, but nothing had been accomplished.

Mr. Edelstein wears a haggard expression. He's a young, athletic man, more concerned with coming up with new games for the kids than with the politics of choosing a coach for one of the many rec center teams.

The boys stand to the side, with Sam at the front. The kids' parents exchange glances, unaware they had not been in the rec center field for the past hour.

Happy with anything that might get someone else speaking, Mr. Edelstein asks, "Boys, do you have something to say?"

They push Sam forward. He proceeds toward the front of the gym. "I think we would like to say something," he announces when he reaches the lectern.

Mr. Edelstein steps from the podium and gestures to Sam to come and speak. There is a murmur from the crowd as Sam adjusts the microphone.

"Hi, everyone," Sam begins. "I'm Sam Austin." Liza and Pete smile as their son continues, "We appreciate everyone wants a chance to coach our soccer team, and we're looking forward to another outstanding season."

Sam stops, unsure of what to say. The team motions for him to continue. "As much as other people want to be in charge of the team, there is really only one person who could coach us."

The audience turns and sees I'm standing at the back of the gym. Some wave to me. I force a smile, embarrassed by the attention.

"Anyway," Sam says as the crowd turns back to him, "while you guys were all fighting, the boys, we went and spoke with Coach Dan. You all know what a strong coach he is and how much better the team was because of him. Well, uhm, we asked him to be our coach again—and he agreed."

There's momentary silence and then rousing applause. Mr. Edelstein returns to the podium and announces, "There you have it. It's the perfect choice. Dan will return as coach. Thank you so much."

I stand in the back feeling the wave of enthusiasm roll through the gym. People come up to me to shake my hand and thank me for being so generous with my time. My only thought is to thank those kids for being so forthcoming and giving me one more chance. I'm not sure what I'm feeling, but I'm glad to feel something, anything but the empty, all-consuming void.

I smile at the boys. They see me, shyly wave, and run off down the hall. I'm left talking to people. I don't have much to say, but I'm not running away.

CHAPTER 48

THE SUN BEAMS ONTO our practice field and the moisture on the grass glistens. The rain stopped thirty minutes before, yielding early enough to allow us to practice. Shadows from the trees cover the edges of the field but don't invade the center circle of grass where the boys have gathered.

It's five minutes before the first practice and the boys are ready to begin. Carter and Leo kick a ball back and forth. They laugh as they talk about school, but it's obvious their primary focus is warming up and getting ready for practice.

Stan stands apart from the others rhythmically kicking a ball up the air. He's juggling using both feet and knees. I stop counting when he reaches twenty touches. He hardly has to move as the ball arcs precisely up in the air. Each time, he waits ready to send it back

Pete and Paul are talking alone. Pete has a clipboard in his hand. I talked to Pete a couple days earlier and told him I wanted to ease back into coaching slowly, and asked whether he and Paul could run at least the first few practices. It's nice to be back, but I'm not ready to be in charge.

Paul blows a whistle, and the boys immediately respond. "On the line, boys," Paul instructs. "It's a new season. Who's ready for some soccer?"

The boys immediately yell and jump to demonstrate their readiness. Paul tells them to prove it by doing thirty push-ups. The boys drop to the ground and begin to count together. They are in unison, and each boy is doing full push-ups. There is no faking and no cheating. Clearly, they've been doing some work in the off-season.

Pete, carrying the clipboard, leads them in warm-up exercises. There's an order to the exercises and the boys begin to tire. Taking that as his cue to switch drills, Pete asks the boys to dribble through an obstacle course he has set up with cones. Each boy navigates through the course, which forces them to move left and right with both feet. Tight turns and sudden shifts in direction pose little problem as each boy gets through the course with nary a knocked-over cone.

I stand on the sideline and marvel at the skills the boys demonstrate in this first practice. I mentally compare each boy to where he was at this time last season. Each has improved, which I surmise is not just due to physical maturity but also must be attributed to effort. It's apparent they have been practicing in their spare time.

After thirty minutes of skills practice, the boys are ready to scrimmage. They get a brief rest and a drink, then split into two teams.

The scrimmage lasts thirty minutes and everyone is sweaty at the end. The level of play during the scrimmage is outstanding and none of the boys spend time messing around or jumping on someone else's back. They are actually attempting to run plays, and when the ball goes out of bounds, they strategize about the next offensive thrust or how to stop the other team from scoring.

I spend the entire practice watching and offer no encouragement or suggestions. When practice is over, they come over to slap hands with me.

The boys walk toward the parking lot. I approach Pete and Paul. "Guys, that was a great practice. The boys were into it. I can't believe how well they're playing. You were organized and the kids responded."

Pete and Paul exchange a glance but can't handle the compliment. Paul says mockingly to Pete, "You are growing up so nicely. I'm so glad you have matured."

Pete rolls his eyes and smacks Paul on the back. "Thanks, Dude. You did the work."

"No, Pete, you're special. You made the kids so much better."

Pete whacks Paul on the back of his head. Paul responds by tripping Pete and then jumping on him. I stand and watch as the two fathers wrestle and roll in front of me.

"I am leaving, you morons. Thanks for letting me come to practice."

As I walk down the steps toward my car, Pete and Paul continue to wrestle. I barely hear as I get to the bottom of the steps, "You are beautiful. I love you."

I climb into my car and smile, realizing the kids are maturing at a much faster rate than their assistant coaches.

CHAPTER 49

THE CLOTHES HANGING ON my side of the closet are a mess. Pants used to be separated in their own section. Same for shirts. Now they are haphazardly hung in no order. I'm trying to select something, but for some reason, I'm struggling with what to wear. I'm only getting dressed for a kids' soccer game, yet I'm as nervous as I once was before a date. I chastise myself for caring.

My reflection in the mirror makes me laugh. What I wear to this game isn't important. I change shorts and put on a different T-shirt under my light-blue coach's shirt. I try a third hat on my head.

None of this makes any difference.

I pull my hat around to face backwards and mock myself by trying to dance in front of the mirror. I'm acting ridiculously, but it alleviates some tension.

My stomach churns. It will help to get back to the field for the soccer game, but I have so much trepidation because I know everyone will be checking me out, trying to decipher how I'm coping.

I glance over at Jill's side of the closet. Her clothes hang in the exact positions they were when she got dressed before Charley's last game. Seeing her things, even momentarily, sends a volcanic flow of emotions through me. Unable to process these feelings, I rush out of the closet.

I miss Jill. I miss being near her. I miss her voice. I miss the feeling of security I had when she was around. There is so much to making a life together, and when it's taken away, all that remains is a void. One gaping, overwhelming hole that feels like it will never fill in.

I cannot decide why I'm so nervous. I haven't been out a lot, but at some point, since the funeral, I've seen most of the people who will be at the game. People will stare at me, but I know it's done out of caring. The glances and forced smiles don't bother me. They simply remind me that nothing has returned to normal.

The game starts in forty-five minutes. Charley and I used to leave about this time to go and warm up before a game. Momentarily picturing Charley striking the soccer ball and sending it into the corner of the net creates a pleasant image, but I force it from my mind.

I walk into the kitchen to the smell of the soup I had eaten for lunch. The pot sits in the sink. There are a few dishes piled next to the sink, but the kitchen remarkably is not a mess. The cabinet next to the sink has the water bottles, and I grab one so I can have some water during the game. I realize I'm delaying the inevitable, so I walk down the steps to my car.

It's unnerving to be driving to a soccer game by myself. I feel I'm doing something wrong. I turn up the dial to make the music blare from the speakers and lower the windows as I make the short drive to the field.

Pete is under the shelter at the edge of the field and appears to have been waiting for me.

"Hey, Coach, how's it going?" Pete asks affably.

"Great day for soccer. Are the kids here?"

"You bet. They've warmed up and are waiting. They have something they want to show you."

Pete and I walk around the field to get to our sideline. He's making small talk. We get closer to our bench, and I see the boys and a couple adults huddled along the fence. They see me approaching. Paul breaks from the group and comes toward us.

"Are you ready for the game?" he asks, appearing a little too excited about the beginning of a game. The other team is shooting at their goal on the far side of the field. I'm thinking our boys should be doing the same.

"Hey, Coach," Pete says as he gets in front of me and stops me from getting to the boys.

"Yes, Pete," I respond as I try to maneuver around him.

"The boys wanted to do something to show how excited they were that you are coaching." He pauses and looks at the team. "I'm not sure whose idea it was, but Liza was the one who got it. Give it time to sink in. The boys are really excited."

"Okay guys, what is it?" I ask as I reach the mass of boys. They are lined up against the fence in a straight line, smiling but appearing nervous.

I wait until Sam, who is standing at the far end of the group, steps forward. All eyes are on him, and he is not entirely sure what to do. He comes next to me and grabs my hand, leading me closer to the group.

"Coach," he begins, He has trouble finding the right words. "We can't tell you how much we appreciate you are coaching us again this year. We wanted to do something to show how much it means to us and that we're thinking of Charley."

I stare at Sam, starting to feel my gut tighten. I have no idea where this is leading. I shuffle my feet nervously.

Sam turns to his teammates and takes a step back. The team splits in half, leaving an opening so the fence is visible. A Pumas jersey hangs on the fence, attached at the shoulders. My knees weaken when I observe Charley's name on the back of the jersey above his uniform number 1.

I stare at Sam and then at Pete and Paul. They smile hesitantly, waiting for my response. Too much swirls inside of me to allow me to react.

Pete steps next to Sam and puts his arm around him protectively. Sam turns to him with a questioning glance. "Liza found it at your house. We all talked about it. We thought it would be a nice tribute."

"Tribute?" I manage to spit out. "I'm not sure how to react."

Sam steps over to me and says, "Come close. You can feel him when you get near to it."

I pull back and walk in the other direction toward the sideline. Without looking back, I yell, "Let's go, we have a game to play!"

The boys are bewildered and slowly trot over to the sideline. I give them brief instructions and tell them who is starting. They run onto the field and shake hands with the other team.

The remaining boys not in the game stand in a huddle as far away from me as possible. They are scared of me and muttering to each other.

The boys line up for the kick, but instead of focusing, they glance over to me. The Connellsville team has the ball and our team won't move. With two quick passes, Connellsville has the ball all the way down field. Unchallenged, their forward lines up a shot and kicks it into the goal. Eli barely moves as the ball flies by him.

My hands rest on my knees and my head is lowered as the lack of intensity registers. I yell out some encouragement and the boys take the ball from the center circle and kick it down to the opposing goal. No one challenges the ball as Connellsville dribbles it over the center line. Again, Connellsville is untested as they move toward our goal. They take a long shot that would have gone in the goal if it hadn't been shot directly at Eli.

"Come on, Guys! Get your heads in the game!" I yell, trying to find something to get the boys to move. They seem stuck.

While I'm seething at the lack of effort, Pete comes over and leans into me. "You know, the boys thought bringing Charley's jersey was a great idea. They were so excited before you got here. They all kept running over to it while practicing to touch it and be close to it. It appeared to give them energy."

I turn my head to Pete and say, "I'm sorry. I wasn't expecting that."

"I know," he responds. "It was probably a little too much. It meant a lot to them."

I watch the ball kicked up and down the field for a couple of minutes, detached from everything happening around me. The game is in front of me, but my thoughts focus on the jersey hanging a few feet behind me. I don't want to see it and I don't want to deal with my reaction to it. But I know it's there and it draws me to it.

Something compels me to turn and face it.

It hangs alone on the fence with nothing else around it. The sunlight reflecting off it causes it to shimmer. The light breeze flutters the jersey.

I turn my back on the soccer game and gaze at the jersey on the fence. My concentration is consumed by the jersey. I stare at it, feeling overwhelmed, scared, yet exhilarated. I walk forward and reach out to touch it.

My fingers caress Charley's name and an indescribable sensation rockets from the jersey and into my heart. My mind clears until my head is filled with memories. Images of our life bang around my consciousness and consume me—Charley, Jill, sports, dinners, games, evenings together, parties, piano, swimming, soccer, wrapping paper, hugs, wrestling, and laughs.

I allow these impressions to take over my thoughts, and I welcome them, unaware of anything happening around me.

Time has no meaning.

My eyes open and I'm aware of people surrounding me. I sense the team is a few feet behind me ... watching me. I motion for them to join me, and they step forward to engulf me. The light touch of many young hands is on my back and legs. I welcome it.

I break free from them and move back toward the fence. Approaching the jersey tentatively, I put my hand out and touch it again. I let it sit there for a moment. Energy, power, memories, and emotion surge through me like a river. I raise my face toward the sun and, with my eyes closed, I feel its warmth.

I need to share this feeling; I turn back to the team and motion for them to come to the fence. The team rushes forward, consuming me and the jersey. We join, entranced by its power.

I keep my fingers touching Charley's name and say to the team, "Guys, you were right. There's energy coming from the jersey. Sorry I wasn't ready for it at first."

No one speaks or moves as we all keep our connection to the jersey.

"Sorry to break this up," Paul interrupts, "but we have a soccer game to play. We're down 3-0. Can we do something this half?"

"Okay, Guys, let's use this energy and play the way we know how," I say. "Everybody put a hand in."

All the kids have one hand on Charley's jersey and the other held out in the middle of the huddle.

I say, "One, two, three."

The response is a unified "Pumas!!"

I'm not sure what was happening when we all connected with Charley's jersey, but we all felt it. The kids certainly believed in its power and ran onto the field in a frenzy. Within five minutes they scored two goals and were running all over the field with renewed exuberance.

The five kids who weren't in the game insisted on standing next to the jersey, soaking in whatever it was giving to them. Whenever I put one of the kids into the game, they charged onto the grass and played with heightened vigor.

The coaching of soccer for me had never been about winning or losing—it was about finding a purpose and playing with passion. All I ever wanted out of this gorgeous gaggle of boys was dedication and a willingness to work to become as good as they could be.

When they won the championship the year before, I thought they had achieved everything possible we could have hoped for. Watching them play that afternoon, I realized there were other levels they could strive to attain. Something possessed them for that half, and it was beautiful to watch.

With five minutes left in the game, the score was tied at three. I pulled little Leo over to the jersey to talk to him.

"Leo, it's your turn. I want you in the game and I want you to show everybody what you have."

I was talking while Leo had a hand firmly on Charley's jersey. He was listening to me, but clearly he was getting more from his connection to the jersey.

It happened quickly after Leo got into the game. He was playing on the left side, and Carter made a crossing pass that hit Leo in stride. The Connellsville players had been tentative the whole half and seemed to be waiting for something to happen.

Leo grabbed the ball in full stride, and when the defender came to challenge him, he moved the ball back and forth between his legs and lifted the ball over the defender's shoulder. Leo gathered the ball in and charged at the goalie. We all knew he was going to score, and he did it by faking a shot to his right and pushing the ball inside the left goalpost.

It was Leo's first goal ever.

It was only the first game of the season, but we knew they were already halfway up the mountain.

Pete hands me the jersey after the game and I tell everyone I won't be bringing it to any more games. They now know they had no limitations, but they would have to find a way to tap into their potential on their own.

I feel the vibration of my phone ringing in my shorts as I walk off the field. Jana identifies herself after I answer.

"Hey, what's up?"

"I wanted to let you know I've had a few meetings with a new potential client. They called me after hearing about the Spinelli case. They're being sued—breach of contract, anti-trust, bad faith. All sorts of good stuff. It's a huge case and I can't handle it myself."

"Jana, amazing news. I told you it was only a matter of time until you started bringing in the big cases."

"It's because of you. You trained me and showed me how to try cases."

"You're being modest. You deserve everything you're getting."

"Thanks, but like I said, I can't handle this case on my own. It's too much. So, I was wondering if you were going to be around sometime. I was hoping you can work this case up with me."

I pause for a moment. This call probably couldn't have come at a better time. I see the kids walking with their parents and getting into their cars to go to their next family activities.

Perhaps it's time for me to dip my toes back in the water.

"Jana, I would love to help you on this case. Can we meet on Monday at the office?"

"You bet. I can't wait to see you there. Thanks, Dan—I'm happy you'll be there for me."

We say our goodbyes and I walk toward my car. I've been here hundreds of times for so many reasons, but today it feels like it might be my first time here.

I clutch at Charley's jersey.

Thanks for looking out for me.

I look up to the sky, take a deep breath, and slide into my car.

ABOUT JAMES ROSENBERG

James Rosenberg is a 3rd generation trial attorney with plenty of stories to tell. Inspired not only by the courtroom stories his father and grandfather used to tell him when he was a child, but also by the wild adventures he's encountered through his own experience as a lawyer. James is fascinated by the intricate, interpersonal dynamics of every trial he's endured. Whether it's the raw emotion on display in court, the tension in the air that builds until someone wins, or the impact that a case's decision has on the parties involved, James is always paying attention and keeping tabs on what's happening.

He also coached his kids in soccer from when they were little until they were able to play in the big games. He never understood why he cared so much about their games—but he did.

The Jersey is his second novel continuing to explore the nature of relationships as he had in first novel, *Legal Reserves.*

If you want to learn more about Mr. Rosenberg and his books please visit his website, JamesRosenbergAuthor.com.

Or check him out on Amazon.com.

THANKS

The Jersey has been an incredible force in my life and reflects the hard work, dedication and inspiration of so many people:

Michele--you have created so many good moments reflected in our stories. You inspire so much good in so many people and much of that is reflected in the book.

Tillie, Henry and Ethan—you have heard the story so many times, but you are the inspiration for the good the book reflects.

Ellie and Shelly—you are the moral center of our universe and everything positive that happens to us.

Dave, Dory, Haley and Thomas—thanks for the constant support, love and the best versions of the clown joke.

Lydia—not only did you see the potential in the story, but you worked so hard to make it possible to share it with others.

Kathy—your editing eye sees all details. Thanks for all of your help.

Annie, Margie, Abbie, Jenny and soccer moms everywhere—you get the boys to games, keep them fed, scream and love every minute of it.

Matt, Marc, and soccer dads everywhere—you yell, encourage and love watching the boys learn life lessons on the field.

Annie, Bernadette, and Amy—you were the guinea pigs, but your support and positivity were more influential than you could ever imagine.

Shelly and Sheila—every day your kind words of support help these stories come to life.

Eric—you know medicine and how it works in the real world.

To the boys—you were awesome when you were eleven and still awesome years later. Now you're pretty much men yet still reflect the innocence of youth. Good luck in everything life throws at you.

Made in the USA
Columbia, SC
12 April 2024